THE FOUR LIVES OF J. S. FREEMAN

Book Three

FREE

Yvonne Anderson

THE FOUR LIVES OF J. S. FREEMAN

BOOK THREE

FREE

Yvonne Anderson

Free (The Four Lives of J. S. Freeman, #3)
ISBN 978-1-946985-12-5

This novel is a work of fiction. Characters, plot, and incidents are products of the author's imagination, and any similarity to people living or dead, whether on Earth or Umban, is coincidental.

TABLE OF CONTENTS

BOOK 3 – FREE

Map of the world Umban   ix
Diagram of Freemansland   xi
Map of the region of Arkentak   xiii

Recap of The Story Thus Far   1

1   To Cararre   5
2   At the Zavazda   13
3   Dissecting Freemansland   24
4   One of Us Is Crazy, And It's Not Me   37
5   The Deal   47
6   What Happened Next   55
7   Twelve Months Later   66
8   Happy Birthday   77
9   Faces From the Past, Facing the Future   88
10 Tired of This   99
11 Unthinkable   111
12 Sinking Sand   123
13 The Deal   133
14 Remediation   143
15 Five Buys in Little Nion   156
16 Nothing Makes Sense   165
17 Indecision   175

18 Purification 184

19 My Third Life Ends 195

20 My Fourth Life. 206

21 Chance Meeting 218

22 This One Thing I Do 229

23 To Freedom 241

24 Finding Home 253

25 Confession. 265

26 Sunset on the Stillwater 277

27 Free Indeed. 290

Umban
NaHora
Tresseiital
Saltcreek Point
Sorona
Walpin
Indopso
Arkentak
Watland
Ellerja
Steefren
Freemansland
Omaseen
Fivepetals
Centre City
Cararre
Nion

Here's a rough diagram of the island Freemansland, nicknamed The Land of Many Mysteries:

Some of this story takes place in a region of Umban called Arkentak. This might help you visualize it:

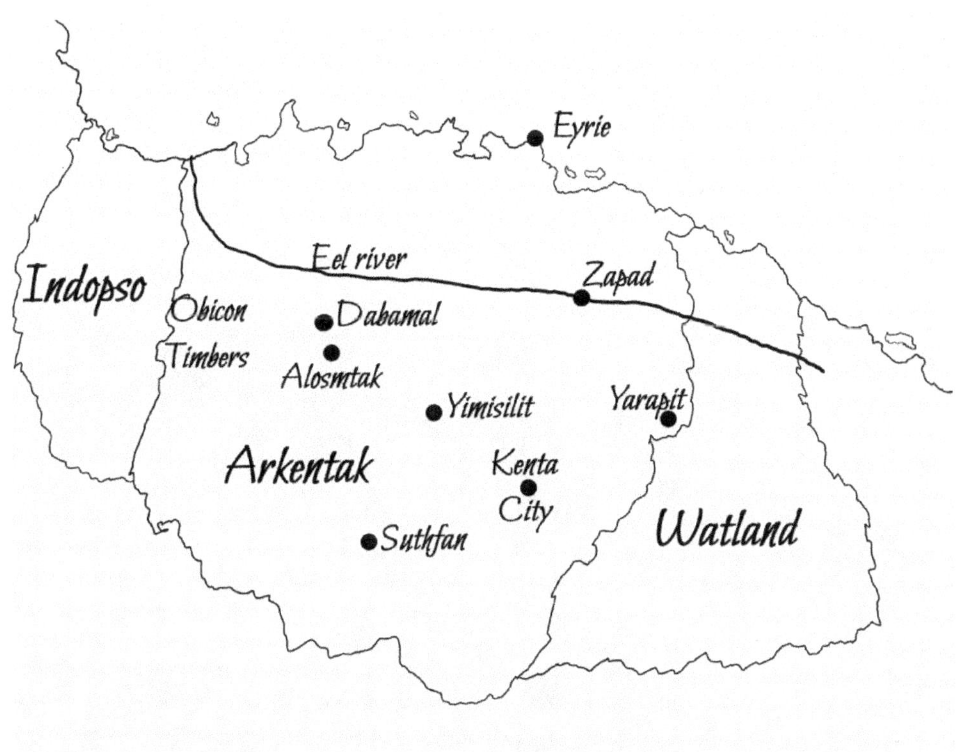

RECAP OF THE STORY THUS FAR

Jemma's first life was rough: motherless from birth and rejected by her father, she mostly fended for herself on the island of Freemansland where she was born. Her one consolation was her twin brother, Jeriah, and her greatest terror was her older brother, Ibro, who did bad things to little girls. One evening Ibro caught her alone, Jeriah came to her rescue, and her father and Ibro both died in the melee.

Thus begins Jemma's second life. Now orphaned, she and Jeriah become wards of the City, the powerful global entity that Jemma holds responsible for everything wrong with the world.

The City sends the twins to the Academy to get a modern education. Their old friend, Mayne Dabo, is also a student there. In order to keep the other boys from bothering Jemma, Mayne leads people to believe that he and Jemma have a marriage arrangement under an old and respected tradition on Freemansland.

Mayne convinces the twins to join the military after graduation, thinking all three will serve together. But to their mutual alarm, they are each sent to different branches of the service.

Being separated from her brother almost sends Jemma over the brink. It's surprising it doesn't, for in her first life, she became infected with two stelli, parasitic worms that live in the brain. A person with stelli is called a stellasede.

As long as the worms are dormant, they do no harm, but when they become active, the stellasede goes mad and dies. Stressful situations are believed to cause the worms to awaken. Yet Jemma survives the strenuous foundational training and begins her military career in peak health.

Jeriah marries and starts a family, causing Jemma to feel separated from him by more than distance. In part because of her loneliness, Jemma agrees to marry Ashgrey (Grey) Standtall, a man of high pedigree, despite the drastic differences in their social status. Seeing the sterling character of the Standtall family, Jemma resolves to put her lawless Freemansland upbringing behind her and embrace this family's nobility as her own. Her third life begins with her marriage.

The fairy tale aspect lasts only as long as the honeymoon, as the world is embroiled in war. Jemma and Grey—still in the military's Information Acquisition Division—are on the front lines. Jemma is nearly killed in a bombing attack. By the time her rehabilitation is complete, her ten-year enlistment is ended, and she is discharged.

Traumatized by the bombing, and with nothing constructive to do with her time, she follows her family's tradition of dealing with stress by drinking. Grey's love intervenes in her downward spiral, and he encourages her to develop her latent creative talents.

She writes fiction for young readers, creating a series about a boy and his twin sister growing up on Freemansland. The books are wildly successful. But her problems are not over.

Her relationship with her brother and his family has been strained since the time she first took up with Grey. Now, her literary success increases the separation between them, as it makes Jeriah's wife, Seena, resentful. Difficulties with her brother are bad enough, but then Jemma's privileged world turns treacherous—Grey's father, a member of the Ruling Council, is murdered, and she learns that other Council members are behind it.

Grey vows to find a way to bring the perpetrators to justice, but Jemma doesn't see how that's possible. These are the most powerful people in the world.

Jemma's writing career is still going strong, but everything else spins out of control. The new regime is turning justice inside-out.

Grey's family is breaking apart. Grey himself is spending far too much time away from home.

Then Jemma's sister-in-law learns of Jeriah's cheating and goes back to Freemansland, taking the children with her.

Jeriah breaks this news to Jemma in a late-night phone call, one of those nights when Grey is away and she's home alone. Her brother admits his infidelities, and when she castigates him, he tells her Grey is guilty of the same thing.

They scream horrible things at each other, and she ends the call by smashing her phone. Distraught, she contacts the liquor store and orders a bottle of whisky to be delivered. But before it arrives, she pulls herself together and decides she won't go down that road again. She's finished with her brother and with everything else from her first and second lives, and that includes alcoholism. She swore to stand tall in her third life, and that's just what she'll do. She tells the doorman to accept the delivery but keep it for himself.

Gray arrives home in the middle of the next morning and finds her still in bed, trying to sleep her depression away. In contrast, he is in unusually high spirits. After convincing her that Jeriah's accusations are wholly unfounded, he tells her he'll be off work for a couple of weeks, and he'd like to take her on a pleasure trip for a few days.

She grieves the loss of her brother, with whom she swears she will never communicate again. But the prospect of a vacation with Grey does much to cheer her. At the opening of Book 3, *Free*, Jemma is preparing for the trip.

❧ Chapter 1 ❧

TO CARARRE

AT MY DRESSING table, I experimented with the hottest new trend for eyebrows.

After penciling a boxy line around one brow and filling it in, I gave my mirrored reflection an appraising look. Wasn't wild about it. I compared my work to the photo of the model I'd been using as an example. Why did it look so much better on her than on me?

Grey passed by, and when he caught my face in the mirror, he did a funny little stutter-step. "What are you doing?"

"Putting on my make-up. What does it look like?"

He came closer and bent to peer at the reflection. "I'm not sure." He picked up the photo I'd been trying to copy. "That might be the silliest thing I've ever seen."

I turned toward him. "You think it's silly?" I waggled my brows up and down.

He chuckled. "It makes an impression, I'll grant you that. But if you like it, go right ahead. I'll just look at your mouth instead." He kissed it.

I slumped in the chair. "I wanted to try something new, but I can't get it to look right." I grabbed a pad, gave it a squirt of Cosmi-Solv, and wiped off my handiwork. "That was a waste of time."

"And eyebrow pencil. If that were ink, you'd have enough there to print a book." At my clothes rod, he went through my dresses as if shopping.

I made a face at him. He had a point, though. I'd already filled two pads with the dark goo and now squirted Cosmi-Solv on a third.

He pulled out one of my favorite outfits, a dark ruby ankle-length culottes suit with double ruffles on the hems. The tailored jacket, trimmed with elaborate gold embroidery, had a long tail but was short in the front. "Now, this shows good taste. And the color goes with my houndstooth trousers, don't you think?"

"Nothing goes with your houndstooth trousers." I applied fresh make-up, but more conservatively.

"So I should wear them and nothing else?"

"If you'd like. Where are we going, anyway?"

He hung the dress on the clothes tree. "Have you ever been to Cararre?"

"I had a book signing there last year."

"Oh, that's right." He went to the jewelry armoire. "Did you see the Zavazda?"

"Cornballs, no. They say you can spend a week of twelve-hour days in that place and not see the half of it." I stood and slipped out of my dressing gown.

He left the jewelry armoire to help me dress. "You're only supposed to tour a small part of it at a time. You'd go into overload otherwise."

"I don't know a thing about art. What are you wearing? I hope not the houndstooth. Next time you're away, I'm getting rid of those horrid pants."

He buttoned me up the back. "What's the matter with what I have on?"

I put on the jacket. "Not a thing." Standing in front of the mirror, I straightened the garments.

He lifted a necklace out of the armoire and put it around my neck.

I smiled at his reflection in my mirror. His frame had filled out a bit over the years, but that was to be expected when a man approached middle age. Despite the extra weight, he cut as striking a figure as ever in his stylish gray trousers and pleated shirt. "Nothing wrong at all. Keep it on if you want."

He nibbled my neck. "Truly, I'd rather take it off..."

⁂

AFTER PACKING FOR a three-day trip, we bought a phone at a local shop and waited while a service tech transferred my codes and settings from my mangled one. From there, we went to the Standtall airfield and boarded the family jet for Cararre.

On the plane, I pulled out my new phone and chose a code.

"Who are you calling?"

A rude beeping jarred me, and I pulled the phone away from my ear, scowling. "Seena. But she's rejecting my call."

He ran his hand over his face the way he did when he was trying not to show his emotions.

"What?"

"I never did like her."

I slipped the phone back into my bag. "Yes, I know. But she's my friend. I want to reach out to her. See if there's anything I can do."

He shook his head. "Let her go. She doesn't appreciate your meddling."

"I don't want to meddle, I want to help." I sagged into my seat. "I have so much, and she has nothing. Now, less than nothing." My throat swelled with a tear-lump. "She was a good friend to me in school. I want to do the same for her."

"She was only good to you because you were beneath her. It made her feel self-righteous to help a poor little waif. But now you've risen above her, and she resents it."

I gaped at him. "How can you say that?"

"Because it's true."

"You don't know Seena. How can you—"

"Think about it and you'll see I'm right. The only thing she ever wanted from you was your gratitude. Now that the tables have turned, she doesn't want to be the beggar picking up your scraps."

I narrowed my eyes. "What makes you so sure?"

"I know the type."

I snorted. "She's not a type. She's my sister-in-law."

"Oh, so you admit you have a brother?"

"Glish, no." I opened a drawer and pulled out a black silk sleep mask. "I don't want to talk about it." I put on the mask and reclined the seat back.

"You were in bed half the day, and now you're going to sleep?"

I ignored him.

"You do have a brother. And you love him very much. You'll get over your tiff before long."

This was no tiff. The things we'd said to each other the night before, I could never repeat. Anger we hadn't known we'd harbored for each other's spouse, each other's family—yes, my bitterness toward him for having children when I couldn't—all that boiled up and spilled out like fiery acid, destroying everything it touched. The bond between us had been eaten away, never to be rebuilt.

Grey couldn't see the tears behind the mask, and I didn't lift it to wipe them away. I let the silk of my CFC privilege absorb them.

WE DIDN'T ARRIVE in Cararre until early evening, so we took in some of the other sights that first day and saved the Zavazda for the next. Grey seemed inclined to baby me that evening, and I was inclined to let him. It reminded me of the beginning of our relationship, when he introduced me to his world.

Though the CFC lifestyle had been foreign to me then, I was so firmly entrenched in it now that I could scarcely remember living any other way. I remembered enough, though, that when I combined my experiences with my imagination, the result made for best-selling stories. By the time I visited the famous Zavazda in Cararre with Grey, my Stillwater books had made J. S. Freeman a well-known name in Centre City and across every region of the world.

In the autocab on the way to the museum the next morning, I reminded Grey I didn't know a thing about art. "I'm not sure why we're even going."

He turned from the window and spoke with sudden animation. "It's about so much more than art. It's about beauty. Architecture, archaeology. Our heritage, our history. Not only as a City, but before. Our pre-history."

I pretended to look around the car's interior. "Where's the camera? Sounds like we're filming an advertisement."

"Not at all. The Zavazda is an amazing place, and I'm excited to finally show it to you. I don't know what's taken me so long to bring you here."

"Our being apart all the time might have something to do with it."

When a cloud of regret crept over his face, I hastened to reassure him. "But we're here now, and I intend to enjoy myself."

"As do I. Look, there it is." He pointed toward a gleaming mass up ahead.

The signature jumble of glittering triangles caught the sun's rays and diffused them into prismatic beams. They formed what at first seemed a lumpy frame of no particular shape. If you looked at it long enough, however, it began to make sense. I couldn't have explained the statement it made, but it seemed to represent something profound.

I didn't come to that conclusion at first. My initial reaction was amazement at its size. Though I'd seen photographs of the landmark, I hadn't imagined it to be so enormous. It was stunning.

I craned my neck to see the top of the many-faceted structure, but we were already too close. "I haven't even been there yet, and I'm already overwhelmed."

"That's the typical reaction. Some people have been known to faint at the sight."

"Then they shouldn't have skipped breakfast."

The cab pulled up to the passenger unloading area, and we got out. I couldn't keep from leaning back trying to appreciate the height of the building as we walked across the plaza, but some of the lumps jutted out and blocked my view of its summit.

Initially, I'd thought the triangles making up the walls were metallic, but now I could see they were of a translucent material in a variety of pale colors. People moving within created ghostly silhouettes.

At ground level, however, the triangles were clear glass, and the building's front was flat, like an enormous window made of a million panes. The plaza on which we walked repeated the triangle theme, with three-sided paving pieces of diverse colors. A few ornamental trees grew here and there, each fenced by the backs of a triad of benches arranged about them.

"What's with the pattern of threes?" I asked as we made for the entrance.

"Everything in the world is based on that number. Solid, liquid, gas. Animal, vegetable, mineral. Proton, electron, nucleus. The three dimensions. Three primary colors. Even time is divided into past, present, and future. You've said yourself that all stories have a beginning, a middle, and an end—"

"Okay, I get the idea." I found his bouncing enthusiasm a bit alarming. "Three is a recurring number in nature."

"It's the number everything is founded on, a reflection of the Creator's triune nature."

He completely lost me there, but I didn't ask. For one thing, I didn't care to go down that crazy religion road. But mostly, we entered the building then, and my senses were assaulted by more than enough sights and sounds to draw my interest.

One of the first distractions was that of two women in the lobby wearing koormas, each with her Kentan "arm," or consort.

I wanted to rush over and slap them senseless. It was those Stridentan zealots who'd brought about the war in which millions had died—most of whom were their own people. How dare they show themselves in the City after what they had done?

Two years ago, they wouldn't have. But a great deal had changed since Janren Stock took over the Ministry of Domestic Peace. Now we were rebuilding their cities, providing for their homeless, contorting ourselves into unnatural positions to accommodate their religious sensibilities. All this, despite the treasonous Kentan leadership's refusal to acknowledge the authority of Centre City. They still considered themselves a sovereign nation, and the City did nothing about it.

The sight of those two well-dressed Stridentan couples made my hackles rise. I bobbed my head in their direction. "Let's follow them and eavesdrop on their conversations. They'll never know we understand their dialect. We need to see what they're up to."

He pursed his lips. "You're not in the Division anymore."

"I know, but—"

"Let it be."

"We won't be obvious about it. I'll just—"

He bent and spoke in my ear. "I said let. It. Be." Then he straightened. "I've arranged for a personal guide. We're to meet her over there." He pointed to a hanging banner saying "Guided Tours."

Though I allowed him to usher me toward the gate, a wave of bitterness rolled over me. "Your father would never have allowed these things to go on."

He stopped and gave me a chilling *don't push me* look. "I told you we will not discuss it."

I looked up at him, eyes narrowed. "What's with you today, anyway?"

"Nothing." His face softened. "We're here to relax and enjoy ourselves. So let's do that." He took my hand and moved forward.

"Sure." I let him lead me. "Let's do that." Then I almost stopped again when I realized how obtuse I'd been.

I will fix it, he'd vowed. And that's what he'd been doing all this time when he was away from home. Trying to fix it.

I gave his hand a squeeze. "I'm sorry, Grey."

"For what?"

"For being such a termagant."

He laughed. "That, my darling, you are not." He continued to chuckle as we approached the gate. "You are caring and concerned. And I certainly don't want to discourage that." His eyes sparkled as he smiled down at me. "I just—"

I smiled back and squeezed his hand again. "I know. Never mind. I'll shut up about it."

He smiled back. "You amaze me, Freeman."

❧ Chapter 2 ☙

AT THE ZAVAZDA

OUR TOUR GUIDE, Exxie Lyth, stood only as high as my shoulder, but she was brisk and knowledgeable. I liked her instantly—even before she asked, "Are you the author, J. S. Freeman?"

When I admitted that I was, she beamed. "I just love your Stillwater books. I bought them for my kids, but I love them too. When's Book 7 coming out?"

"Later this year, thank you for asking."

"Tell me." She inched closer and spoke in a conspiratorial tone. "Do Tia and Harmay get together eventually? They do, don't they?"

I chuckled. "You'll have to wait until next year, when we release the last book."

Harmay, of course, was Tuu's best friend, and yes, I modeled the character after Mayne. But if you want to know if he and Tia get together, you'll have to read the Stillwater series yourself. I'm not giving any spoilers here.

Exxie made an exaggerated sigh. "I knew you'd say that. Are you going to give Tia's brother a love interest?"

"Do you think he needs one?"

"Of course. Everybody does, don't you think?" She turned a plaintive gaze up at Grey. "Is Tuu going to fall in love?"

He had been watching the exchange with smiling eyes and now raised a hand in mock distress. "Don't look at me. I have no inside information."

"Well, then, I guess I'll have to wait." Exxie gave an exaggerated sigh, then motioned for us to follow her. "Let's begin our tour."

EXXIE SHOWED US some highlights of the labyrinthine museum, beginning with a small display of early Jamaharian artifacts and progressing through selections that reflected the uniting of the nations under the umbrella of Centre City.

All the most famous works of art were here. For each, Exxie gave the history of the creation of the piece, a short biography of the artist, and other interesting tidbits. I'd seen photos of most of these works before, but I was surprised at how moving it was to stand in the presence of such masterpieces.

Next, we went through exhibits showcasing art of specific regions. Again, Exxie's commentary gave it all depth and meaning.

Though I didn't usually appreciate art, I was affected by the commonalities in every cultures' works. Wherever the artists lived, they all struggled to maintain their people's heritage even while melding with the City in order to survive and thrive. The masterpieces touched me deeply, shouting out the truth that all the peoples of the world were united by a common humanity more than by political treaties.

I must have told Grey a half a dozen times, "I'm glad we came. I see why you brought me here."

I think the morning's tour left us all emotionally drained. To fortify ourselves, we went to the mall on the basement level, where culinary artists from around the world sold the fruits of their labors.

As we entered the concourse, Exxie turned to me. "Do you have any preferences as to cuisine?"

I shook my head. "I like just about everything, as long as it never walked on hooves."

She looked up at Grey with a perplexed expression.

He smiled. "We prefer fish or poultry over other meats. What do you recommend?"

"Have you ever had mirtositi?"

We answered together, "We love it."

Exxie grinned. "Well, then, it's settled." She hurried down the concourse like a woman on a mission. "We have one of the world's best mirtositi artists here today, Jano. It's her son Lodo's shop, but Lodo's wife went into labor this morning, and he's with her at the hospital. Jano's filling in for him."

I'd heard of Jano, and followed willingly.

Though the mirtositi stall was closed when we arrived, Exxie called through the gate into the darkened room in the Nionese dialect, "Hello, is anyone there?"

Of course people were there. We could hear voices and see lights on in the back.

In a moment, the front section lit up, and a woman in Nionese chef's robes bustled toward us, frowning. She wasn't much taller than Exxie. "You are early, Mrs. Lyth. You come before we open." She unlocked and pulled back the gate. Her sweeping *come on in* gesture jarred against her brusque words. "Art cannot be hurried. Do not be impatient."

Exxie led the way into the dining area. "We are happy to wait, Madam Jano. We merely wanted to make sure we got a seat."

Jano harrumphed. "You have your seats. Now, sit and wait." She turned away with an air of disgust and disappeared into the back.

We sat at a long counter, and Exxie grinned. "Don't be fooled by Jano's charm. She comes across as a sweet old thing, but she's really quite disagreeable."

Grey's laugh reverberated in the empty room. "Let me guess. You're related?"

"You're onto me." Exxie winked. "She's my aunt. I love her to pieces, but mostly because of her mirtositi. She really is as grumpy as she appears."

A few moments later, two young assistants came out bearing a number of containers and utensils. They gave us polite nods as they arranged them in a meticulous order, making sure every object was perfectly straight and in a precise position. One of them opened the door and turned on the "Open" sign, then they all scurried into the back again.

Other customers came in, talking about Lodo and the reputation of his mirtositi, and how rumor had it that his mother was one of the world's premier mirtositi artists.

Jano came out with a long, sharp knife in her hand and a scowl on her face. "Lodo is not here. I am creating the mirtositi today. You not like it, you not need to stay." She gestured with a wave of the glittering blade.

One of the customers stared. "Are you Jano?"

"I am. Who are you?"

Grey and I exchanged sideways glances. We hadn't expected entertainment with our meal.

More customers had filed in than there were seats at the counter. An assistant was sent to stand at the doorway and turn people away, and Jano told those who stood around that she served no one who wasn't seated. "If you want to wait, you may. But move out there." She waved her knife toward the door.

The standing crowd left in ones and twos, muttering. But she never looked their way again. She was too busy accosting us at the counter. "You citizen?" She asked us each in turn—except for Exxie. Once she had an answer from everyone else, she addressed us all. "If you citizen, you pay three hundred fifty urexi. You who are not, it's one hundred. Pay Tremo here." She waved toward an assistant. "Everybody pay. Three fifty, or one hundred. But you, woman—" she pointed her blade at Exxie, and it came awfully close. "You no pay. Your money no good here."

Two of the citizens got up and left in a huff, apparently offended at the uneven prices. Two more took their places from the group outside, apparently willing to pay the cost. Grey seemed amused as he surrendered the funds. "I sure hope this is good."

Jano perked up. "Who said that?"

"I did." Grey raised his hand. "I've heard you're the best. Let's see if you are."

She scowled at him. "You big man think you know mirtositi? I shall show you mirtositi." She surveyed the bewildered line of faces at the counter. "Prepare yourselves. I am an artist."

She went to work. With deft movements too quick for the eye to follow, she spread sticky nionarz on a mat, arranged rows of colorful ingredients over it, and rolled it into a log. It took her two seconds to slice the roll and put one piece on each of ten small square plates, which her assistant, Tremo, distributed to each of us at the counter, along with dipping sauces.

I'd had mirtositi elsewhere, but never like this. Before I'd worked the last delectably-seasoned grain of nionarz from my teeth, a fresh plate appeared before me with another offering. A third assistant provided a tiny, stemless glass of Nionese wine, which was potent enough that the small size of the vessel was appropriate.

For the next twenty minutes, we sat in a whirlwind of food coming and going, plates being cleared, ingredient platters removed and more brought in, all performed with military precision. As she worked, Jano kept up a constant chatter describing some of the ingredients, giving the creations fanciful names, insulting one customer or another, and praising her own skill. She never spoke to her assistants, nor did she glance at the growing audience outside.

By the time the amazing performance was over, I couldn't have squeezed another grain of nionarz into my belly.

As the assistants cleared away the last of the dishes, Jano turned to Grey. "Well, big citizen man. Was that a good lunch?"

By way of answer, he rose from his stool and applauded. The rest of us followed suit, and Jano bowed. "Thank you. You are all true connoisseurs of the art. I hope you will tell your friends." She turned and scurried into the back.

I was pretty sure she was blushing.

After sharing such an experience, those of us at the counter might have felt like close friends, but we couldn't linger. The assistants hurried us out to make room for the next group.

"Why didn't she take your money?" someone asked Exxie.

"I guess she liked my looks."

The ten of us made our way through the press of the crowd around the door and out into the wider part of the concourse, commenting and exclaiming about the experience. Some exchanged contact information so they could keep in touch.

Exxie turned to Grey. "Are you ready to go to the research wing?"

Before he could answer, the assistant Tremo came running toward us. "Mr. Big Man, Miss Freeman!" He stopped before us, breathless. "Madam Jano would like to see Miss Freeman. Please, if you would come with me?"

To the stares of the others, we followed him into the shop and all the way to the kitchen.

The fishy smell back there was delightful. Considering the artist's severity, I wasn't surprised everything was immaculate despite the frenzy of activity. I was surprised, though, to see a stack of books on a small table. My books. All six that had been published.

More surprising yet was the sight of Jano coming at me, not with a knife, but a pen, and a grin the size of Exxie's. "Miss Freeman. I am a huge fan of your work. Would you please sign my books?"

⁂

AFTER THAT REMARKABLE experience, Exxie took us on a hike for what seemed like kilometers into a part of the building labeled "Research." There, she turned us over to the care of a lanky man named Dr. Semilum.

His brown eyes sparkled with intelligence, but his ill-fitting clothes indicated a distinct lack of concern for fashion. The rash of crumbs littering his full beard was a bit distracting as well.

He greeted Grey politely but without interest. To me, however, he gave his full attention. "Miss Freeman." He eyed me as a scientist views a specimen. "You are an artist, not a historian. You allow your work to violate the truth."

What was that all about? In a rush of anger, I looked him in the eye. "I am no artist, Dr. Semilum. I merely write children's books. And I never claimed them to be historically accurate."

Grey put his hand on my shoulder. "My wife is an artist to be sure. But I agree that her artistic renderings may not conform to the historical record."

Grey read my manuscripts as I wrote them. His encouragement was always enthusiastic, and I never got the impression his praise was anything less than sincere. But he had expressed reservations about the way I played on the supernatural legends and took liberties with reality.

"That could never happen," he'd say, or "The wild people of the wood aren't really as you describe, are they?" I'd tell him it was just a story. It wasn't supposed to be real.

I portrayed Freemansland the way people liked to imagine it. The way *I* liked to imagine it.

I took courage now from his hand around mine, and from the recent praise by Jano and Exxie. "My books are very popular. What do you know about Freemansland anyway, Dr. Semilum?"

He drew himself up. "After three decades of research, more than anyone, I should think. I have spent more time on the island—and in it—than you have."

I frowned. "*In* it?"

"I am sorry." Grey squeezed my hand. "I should have told you earlier about this part of the tour, but I hoped to surprise you."

I turned my frown on him. "What are you talking about? What's going on?"

Dr. Semilum answered for him. "Your husband asked me to give you a preview of our upcoming exhibit and show you some of the things we have learned. So that before the new Freemansland Hall opens, possibly next year, you might perhaps share with us some of your knowledge. Though I am frankly skeptical about the usefulness of that. We are scientists here, not given to silly imaginings."

My mind struggled to keep up. "Exhibit? You mean you're planning to have a Freemansland Hall here at the Zavazda like what you have for the other regions?"

"Of course." He spoke as if I were a backward child in need of special tutoring. "We have the same concern for Freemansland as we do for any other part of the world under our jurisdiction."

"Ah." Things were starting to make sense now. "You're saying you aren't content to just blow a hole in it, but now you're taking it apart to see what's inside?"

The lower part of Dr. Semilum's face contorted in what I first took as pain, but then it took shape as a slow smile. "That is one way of putting it, yes. Exactly so. The creatures clinging to the surface of that unique structure do not know all that is within. But under my direction, the City is learning. And, as always, we wish to share our knowledge with the rest of the world. That is why the Zavazda exists. To share beauty and culture and knowledge with everyone, for the enjoyment and enlightenment of all people."

I crossed my arms and glared at Grey. "So that's what this whole trip is about? To trick me into coming here for a lecture about what it is to be a Freemanslander? Whatever happened to being honest with one another?"

Grey put a gentle hand on my arm. "I wanted to give you a special treat. And you have been enjoying yourself, haven't you?"

I shrugged, keeping my arms folded. "Until now, yes, but—"

"That is my whole agenda. For you to enjoy the experience. I had the opportunity to meet Dr. Semilum recently. When he told me about his work, I thought you might like to see it for yourself. If you're not interested, we can leave. There are plenty of other things at the Zavazda we can look at instead."

He had such a boyish, pleading look, I almost smiled. "Of course I'm interested." I uncrossed my arms but kept my frown. "It's the way you sprung it on me that I don't like. You know how I feel about surprises."

"I know. Or, I should know. But I forget sometimes."

I glanced at Dr. Semilum, whose eyes had been darting back and forth between us with a clinical interest that reminded me of someone. "Do you know Eglor Pigeon?"

His smile returned. "My cousin. He, too, is involved in a study of your island."

"Yes. Of the stelli that inhabit it." I nodded. "He's told you about me, hasn't he?"

"Of course not. That would violate privacy laws."

I laughed. "Privacy laws cover doctor-patient privilege, so your citing them means you know he's my doctor. Which tells me that he's told you about me."

He flushed. Deeply.

I continued without pause. "But I don't mind. He's offended me so many times in so many ways, I've developed calluses against it."

A glance at Grey told me he was enjoying the exchange. Encouraged, I went on. "So what have you learned? I'm ready for the tour through the mysterious bowels of Freemansland and a lecture about the creatures that cling to its surface." I wrapped my arm around Grey's, feeling ready to stand up to any arrogant pigeonhead.

Dr. Semilum stroked his beard—dislodging the crumbs, to my relief. "You are as enigmatic as I had been led to believe, and as volatile."

"Led to believe by your cousin, with whom you have never discussed me. Of course."

That weird smile reappeared. "Led to believe by my study of your birthplace as well as your writings."

"Yes, I suppose your study requires you to read my silly imaginings."

"You do have a way, Miss Freeman, of distorting one's words."

"We're all friends here, aren't we? Please, call me Mrs. Standtall."

Grey chuckled. "I think it's time for you to show us the things you told me about, Semilum."

The scientist perked up at the suggestion. "Yes, of course."

He led us down a corridor and into a room the size of a warehouse, and with similar decor. Open beams overhead, bare floor, shelves here, boxes and bins there. In the center, simple light fixtures hung down above a bank of computers, a couple of which had people perched on stools in front of them. The scent in the room held a familiar taint of seaweed, mold, fish, and hairpine, along with a hint of ersatz crim.

"Your life's work is the study of Freemansland, but you settle for Laffcrim?"

Dr. Semilum's eyes widened. "Why do you say that?"

"I have a nose for these things."

He almost smiled. "It's my employees. They prefer the flavored crims. Personally, I prefer tea."

"Why am I not surprised?"

"I think you are a reader of people as well as writer of books."

Grey squeezed my hand. "The one skill is useful in practicing the other. When you told me about your research, Doctor, I didn't envision such an inventory of artifacts."

"Nor did any of us anticipate they would tell such an interesting story." The doctor led the way to the center of the room. "I shall show you." At the computer bank, he said sat in front of a keyboard. "Let's pull up a stool."

We each sat.

After a few keystrokes, a large screen rose from behind the computer, giving us a clear view of what he pulled up. Then, with the animation of a man warming to his favorite subject, he told of his studies, showing image after image of what he described.

A shortened version would go something like this:

❧ Chapter 3 ❧

DISSECTING FREEMANSLAND

UNTIL ABOUT A century before Grey and I visited the Zavazda, the City Fathers knew very little about Freemansland. It had been seen from the air and from the sea, but few had visited. Those who had, found it inhospitable.

Foul-smelling waters encircled steep, wooded slopes where nothing could live but wild things. The only flat ground was the ice-encrusted top upon which no life was found.

The weather was equally unbearable. When explorers came, they found the lower parts too steamy for man or beast (though both lived there), and the top, accessible only by air, was too cold. No one from the City had ventured onto the middle layers, so they didn't know the climate there was more temperate.

The inhabitants were wholly uncivilized. They spoke a crude dialect of the common language but would rather kill a stranger than converse with him. Deadly beasts ran rampant. Armies of insects bit and stung. Some of the vegetation was poisonous. The place was the stuff of nightmares.

Once the rest of the world had been brought under submission, though, this mystery posed a challenge the City could no longer resist.

Envoys attempted a couple of peaceful forays, but each was met with determined resistance. The natives slaughtered the third embassage and sent their violated bodies out to sea in the dinghy in which they'd arrived.

That was the last insult. The City's next contact with Freemansland was with a missile.

The admiral aboard the City destroyer that launched it was amazed to find, rather than creating a pile of natural rubble, he'd blasted into a hollow structure. The soldiers on the personnel carriers landed in waves. The population was so stunned by the blast and overwhelmed by the invaders' numbers that they capitulated without much struggle. The gaping hole into the interior was sealed off and placed under guard, and another army was sent—an army of scientists—to investigate.

Their findings changed their understanding of the history of the entire world.

YOU CAN'T ARGUE with the evidence, according to Dr. Simelum. I expect he's right. But you can argue with the way it's interpreted.

The evidence clearly shows that the island now known as Freemansland was not a natural phenomenon, but a marvel of engineering that left the finest City minds breathless with awe. The materials forming its shell were known, but how it had been built, and for what purpose, and by whom, and when? Those questions could not be answered.

Scientists often date things by comparing them to similar objects of known or estimated origin. An item's purpose can be similarly ascertained. But Freemansland was unique. There was nothing to compare it to.

It was plain that at one time, people had lived within it as well as on it. But the artifacts they'd left behind, their advanced technology and written language, were as unique as the structure itself.

Evidence existed elsewhere of civilizations that pre-dated modern history. Some sort of cataclysm had wreaked global destruction, and the world's current population descended from the survivors. For that reason, some speculated that the massive six-tiered structure was a remnant of a previous society.

Others, pointing to the fact that nothing in the world even remotely resembled it, believed it had been built by visitors from another planet. I found that theory preposterous, but Simelum insisted it wasn't as unlikely as it may seem. "We have found ancient writings in Arkentak and the surrounding region that speak of the Visitors, the Strangers. The references are so vague we cannot be certain what they mean, but the description of these Strangers does not quite fit any known race."

I wasn't convinced. "How are they described?"

He did a quick search on the computer and pulled up an image of a fragment from an ancient book. I couldn't read the writing, but Simelum pointed to a section. "Right here, and I quote: 'Small, dark men of unusual strength, with eyes of bright glowing colors.'"

"Glowing eyes?" I narrowed mine. "Like the wild people of the wood on Freemansland?"

Dr. Simelum shook his head. "The words are *bright glowing colors*, but in the case of a stellasede, it is the sclera, the whites of the eyes, that sometimes appear luminescent, not the corneas. This doesn't describe the phenomenon you're thinking of." He glared at me as if impatient with my stupidity. "Moreover, the writings were not found in Freemansland. And that is the only place stelli are known to exist."

"They had to have gotten there from someplace, didn't they? Were they brought here by space aliens as well?"

Simelum frowned. "We are talking about science here, Miss Freeman, not science fiction—"

"Mrs. Standtall."

He pursed his lips. "The evidence seems to indicate that at some point in pre-history, our world was visited by human-like entities from a different world. Unlike fiction writers like yourself, I do not depart from the facts. Following the evidence to see where it takes us is no less fascinating than the sort of fabrications in which you indulge."

Grey must have sensed I was near the point of lashing out, because he put a calming hand on my shoulder. "I am not saying you are mistaken, Doctor, but if this is all the evidence we have for a visitation such as you describe, it is rather thin. What was it you told me earlier about the history of Freemansland?"

"Oh. Yes. There is no question that at one time, it was used as a penal colony."

I sighed. "Everybody knows that."

"Common knowledge is not always accurate. But in this case, we have found evidence to confirm it." He brought up images to illustrate. "In ruins on the uppermost tier of your strange homeland, we have found records of who was brought there, under whose authority, and for what reason. We have learned that at the time the prison was established, engines within the structure generated energy and projected it in a field of some sort around the entire island that gave the highest altitude a more temperate climate."

Okay, that was a surprise. "You mean Harsh was not always frozen?"

"If by *Harsh*, you mean the upper tier, then yes. What we call Tier One was formerly protected by an energy dome that allowed for a denser atmosphere and warmer temperatures than are naturally present. The residents—inmates, if you will—raised livestock and crops to feed and clothe themselves. Perched up there on top of the world, so to speak, on a pinnacle surrounded by ocean, they could not escape. So there were no guards, no overseers, no government apart from what they instituted themselves."

Grey radiated excitement. "This is where it gets interesting."

"I find it all interesting." I pointed to the image on the screen showing a record of a harvest of some crop for a year unknown to me. The writing was hard to make out, but it was similar enough to our modern language that it wasn't entirely gibberish. "And more concrete than your wacky space alien theory. You say you know who these people were? That is, my ancestors?"

Dr. Simelum nodded and pulled up something that looked like comparisons of DNA sequences. "For decades, we've known you people were related to the Kentans."

"What?"

"But we didn't know how that was possible, nor how close the relation." He highlighted one sequence. "This is your DNA."

I started to object, but he interrupted me. "We obtained this legally, when you were a ward of the City. Therefore, it is City property." He highlighted another graph. "This is taken from a native of Arkentak, one of the Kentan priestesses. The markers indicate a close familial relationship." Whether that sample was legally obtained, he didn't say.

I could see the similarities he pointed out, but how could I know the samples were really what he said? "I don't know much about reading these things."

"I suppose not. Here, let me show you DNA from other sources." One sample after another came up on the screen. "This is taken from a man of Watlandish heritage. This, a female from NaHora. Here is a sample of Nionese material. And this is from a horsefish."

Grey chuckled. "Why include that?"

"To show the differences between human and animal. I am no geneticist myself, but anyone can see that yours, Mrs. Standtall, shows a close connection with that of this Kentan woman. Genetically, you are cousins."

I could see what he was saying. "Okay, so my Freeman ancestors were Kentan. That's no shock. When I lived and worked in Arkentak, I could see the physical resemblance. What does that have to do with space invaders?"

"I never said anything about an invasion."

"I thought you did."

"Contact. Interaction. We have no evidence of aggression."

A sudden wave of weariness rolled over me. Too much emotion, too much food, and annoyance at this prickly pigeonhead made me want to go off somewhere to be alone. "Whatever. My ancestry is plainly not extraterrestrial." I gestured at the images on the screen. "Can we move on? You say you're planning an exhibit of art from Freemansland? I wasn't aware we had any artists."

"You are one yourself."

I sighed. "All right, I can come and do a book signing or something. That would take one room, not a whole Freemansland Hall."

Dr. Simelum turned to Grey. "Is she always so obtuse?" Without waiting for an answer, he pulled up more images. "What do you call this? And this? And what about this?"

"A jacket," I said. "A bag. A dragonskin chair. That's more of an industry than an art."

He shook his head. "And these?"

"Whisky bottles. Or wine. Usually whisky."

"Such as you won't find anywhere else in the world."

I shrugged. "I suppose not. But the only reason people created their own distinctive bottles was so other people would be less apt to steal them. It was like a label or a brand, so everyone would know what was yours."

"I see." Dr. Simelum nodded. "You are saying the art of Freemansland has a practical use, but you do not recognize it as art for art's sake."

"You could put it that way, yes."

"Why do you write? What is the practical purpose?" His smirk seemed to suggest he'd caught me in an inconsistency.

"It gives me a reason to get up in the morning."

His heavy brows rose.

"It keeps me from drinking myself to death. It reminds me I'm a citizen, not a besotted Freemanslander."

"It is a practical endeavor, then?"

"Wholly."

He smiled. "Interesting. I had no idea Freemanslanders see art in that way. What do you know about some of your people's other art forms? Pottery, distillery, leather working?"

I hoped to shock him with my answer. "I know how to kill and skin a dragon."

But his response disappointed me. His eyes widened in interest, not alarm. "Perfect! We have some artifacts you might be able to help us identify." He left the computer and hurried across the room. "Come along."

I looked at Grey, who seemed intrigued. We followed him.

This all had my head spinning. What did the ridiculous talk about extraterrestrials have to do with my supposed kinship with the Kentakans, much less the art of Freemansland? Dr. Simelum talked as he walked, but though Grey and I followed with our feet, I was too distracted to follow what he said.

After a moment I figured out he was talking about a reproduction the museum was making of something on Freemansland. My first thought was the miniature model of the island that Grey had commissioned for my aquarium, but then I realized he was talking about a room.

That was silly, as Freemansland buildings had only one room. If you needed more space, you built an outbuilding, like ablutions, or a storage shed, or—

That's when I caught on that he was talking about a dragon hunter's skinning shed, and had just asked, "Have you ever seen one? You describe the one in your books quite vividly. I confess we have modeled our reproduction as much on what you have written as on what we have found."

Entering a hallway on the other side of the main room, he turned. "I am aware, however, that the details you relate in your books cannot be counted on for accuracy, however intriguing it may all be." When we'd caught up, he led the way into a small room off the hall.

I answered as I entered. "I don't recall going into any detail as to the layout of a skinning shed." Once inside, my heart almost stopped at the horrible familiarity.

Grey took my hand and gazed around. "Did your father's skinning shed look like this?"

I clung to his hand. "Yes. Very much like it."

The room smelled familiar, too. It was as if they'd removed an actual skinning shed from Freemansland, board and stone, and put it back together here.

The doctor spread his arms. "So this is an accurate reproduction?"

I took shallow breaths, trying not to inhale the scent of the waterfir wood, the blood and dragon fat soaked into the skinning table, the memories... "Yes. I believe it is." My stomach churned.

"You believe so, or you know? Do you know from experience?"

I swallowed. "Like my Tia and Tuu characters, my father was a dragon hunter."

His face lit up. "Truly? Did you ever have the opportunity to see him at work?"

"Of course."

"Wonderful. Could you—" He held up a finger. "I wonder if you can identify something for me. Please wait, just one moment. I shall fetch it."

He almost ran out, leaving Grey and me standing there. I think we were both a little stunned by the professor's excitement.

Grey turned around, making a full circle. "So this looks like where your father used to work."

I tried to ignore my rising unease. "It's uncanny. It could be the very place. Table in the middle, with the trough to catch the fluids. Even the bucket under where the trough empties. Supply shelf with knives and towels."

"Those are towels? They look like grass mats."

"They are, more or less. But absorbent. We call them towels." *We?* "I mean, *they* call them towels. First time I saw a cloth towel, I didn't know what it was."

Dr. Simelum returned with a box in his hand. "One of our archivists brought in this tool, but we don't know what to make of it." He set the box on the table and pulled out the object. "It was found in the remains of what was probably a skinning shed—the very one we have reassembled here, in fact. Can you tell us what it was used for?"

"It's a fire siphon."

He blinked at the object in his hands, then at me. "Explain, please."

"When you're skinning a dragon, the first thing you have to do is siphon out the firewater. It flames about one second after being exposed to oxygen and burns at almost 4000 degrees. If it spills onto the table, you and your shed will be ash in no time. May I?" I reached for the siphon.

He handed it to me, and I described how it was used. "You lay the dragon across the table on its back and prop its mouth open." I glanced at the supply shelf. "I don't see a wedge, but ordinarily it would be up there with the knives."

"What does it look like?"

"A smooth, sturdy stick with a Y-shaped fork at both ends."

"So it's not a wedge shape?"

I shook my head. "No, we just call it that. Wearing gloves such as what you have over there on the shelf, you pry apart the jaws and wedge the mouth open. You need gloves because the teeth are so sharp. Even though the dragon's dead, it can still hurt you. Or kill you, if you're not careful with the firewater."

Dr. Simelum seemed fascinated. "I've never seen a dragon."

"You've studied Freemansland for three decades but never saw a dragon? You must never have actually lived there."

His eyes widened. "I never lived on the stillwater. What a thought! I spent most of my time inside the structure, though occasionally I ventured out onto the fourth level, the one you call Coldclime. Dreadful, dreary place, and too cold for dragons. It rains all the time. I cannot imagine how awful it must be on the lower levels, with the intense heat." He shuddered. "So you prop open the beast's mouth. What do you do with this?" He fingered the long, thin tube. "It is as fine as a needle."

"You locate the glands on either side of the mouth, just under the nostrils. You insert the siphon into the duct, work it down as far as you can, then pump."

I squeezed the trigger to demonstrate. "Slowly. The liquid is a pale blue color, just dark enough that you can see if you're in the right sac. If you pull up a red liquid, it's blood. White is fat—they have a lot of fat in the head area. You better hope it's blue the first time, because you don't want to go poking around and perforate the sac, or the firewater can seep out."

Dr. Simelum beamed. "This is wonderful! The incendiary liquid is drawn up through the catheter. What is the tube made of, incidentally? It's a very unusual material."

"Dragon rib bone."

Grey's brow furrowed. "How can you make something so flexible from bone?"

"Dragons have two sets of ribs. The outer set are fairly firm. The inner ribs are thinner and, as you can see, quite pliable. Tough, though. Very tough."

Dr. Simelum ran his hand around the circular disk in front of the trigger. "This looks like dragonskin."

"The wooden shield is covered with skin to make it flameproof. If a speck of firewater flies onto it, your hand will be somewhat protected from the flash. Dragonskin is impervious to flame, you know."

Dr. Simelum lightly tapped the sight tube. "This looks like a tiny telescope."

I nodded. "You look through the lens when you siphon the firewater, so you can see the duct without having to put your face near."

"And the liquid goes into that reservoir?"

"That's correct. When the vial is full, you wrap it in a thin scrap of dragonskin." With the siphon on the table, I demonstrated. "You ease the tube from the vial and at the same time, slide a disc across the top. Ordinarily there would be one here on this loop, but it's missing on this one."

I continued. "Then you seal it with these clamps so no air can get in, and ease the vial out. It's a good idea to hold the siphon as far away from your body as you can in case a drop of fire escapes in the process."

Grey seemed almost as intrigued as Dr. Semilum. "And it bursts into a four-thousand-degree flame the instant it's exposed to air?"

"Not the instant. You've got about a second from the time it hits oxygen until it blows. Some dragon hunters keep a bucket of water on the table in case of drips. A quantity of water will neutralize the liquid if it's only a drop or two."

Dr. Semilum examined the device. "Wonderful. Wonderful. I have puzzled over this for years." He actually smiled at me.

The strange feeling that assaulted me as soon as I'd stepped into the room had not lessened. If anything, it continued to grow. I'm not sure how to describe how I felt—light-headed and heavy at the same time. Explaining the use of the siphon gave me something to focus on and hold the sensation at bay, but the longer I stood there, the more I wanted to get out.

And at Dr. Semilum's creepy smile, panic crept up on me.

He stepped toward the barrels beneath the supply shelf. "We found salt residue in these. I assume salt was used in the skinning process somehow?"

I shook my head, clenching my jaw against the queasiness the motion produced. "For curing. Tanning." My ears rang and my voice sounded distant.

Or in a barrel.

"Not for skinning."

Dr. Semilum lifted the lid of one of the barrels. "Have you seen the procedure? Can you—"

I tasted the salt in my mouth and felt the burn in my eyes. Dr. Semilum's voice became Ibro's harsh laughter. Feeling the savage grabbing of horrible hands, I screamed.

Or at least, that's what Grey told me. My memory of the events ended with Dr. Semilum lifting the lid of the salt bin.

Grey says I ran into the hall, and when he tried to stop me, I attacked him, screaming obscenities. To avoid being kicked and clawed, he grabbed and restrained me from behind.

That's when my stomach expelled the remains of Jano's artistry in a most unaesthetic spew, and I passed out.

❦ Chapter 4 ❦

ONE OF US IS CRAZY, AND IT'S NOT ME

D R. SEMILUM WANTED to call for an ambulance, but Grey was afraid the emergency personnel would upset me even further.

He was probably right.

"I'll be okay," I said, seated on the floor in the hall with Grey crouched beside me. "You said yourself visitors to the Zavazda can sometimes be overwhelmed."

Dr. Semilum spoke up. "I've never known a visitor to vomit."

I didn't get the impression Grey was convinced I was all right, but he seemed unwilling to argue in front of Dr. Semilum. "We'll go back to the hotel. If you show any more signs of stress, I'm having you looked at. And I mean *any* sign."

"It was just a little indigestion." I scowled. "You're making too much of this." But I didn't try to stand, because I was pretty sure my legs wouldn't support me.

By the time the maintenance crew came to clean up my mess, Grey had gotten me to move to a chair in the larger room. After a short rest there, he took me back to the hotel.

When we'd arrived at the Zavazda that morning, it had seemed enormous. Now, it seemed to never end. Never. I wanted to get out. To get home. Where was home? I clung to Grey's arm, to the only reality I could count on. His solid strength. His goodness. His love. I walked in that and refused to let my mind wander anywhere else.

All was well, because Grey loved me. Ibro couldn't hurt me. And if I kept walking, I'd be out of this horrible maze eventually.

Grey put his lips to my ear. "How are you doing?"

"Good." I nodded. "Really. Whatever happened back there, I'm over it."

Except I wasn't.

I gave his arm a squeeze. Beneath the sleeve, that arm was scarred. The hidden disfigurement reminded me of his noble character.

I was scarred, too. What did my hidden disfigurement speak of?

⁂

"THAT WASN'T THE brain worms waking up," I told Grey in our hotel suite, "if that's what you're worried about."

His brow furrowed. "I want to believe you. But how do you know? How do you know you haven't had other incidents? You spend so much time alone. You could have blackouts and not know about it, couldn't you?"

"I did have another incident."

When his eyes widened in alarm, I hurried to add, "After you cut your hand, remember? When the doctor was pulling glass out of you."

"I thought you just fainted at all the blood."

I shook my head. "It was a memory jumping out and mugging me. Same as it was today. I can feel them coming, but I can't stop them."

"A memory?" He led me to the settee. "For it to cause a reaction like that, it must be a horrible one. Do you think—" He kissed my forehead. "I don't know the best thing to do in a case like this. I'd like you to tell me about it, but I don't want to push you."

I'd told Grey a great deal over the years. Almost everything. Not about Mayne. And not about the circumstances under which Riah and I had become wards of the City. That, I hadn't been able to put into words.

He was still talking. "But I think you should tell me. Whatever happened, it's too hard for you to bear alone."

Riah carries it with me, I wanted to say. But no, Riah was dead to me.

Riah was dead to me.

Trembling overtook me, and I wept in Grey's arms. One scarred, both powerful. Both held me. My face pressed against his breastbone, behind which a heart beat with love for me. *For me... for me... for me,* it beat.

I wanted to get inside him, to be absorbed by him, to be truly one with him. To be far above and beyond the Freemansland of my birth, my violation. To be a Standtall through and through, to no longer bear the stain of my birth, my pollution.

Behind my closed eyelids, scenes of Freemansland paraded, scented by a residue of vomit. Around my vile, quaking body, cashmere sleeves. Absorbing my tainted tears, fine Nypegian cotton shirting.

We were two people, one stained, one pristine. We would always be two people. I would never be clean. I would always smell like vomit.

I cried so hard, I think I'd have thrown up again had there been anything in my stomach. I seldom cried, but now I was doing it again, twice in one week. Maybe my brain worms *were* waking up. Maybe this was what it felt like to die.

GREY WAS PATIENT. He let me carry on like a hysterical child until I ran out of steam and my sobs faded to whimpers that ended in hiccups.

Then he peeled me off of his wet chest. "Let me get you some babunja tea."

I made no objection when he rose. *Better change your clothes while you're up*, I wanted to say, but I hadn't the strength to speak.

I didn't have the strength to stay on the settee alone, either. So after a few seconds, I got up and followed him, snuffly and weak and thick-headed.

He searched the cabinet and drawers in the small kitchen area. "There's no babunja here, and I didn't think to bring any. I'll have some sent up."

When you're a CFC, you can get anything you want.

So why did this wonderful man want me?

We both changed clothes. I had some tea. After I calmed a little, I wanted Grey to know. Even though I was afraid it would change things between us, I wanted to tell him, and he said he wanted to hear it.

So I told him, slowly and in small, carefully worded pieces, about that day. The day my first life ended.

I shared with him my most horrible secret. That not only had I caused my mother to die at the time of my birth, but I was also responsible for the death of my father. Papa came to the defense of my brother when Jeriah tried to protect me from Ibro. He'd died as a result.

Both of my parents were dead because of me.

IT CHANGED NOTHING between Grey and me. He didn't love me any less, and I couldn't possibly have loved him more.

But things changed between us anyway. Not because he learned the worst of my awfulness, but because of what he'd learned earlier.

He'd taken me to the Zavazda so I could see and hear for myself what he'd discovered there. But we'd never gotten to it, because Dr. Semilum took me to that recreated skinning shed first.

Grey explained it to me later, after we returned home. Once he was confident I was in my right mind, that my stelli were not on the move.

I guess that incident at the Zavazda shook him up pretty badly. Poor Grey.

What he told me next, though, shook me up. I won't say *poor me*, though. I'd been shaken from my earliest memories. But Grey, despite his education and experience, was sheltered from reality. He hadn't learned that we all have brain worms of one kind or another.

A couple of days after returning from the Zavazda, we sat in the media room with a grappleball game playing on the big screen. "So," Grey said, "you never heard the rest of the story."

He'd been listening to the game through an earpiece so the sound didn't distract me, and I sat nearby, drafting the final book in the Stillwater series. Though it would be a couple of years before it was published, I was eager to wrap up the whole, long story and let the characters move on. They couldn't remain children forever. Besides, ever since Mimma had suggested that I write novels for adults, I'd been itching to try. I even had a story line forming in the back of my mind.

It surprised me when Grey pulled out his earpiece and spoke to me. I glanced up at the game, still playing on the screen, then back to him. "What story?"

"About the relationship between Arkentak and Freemansland."

"Seriously? You want to talk about that instead of watching the game? Isn't this the MegaMatch?"

He made a face of disgust. "It is. But I've seen better grappleball played by academy kids in the Ellerja Games. The Claws are falling apart, and I can't stand to watch."

"So why is it still on?"

"I keep hoping they'll turn it around."

I knew little about the sport, but by way of making conversation, I repeated what I'd heard others say in years past. "Perhaps they should save their celebrations for after the game instead of partying the night before."

His eyes crinkled. "Perhaps."

Was he laughing at my comment?

"But seriously, I'd rather talk with you about Freemansland than watch the MegaMatch." The smile spread from his eyes to his mouth. "At least, this particular MegaMatch."

"Well, then, let's talk." I closed my computer and stood. "But first, I could use some crim. How about you?"

"Sure, thanks."

I made a pot and brought it in to where he frowned at the video screen. Then, sipping from my steaming cup, I listened to his strange story.

And I do mean strange. I could hardly believe what I was hearing.

He always had an interest in out-there stuff like religion and philosophy, so it's not like this was our first conversation that went in that direction. But it was the first time he put it in terms of truth—*This is what I believe*—rather than theory—*This is what some people say*. And I don't mind telling you, it made me uncomfortable.

According to his theory, Freemansland was built by an unknown culture prior to some sort of calamitous event that caused it to be abandoned. A hundred years or so after that forgotten calamity, the Kentans were visited by a people who looked much like us but were from another world—the small, stocky, bright-eyed aliens Dr. Semilum talked about. Crazy, right?

These supposed aliens allegedly told the Kentans—how they communicated with them, he didn't say—about some god of theirs.

They claimed he was not merely the god of their world but of all the universe. He'd supposedly created everything, everywhere. And he wanted everyone everywhere to acknowledge him as the supreme authority. Kind of like the City Fathers, except one individual rather than a triad of men, and ruler of every planet and star, not just one world.

The creator and lord bit wasn't too hard to deal with, the way he explained it. That is, I didn't believe it, but I could see how a person like Grey, with a bent toward mystical stuff, might decide some deity had created everything. I had never been wholly satisfied with scientists' explanations of the origins of the world. Even they admitted they didn't know how matter and energy and everything came about and were more or less guessing. It seemed just as plausible to think some power had created it. It had to come from somewhere, after all.

The problem was, he claimed this deity was not an impersonal power out there in space that left his handiwork to run on its own. No, Grey insisted this god was a person. Not a human like us, but a personality, a being that was not only aware of what every aspect of what his creation was up to at every moment, but who actually cared about it. Supposedly, he had intimate knowledge of, and loved, every individual person on every planet.

I crossed my arms. "Why would any god care about the likes of us? We're all idiots."

Grey's eyes crinkled. "True. But God is like a father. He knows his children's limitations, yet he loves them anyway."

"Humph. There's fathers and there's fathers. And if this god of yours is anything like *my* father, he'd leave us alone to kill ourselves. Which is pretty much what he's doing. I don't see how you can say he cares."

"Well, he apparently cares most about the people on a different planet." Grey shut off the television. "This game is not worth watching." He left his chair and sat beside me on the sofa. "I don't know why, but for some reason, this God took a particular interest in a planet called Earth and established a relationship with the people there."

"I don't imagine they appreciated it."

He gave me a puzzled look. "Why not?"

"I know you loved your father, but you wouldn't want him looking over your shoulder all the time, would you? Not that I believe any of this is true, but let's pretend. If I were them, I'd want him to go away and leave me alone."

"Apparently, that was more or less their response." Grey shrugged. "I don't know the details, but somehow the people weren't paying attention to what this God was trying to tell them. They lived much like we do in this world, hating one another, hurting and killing people, lying and being untrustworthy."

I tried to envision a fatherly god. "Not standing tall."

"Exactly. The people were so terrible that even when they wanted to do good, they couldn't." A sadness seemed to come over him. "A few wanted to be good. But no matter how hard they tried, they couldn't live up to their God's perfect standard."

I nodded. "Like you felt when you weren't able to save your father."

His face softened. "Something like that, perhaps."

"That's quite a story. But what does it have to do with Freemansland?"

"Well." He put his arm around me. "I know you think this whole thing is strange."

"Ridiculous might be a better word."

"I know, but just listen. Somehow, the people were so bad God couldn't have a relationship with them anymore, but he wanted to. So—" Grey gave me a questioning look. "You're going to think I'm crazy."

"I already do."

That's when he proceeded to tell me this god character was somehow made of three people, like the City Fathers are three people. But not like that, because it was one being, but three people. And one of them went to Earth, looking and acting exactly like an ordinary person, even to the point of being born as a baby. Except he didn't have a human father. His father was another of the three people that made up the god.

And when he was grown, this man-god, or god-man, whatever it was, allowed the wicked men to murder him. In some way I couldn't begin to fathom, his death was supposed to pay for all the wicked things that everyone had ever done and ever would do. And then, after he'd been dead for three days, he came alive again to demonstrate that he was a god and had power over death. And the reason he did it was so that anyone in the whole world who believed he really was god and worshipped him as such, would be absolved of every evil thing they'd ever done, and so be brought back into a forever relationship with the father-god who loved them.

By the time Grey got to that place in the story, I was hopelessly confused. "That still doesn't tell me what that has to do with Freemansland."

He gave a small smile. "I'm getting to that. I don't know how it happened, but somehow, some people on another planet heard about this. They were just as wicked as the people on Earth, and just as unable to dig themselves out of the hole they were in. When they heard about this God, they got all excited about the possibility that they could know him too. And somehow, that happened."

I lifted my brows. "What happened?"

"They believed the story, and they came to know this God. They didn't just know *about* him, but they *knew* him. He forgave them for everything they'd ever done, and their lives were changed. And they went to other planets to tell them about all this."

"And I suppose one of the places they went was Freemansland?"

Grey shook his head. "No, Arkentak. Quite a number of the people believed. And they quit worshipping the goddess Striden, because this God is superior to her. He's greater than anything."

"You're speaking in present tense."

"I am. But back to the past. The Kentans used that abandoned man-made island as a prison, and some of the prisoners were those exiled for rejecting their goddess. I don't think that was the only kind of criminal they sent there, but it seems many of them were. And the Sonmanist religion of Freemansland is the remnant of their beliefs. It's probably unrecognizable by now, but that's its origin."

He seemed to wait for me to say something, but I was too rattled to speak at first.

I finally found my tongue. "The Sonmanism of Freemansland came from space aliens."

"It does sound pretty funny when you put it that way, but—"

"Funny? I'm not laughing." I stood. "I'm going swimming. And I hope when I get back, you'll tell me this whole story is just a joke."

I was afraid he'd get up and follow me, but he didn't. He stayed where he was and called after me, "It's true, Freeman," then turned the video screen back on. Without the headphones. "You'll see that for yourself one day."

Sure, I muttered as I strode into the bedroom to get my swimsuit. *When fish fly.*

ꙮ Chapter 5 ꙮ

THE DEAL

A FEW DAYS after our bizarre conversation about the religion from space, Grey had to go back to work. When he was sent out of town a couple of weeks later, my breakdown at the Zavazda was a distant memory.

For me, at least. Or so I told myself. But as he prepared to leave, his whole body radiated concern. "You sure you'll be okay?"

"Of course. I'm always okay with you leaving. Anyway, I'm traveling too, day after tomorrow, remember?"

"Oh, yeah. That writing workshop in Mount Peel. I'll call you every day, if I can. If you don't hear from me, text me, all right? Just to let me know you're okay. At least once a day."

I narrowed my eyes. "Why are you so worried about me all of a sudden?"

"You know why. Because of the way you got, you know, so upset last week. And because you're in mourning for your brother, and—"

"I don't have a brother."

"That's what I'm talking about. You need to make up with him. You've been moping for—"

"I said I'm fine. If you're going, then go. Don't harass me."

He pulled out his watch and took a look. "You're right, I need to go." Then he picked up his bag. "But it's not harassment. When someone tells you what you need to hear, it's called love."

I shook my head. "Harassment."

"I love you, Freeman. Think about what I said. About your brother, and also about God."

"My name's not Freeman. I don't have a brother." I opened the door for him. "And I don't believe in space aliens."

He went through the door. "I'll call you."

It irritated me that he was right. About my brother, that is, not about the space god. I really was in mourning. I wanted to call Riah, to hear his voice. Better yet, a video call. I thought about him constantly. But I wasn't a Freeman anymore. I was Mrs. Ashgrey Standtall. I was a CFC. I was sober, a devoted, faithful spouse, and I didn't have a twin who was neither.

And that god stuff? When Grey and I had last talked about it—which had been a couple evenings before, after which I'd asked him not to bring it up again—I'd said, "If this god is such a great and powerful person-like thing, don't you think he'd communicate like a person? I mean, when we want to share knowledge with a large number of people, we write a book, right? Why can't this god do something like that ?"

Grey had smiled. Smiled! Which made me groan. "Oh, now you're going to tell me he *did* write a book?"

"There is a book that's attributed to him, yes."

I put my face in my hands. "Of course there is." Then I spread my fingers and peeked through them. "You're making this up as you go along, right? "

He shook his head. "I've seen it. Portions of it, anyway. At Dr. Simelum's research lab at the Zavazda. The originals are still in Freemansland, but he's taken scans, made duplicates. Soon as I get the chance, I'm going to try to get a copy for you. It's amazing. Once you read it, you'll see what I mean. All this will make sense to you then."

"All right. You get me the book, and I'll read it. Until then, I don't want to hear any more about it. Deal?"

He hesitated.

I raised my eyebrows. "Deal?"

"You have to promise to read it."

"If you get me a copy, I will. And in the meantime, we won't talk about it anymore, okay?"

He nodded. "Okay. It's a deal."

As I said before, things were different between us. Something had happened. Grey had changed. And he attributed it to this alien god.

But he was a man of his word, so I was confident he'd never bring up the subject again.

☀

MIMMA DECIDED THAT this year, the Standtall family should celebrate New Day at their Crater Lake estate on the island of Steefren. Apparently Silver and Pearl had convinced her to leave frozen Centre City during the winter months and spend the holidays in the sun.

I approved of the change in venue and looked forward to the outdoor activities Mimma had planned. As the time approached, however, an unseasonable tropical storm formed in the region. At first, it looked like it would miss us. But it made a sudden swerve toward Steefren shortly after we arrived, turning the planned agenda on its head.

As if that weren't enough to dampen the biggest holiday of the year, a virulent respiratory virus spread throughout everyone at Crater Lake—family, servants, and guests alike. Because the storm had suspended all travel between Steefren and the mainland, we had no access to medical care.

Ordinarily, at the first sign of a sore throat, we would go to a technician who would isolate the specific virus and tailor a treatment to target it. With the proper medication, the infection would be gone in twelve hours. But being isolated by the storm, we couldn't prevent the virus from spreading throughout the estate unchecked. Of the approximately fifty people at Crater Lake that holiday, only five or six remained healthy. I was not one of them.

Our fourth day there—the second since I'd gotten sick—I spent the entire afternoon in the bedroom, writing. And going through a ream of tissues.

Grey, hoping to avoid infection, kept to himself in the sitting room of our suite. I'm not sure what he did all day, and I was too miserable to care.

I was in the midst of drafting the adult book I'd been mentally plotting, and the story was as bleak as my environment. Outside, the screaming wind flung waves of rain against the house. The storm shutters protecting the windows blocked both the view and the daylight. Emergency generators provided us with basic needs, but the reserve lighting was dim.

My mood was darker than the gloomy corners of the room when Grey came in. "I've been listening to you cough. I hope you don't feel as bad as you sound." He handed me a glass of water.

"Thanks." I took the water and sipped it. "But I think I need something stronger than that." I coughed, holding the glass carefully to avoid spilling it, then took another sip. "I may sound bad, but I feel worse."

I set the glass on the nightstand, then closed my computer. "I can't write anymore. I need to sleep, but every time I try, I wake up coughing."

"Let me fix you an old family remedy. It won't cure you, but it will help you sleep soundly enough to forget your misery for a good twelve hours."

I shoved my computer to the foot of the bed. "I could go for that. Bring it on."

"I'll be back with it in a few minutes."

Though it was early in the evening, I got ready for bed, and he returned a short time later with a mug on a tray.

I sniffed the steam. Even with my clogged sinuses, I could smell a combination of babunja and alcohol as well as hints of spice. I tried a taste, but it was too hot to drink. "Oh, I don't want to burn my mouth."

"No," he said, "but drink it as soon as you can. It works best when it's piping hot, and it tastes worse when it's cold."

"It doesn't smell bad, from what I can tell. Pretty good, in fact." I inhaled the steam, but then had to set down the cup to cough.

He picked up my computer from the foot of the bed. "How's that new book coming along? Do you mind if I read it while you're sleeping?"

I finished coughing, then took a taste of the concoction. It wasn't terrible. "I'm probably two-thirds done with the first draft. Maybe it's because I'm feeling so bad, but I'm stuck. If you want, read it and see what you think." I took another sip. "So this is an old Standtall remedy?"

"No, from my mother's side of the family. The Standtalls don't get through our troubles by sleeping, we tough them out. Or so Papa used to say, even as he allowed Mimma to give him a cup."

I smiled. "I liked your father. And Mimma's the best." I inhaled the steam, then took another sip. "And this stuff's not bad."

The remedy worked. When I awoke sixteen hours later, my symptoms weren't gone, but I felt rested and ready to face anything.

After a shower, I went into the sitting room, where I found a pot of fresh crim on the sideboard. As I poured myself a cup, Grey came in with a tray. "Hungry?"

"Starved."

"I heard you in the shower, so I went and got you a little something. The kitchen staff is all sick, so it's not much. Just a couple of stale rolls and some fruit."

He laid the tray on an accent table, then sat across the room while I ate. "I read your manuscript. Just finished it this morning."

I didn't reply until I'd swallowed a mouthful of honeyed roll. "I'm afraid I'm in over my head, writing for adults. Do you think it's worth finishing?"

"I'm not sure how to say this, Freeman." He leaned back in his chair and crossed his legs.

"That's what I was afraid of. Well, if I'm not cut out for real novels, I can stick with children's stories."

"Don't put words in my mouth."

I stuck more food in mine and let him continue.

"You know I've always encouraged you to write. From the time you were a student in my class, I've said you have a way with words. And the success of your Stillwater series proves I'm not the only one who thinks that."

I nodded and chewed.

"But this story— Does it have a title yet, by the way?"

I shook my head and swallowed. "I haven't come up with one. But no matter. I doubt I'll ever finish it, so it doesn't need a name."

"Why don't you want to finish it?"

"I'm in over my head. I was kind of writing it for Mimma, you know. And for your father. I wanted to portray people like them who loved one another so completely, who were faithful through thick and thin. I wanted to show the depth of her pain when he died, how losing someone you love like that is a tangible pain, like losing a real part of yourself. People die in stories all the time, and sometimes it's sad, but I wanted the reader to really feel it. I wanted to celebrate goodness of character. To elevate the nobleness of a relationship like your parents' above the cavalier crassness of what most people call love. Does that make any sense?"

The corners of his eyes smiled. "It makes beautiful sense."

"But I can't do it."

"I disagree. Even though it's just a first draft, I'm already seeing all that in your story. You definitely *can* do it."

I shook my head. "No. I can make the reader feel their love, because—" I smiled. "Because I know that kind of love."

He smiled back.

"But I can't make anyone feel her pain, because I've never felt it. Not really. I've never lost my true love. I can describe what I've seen Mimma go through, but I can't truly portray it because I haven't truly experienced it."

"I pray you never do." I think his eyes filled with tears, but I couldn't be sure because my own vision blurred.

He cleared his throat. "I'm going to make a prediction."

"What's that?"

"You're going to finish that novel. Maybe not right away, but when you're ready, you'll finish it. And Brick House will publish it. And it will win a Centre."

That sent me into a fit of coughing.

Every fourth year, the Centre City Awards Committee, comprised of academics and officials from all over the world, bestowed awards in various fields. Such a prize was officially called the Centre City Award for Excellence in Literature (or whatever the category) Exceeding the Expected, but no one called it that. For all but the most formal purposes, it was simply called a Centre Award.

When mostly recovered from coughing, I choked out, "That's funny, Grey. I was born on Freemansland."

"What does that have to do with anything? Excellence is excellence. That's all they look at."

I coughed some more. It wasn't like him to be sarcastic, but he couldn't honestly think the awards were anything other than political.

Grey gave me a glass of water to soothe my throat. "I'm serious. The bones are that good. Once you've got it fleshed out, it will leave people gasping."

Now that I was awake after that wonderful, long sleep, all my congestion had awakened as well, and dealing with it prevented me from arguing. But, warmed though I was by his praise, I didn't see how that story was all that special.

MIMMA WAS NOT among the few who escaped the respiratory virus. Always the gracious hostess, however, when the medical technicians finally reached the island with their equipment, she insisted on being the last to be treated. In the meantime, she made use of the old family remedy and slept her worries away.

There was a problem with that tactic. It's good to sleep when you're sick, but if you lie in bed too long, pneumonia can set in. By the time the doctor arrived to examine her, both lungs were full, and the infection had spread throughout her body.

A week after New Day, Mimma's days ended.

As her oldest son, Grey served as First Survivor.

It was a horrible time. But within a year, I was glad she was gone, so she didn't have to see what happened next.

❧ Chapter 6 ❧

───◆───

WHAT HAPPENED NEXT

───◆───

TEN MONTHS AFTER Mimma died, I spent the morning with my publicist preparing for the upcoming release of the last book in the Stillwater series. This included a guest spot on the popular talk show, *The City Slate.*

Before the show's filming, I had lunch with Jena Trebb, the illustrator and cover designer I'd worked with from the beginning, and two writer friends, Krin Mossa and Abi Plank.

Krin picked the croutons off her salad. "Why can't I remember to ask them to not put these on? There's no point in eating a salad if you're going to put bits of fat-slathered starch on top."

I picked up my sandwich. "I like croutons. They're crunchy and good." I took a bite and added, with my mouth full, "Kinda like this sandwich."

Jena watched me chew, her bean-protein wrap untouched on her plate. "I think you've ordered a fish sandwich every time we've had lunch together. Is that all you ever eat?"

Abi had a bean wrap, too. "All that bread isn't good for you." She nodded toward Jena's lunch. "With a wrap, you get the good insides of a sandwich but without all the carbohydrates."

Having finished dissecting her salad, Krin drizzled on a little vinegar. "Jemma doesn't care about that. She can eat anything and still look like she's twenty. How do you do it, kid?"

"I swim a lot. But mostly, I eat lots of fish."

"But the fillet you're eating is breaded and deep fried." Jena shuddered. "That should put fat on you by the layer."

I shrugged. "I eat what I like. I figure if it doesn't make me sick, it's not going to hurt me." Why did they always have to make such a big deal about these things?

I was relieved when Abi changed the subject. "I wish you were coming to the party tonight. It's going to be fun."

That was something else I couldn't understand: how anyone could enjoy the loud music, shouted conversations, and crush of people at a Centre City party. Sometimes I went to one because it was expected, but I bowed out whenever I could. "I already told you. We're having a party of our own, for Grey's birthday."

Krin pretended to pout. "And we're not invited?"

"It's small, family only." Actually, the only guests were Bark and Pearl, and all we were doing was going out for mirtositi.

"Family?" A wicked smile spread across Krin's face. "Does that include your actor brother-in-law? Oh, please, invite me!"

My phone rang, and I pulled it from my bag. "Maybe next time." I frowned at the phone. It said the call was from Ministry Security. Not Grey's work number, but some generic Ministry Security code I didn't recognize. "I don't know who this is, but I'd better take it."

The male voice answering my hello was deep and businesslike. "Mrs. Standtall, this is Ren Gans from Ministry Security. I and my partner, Kalto Beam, are outside the restaurant. We need you to leave the table and come with us, please."

My stomach did a flip, and the taste of my sandwich turned sour in my mouth. I turned to look out the window. Two men in uniform stood outside, one of them talking on a phone.

"I'm sorry, what?"

"We're sorry too, ma'am. Your husband has had an accident, and we're here to take you to him."

My vision dimmed, my ears rang, and I swallowed hard against the nausea that threatened to overtake me. "I see." A slow breath helped me regain control. "Thank you. I'll be right there."

The ladies stared at me, and Jena said, "What was that all about?"

"I have to go." I slipped my phone back into my purse with shaking hands. "Would one of you be so kind as to take care of my bill when it comes?" I stood. "I'll pay you back. Just let me know what I owe you."

I was already on my way to the door when Jena called, "Don't worry, hon. I've got it."

⁂

I WONDERED HOW my legs held my weight as I exited the restaurant. I hovered on the edge of collapse, physically and emotionally. All I could think about was Grey's father in that death chair. Except in my mental image, it was Grey who sat there.

One of the men nodded to me as I approached. The other stepped toward a waiting car and opened the door. Neither spoke.

Neither did I as I got into the back seat. I was glad to sit.

One of the men closed the door. Still wordless, they both got in the front, leaving me alone in the back.

A wave of panic rolled over me. I pawed at the door, searching for a window control. I needed air.

The car moved forward, and my stomach churned. "Is there any way you can open a window back here?"

Neither turned around. "Sorry, ma'am."

I leaned my head back and breathed slowly, trying to control the nausea. To focus on Grey instead of my churning stomach. They said he'd had an accident. They didn't say he was dead. If he was injured, he'd need my support. I needed to be strong for him.

I thought of Mimma. She had always been a rock.

Even in her death chair, she hadn't sagged.

I was a Standtall by marriage, too. Just as she was. I would be a rock for Grey. Whatever happened, I would be a rock. For Grey.

So I told myself as the car threaded through the streets of Centre City, carrying me to... my guardians in the front seat had never told me our destination, and I didn't ask.

Nor would I ask. I would be Mimma, for now. I would be patient. I would be serene. I would be a rock.

I wanted to bash one of those heads in the front seat with a rock and demand that he tell me what was going on.

I breathed slowly. My stomach ceased its churning, its contents lying like a lead sinker in my gut.

We rode like this for over an hour. I watched the minutes on the dashboard clock roll over, one by one, seventy-two times. The Security men never spoke, but they seemed to text each other several times.

What was it they weren't telling me?

The car turned down the road leading to the military hospital where I'd been taken after the bombing. If it was a hospital, not a morgue, that meant Grey was alive, didn't it? But there was probably a morgue here, too. I'd have to wait and see where the car ended up.

Ended up. Where *would* this all end?

If it were with Grey in a death chair, I'd officiate as First Survivor, accept the death beads, then take a gun and splatter my brain worms all over the room.

If he lived, I'd be a rock for him. No matter what. He'd do the same for me.

The car pulled up to an entrance marked Citizen Emergency. The backseat doors remained locked until after the Security men were both out. Then the lock disengaged and one of the men opened the door.

Between my two guardians, I walked to the entrance. The doors opened, and two more Security men gave my cohort a nod before turning their expressionless faces to me. One said, "Please come with us, ma'am."

I went, standing tall. My legs did not wobble. I was a rock.

"JEMMA." BROSE L'NEE looked up at our approach. He spoke to my chaperones. "Thank you, gentlemen. That will be all."

The men nodded, turned, and headed the other direction. Not that I paid them much mind, for Brose had my full attention.

He was Grey's immediate supervisor, and a good man. I had met him and his wife, Nelia, at a Security party a couple of years ago, and Nelia and I became friends.

"Brose, what—"

Before I got the words out, he wrapped me in a hug. "I'm so sorry, Jemma. I don't know how this happened."

My rocky patience threatened to crumble, and I pulled away. "How *what* happened? What the slime is going on?"

I flushed at my slip of the tongue, but he didn't react. "Ashgrey is in surgery. It's going to be awhile. Come sit down, and I'll tell you what I know."

He brought me into a small waiting room where a newsfeed played on a video screen mounted high on one wall. A small woman about my age looked up when we entered. Her clothes were simple, her appearance rumpled, her face strained. Seeing me, she stood.

Brose introduced us. "Jemma, this is Ina Kerb, one of our investigators. Kerby, Jemma Standtall."

I shook her hand. "Kerby? Grey mentioned you not long ago, but I didn't realize Kerby was a woman."

Her brows rose—ordinary, non-CFC brows. "He mentioned me?"

"He told me his co-worker Kerby had a litter of goshonds ready for adoption. He asked if I wanted one."

She perked up a little. "Do you?"

Who cares? I wanted to scream. *Tell me what happened to Grey!* But Mimma would be kind enough to answer the question. "No. He's been trying to talk me into getting a kyukur for the longest time. Says they're not only protection but good company as well. But I don't like the thought of keeping an animal in the house."

Brose gestured to a row of chairs. "Let's sit down."

I took a seat. "Tell me what happened, Brose."

Kerby put her hand on my arm. "Let me tell her. I was there."

"You were where?" I struggled to stay calm.

"Your husband and I went to the Tarquin district to check out a lead. Walking down a street, we passed a doorway. A man stepped out of it and shouted, 'Hey! Standtall!' We both turned, and the man—" She swallowed. "He shot Ashgrey. Soon as we turned around. Fired three times before I could react." She took a breath. "Ashgrey fell. I tackled the man and disarmed him." Her voice broke. "I'm so sorry. It all happened so fast."

"Who was this guy? Where is he now?"

Brose answered. "He's in custody. Has head injuries from Ms. Kerb slamming him against the pavement to subdue him, but we'll question him when he's able to answer."

Hard to believe the diminutive Kerby could incapacitate an armed man, but of course she was well trained. My stomach was flipping again. I took a slow breath. "Ashgrey's alive, though. He's in surgery, right?"

Kerby's eyes filled, and Brose answered for her.

"It doesn't look good." He took my hand. "He was shot in the face, Jemma. All three times. It's a miracle he wasn't killed instantly."

I pulled away and gripped the chair arms with both hands, trying not to visualize what he was saying. Shot in the face... I wanted to put my head down to keep from passing out, but my lunch would come up if I leaned over.

Brose was talking, but I couldn't hear him through the buzzing in my head. I stared at the floor, focusing on a piece of dirt someone had tracked in. Not dirt, it was a tiny stone. Flat along one edge, with a—

Brose's hand was on my arm. "Jemma? Are you all right?"

I played back what he'd just said. I hadn't listened, but it still sat in my mind. *The City's best neurosurgeon is on his way here. In the meantime, the doctors on staff are trying to keep him alive, keep him stable. All we can do is wait and hope.*

I stared at the little piece of stone. *I will be a rock for him.* "He's still alive. As long as he's alive, I'm okay."

Kerby put her hand on my other arm. "Is there anything I can do for you?"

"I'd prefer that you both not touch me." I shook off their hands and crossed my arms. "Thank you."

I think they exchanged glances, but I kept staring at the pebble.

Kerby rose. "I can't stay. I have to go through the post-violent-act protocol, but I wanted to see you first. Explain what happened."

I nodded but didn't look up.

Brose stood. "You're right, Kerby, check in with the counselor, then go home. I'll let you know as soon as we learn anything."

He embraced her in a professional way. "You going to be all right? Do you have someone to stay with you? You shouldn't be alone."

"Thank you, Mr. L'Nee, but I won't be alone."

Glancing up briefly, I caught the weak smile she tossed my way.

When I didn't lob one back, her face turned grave. "I'm sorry, Mrs. Standtall. I reacted as fast as I could, but—"

I forced myself to sound pleasant. "I know you did. I don't blame you. And please, don't blame yourself." I swallowed. "I'm sure this is very hard for you." I couldn't imagine the horror of what she'd just seen, but I had no more words for her. I had none for anyone.

She bit her lip and nodded. "Thank you."

I resumed my study of the floor by my feet, and she left. Skittered out. Like she wanted to stay but shouldn't, wanted to say something but couldn't. Wanted to escape, but her legs were too short to do it gracefully. Skitter was all she could manage.

I tried to visualize what she'd told me, but the image—the missile slamming into my husband's face (even now, I cringe as I say this), his body falling, the flesh, the blood, the—I wouldn't allow the picture to form.

Instead, I pictured the mousy little Kerby. Child-sized. Girlish face. Straight, stringy hair hacked just-below-chin-length and tucked behind the ears. With my Ashgrey? No. I knew what attracted his eye, and she wasn't it. She was a co-worker, nothing more. Of that, I was confident.

But she had been with him. They had walked together. Talking casually. Comparing notes. Maybe sharing a private joke. A subtle one, the only kind Grey appreciated.

And then Grey on the ground, a felled tree, and little Kerby springing like a wild rikicat to defend him. No, not a cat with claws and fangs. A marsh bear. In miniature. Knocking the man off his feet—I knew the moves she must have used, for I'd been trained in them myself—the gun from his hand, his head against the pavement—adrenaline rushing, not knowing what she was doing until it was done, and then...

Grey on the ground, with his face—

That pebble on the floor. Had I tracked it in? No, the soles of my shoes were too smooth to pick it up. It could have been here for days. How often did they clean the floors in this room?

"Is there anyone you'd like me to call?"

I looked up. Brose still stood, his expression pained.

"No." I shook my head. "Thank you." Then a thought eked its way into my consciousness, and I reached for my phone. "Thank you for reminding me." I selected my publicist's number.

She picked up on the first ring. "Jemma? I'm on my way to the studio. I'm not late, am I? No, it's not even half past yet, and we're not due until—"

"Change of plan." I interrupted her. "I'm not going to make it. You'll have to do the interview for me."

"What? No, Jemma, I can't do that. It's *you* they want. Nobody cares about—"

"Can't be helped. Something's come up. Just cover it for me, would you? I'll explain later. Thanks." I hung up before I broke down.

Brose eased into the chair beside me. "I could have done that for you. If there's anyone else you need to call, let me know."

I nodded, breathing slowly, trying to regain control.

ALMOST TWO HOURS later, the video screen on the wall announced the upcoming visit of world-famous author J. S. Freeman as a guest on the evening's edition of *The City Slate*.

I'd been blocking out the noises coming from the screen, but the sound of my name caught my attention.

The show would be filming now, but without J. S. Freeman. They'd better change their announcement. The call to my publicist reminded me I had another appointment to cancel.

Brose had gone to stretch his legs, but I wouldn't have asked him to make the call for me anyway. Not sure exactly what I would say, I pulled out my phone and called Bark.

The call went to voicemail. I disconnected without leaving a message and called Pearl instead.

Voicemail again.

Back to Bark. Two rings, then, "Hey, Jemma! Through filming your spot already?"

"No." I swallowed. "I, ah, I'm not at the studio. I'm at Walpin Rush."

"Walpin Rush. You mean like the military hospital?"

"Yeah, like that. I'm here with Ashgrey. He's, um— That is, I'm not really with him, I'm here because he's here, and—" I took a breath.

"Jemma?"

"You really need to come, Bark. You and Pearl. You need to be here."

A short silence. "Okay. That's absolutely okay. What happened? You're okay, though? You said you're there with Ashgrey, but you're okay yourself?"

I nodded. But we weren't on a video call, so I needed to speak. "I'm all right." What a lie. I was anything but. "I'll tell you about it when you come."

"What— Okay. I'll be there—we'll both be there, in... looks like about forty minutes. Is that okay?"

"Yes, and if you say okay one more time, I'll scream in your ear and deafen you."

"That wouldn't work. The phone filters out dangerous frequencies."

I had to smile. "Just get here, would you?"

I put my phone away as Brose came back carrying two disposable cups full of something. "I brought you a crim."

"Thanks." I took the one he offered and tried not to make a face at the odor wafting up in the steam. Whatever that stuff was, it wasn't crim. "Looks hot." I set it on a nearby table. "I'll let it cool. What do I owe you?"

"Nothing." He took a sip of his own and made a face. "Yeah. It'll scorch ya. Well, Ash's status is unchanged. The neurosurgeon's still in the air. Meanwhile, our boy's hanging in there. They've got a reconstructive guy coming in too."

"I just talked to his brother. He and his wife are in town for a visit. We were supposed to go out tonight for his birthday."

"Oh, yeah. His birthday was tomorrow." Brose let out a long sigh.

"His birthday still is tomorrow, unless they've changed the way the calendar works." I stood. "Bark won't be here for over half an hour, so I'll take a walk before he comes."

"That's good. You could use a break."

I picked up the cup and took it with me. At the nearest restroom, I emptied it down one of the sinks. As it ran out of sight in a steaming trickle, I pondered my life going down the drain with it.

I tossed the empty cup in the trash receptacle and glared at the forty-year-old woman in the mirror. She looked haggard. Angry.

I experimented with expressions, trying to duplicate Mimma's face of loving grief. There, that was it. Yes. That expressed the sort of patient devotion she exhibited. Strength in a sea of stress.

I practiced keeping the expression while speaking. "Thank you for coming. I am Jemima Standtall. And I am a rock."

❧ Chapter 7 ☙

<hr>

TWELVE MONTHS LATER

<hr>

I COULD WRITE AN entire book about the events of the year that followed, but truly, I haven't got it in me.

Nor would it move the story forward, and move forward we must. Even as it stands, it will be a race to see which we reach first: the end of this tale, or the end of me. So we must move on.

Bark called me about twelve months after the shooting. "Pearl and I would like to have a birthday party for the brudder. Nothing big, just close family, maybe a friend or two. Think he's up for it?"

It was a video call, and I tried not to frown as I hesitated. "I'm not sure. His birthday is certainly something to celebrate. It's huge. But—where are you thinking of having it?"

If he sensed my irritation, it didn't register on his eager, boyish expression. "Here at our place in Drevadell. I know, it would be a tiring trip for him. But that leads me to the rest of my plan."

I reclined on the settee where I'd been watching my fish, trying to remember what it was like to be carefree on Freemansland. "It would be quite a trip for both of us."

It made me weary just thinking about the stress, not to mention the enormous chunk of time it would take from my already-strained writing schedule. And the fact that I'd never liked parties under any circumstances. But I didn't want to appear ungrateful.

"Pearl and I were thinking—well, this was her idea, not mine. I love it, but it never would have occurred to me to make the offer. She's the thoughtful one."

Was this conversation confusing, or was my brain too tired to follow it? "Make what offer?"

"The other part of the plan." Bark's expression and voice simmered with suppressed excitement—much like Grey used to be when he had a surprise for me. "Like you said, it'll be a big trip. You'll probably want to bring him a couple of days early, so by the day of the party, he'll be rested up enough to enjoy it."

"Yes, that would probably be wise…"

"And then the next day, after the party, what do you say you leave him here with Pearl and me for a while?'

I blinked at the beaming face on my screen. "Huh?"

"Let us give you a break. You can go wherever you want, do whatever you want, for as long as you want. Take a week, take a month, take—"

"Bark, you don't know what you're saying."

Pearl leaned in then. Apparently she'd been sitting nearby, but I hadn't seen her until now. "We'll help you the first couple of days you're here so we can see the routine. And if you're not completely confident about leaving him, you don't need to, of course. But please, let us help you. You'll wear yourself out going it alone."

"Besides." Bark grew serious. "It isn't good for him to be so dependent on you for everything."

"I'm not alone. I have help a couple days a week. And he's getting more independent all the time." A thud from the bedroom made me pause, every nerve activated. "Slime. I mean, glish. Hang on." With some difficulty, I rose from the settee. My hip ached, my shoulder throbbed, and nothing seemed to work the way it used to.

I kept up the conversation as I walked toward the back of the house. "Sounds like he's up. We had a bunch of tests and were with doctors all day today, and I'd hoped he was worn out enough to sleep without me having to drug him. I just hate doing that, but he usually won't even lie down otherwise. Hang on a sec."

In the bedroom, I turned on the light. Grey lay half out of the bed, caught in the safety rail. He'd apparently flung his hand onto the bedside table that held his airflow device, knocking it down. That must have been the thud I'd heard. The mask lay on the floor as well, as if he'd pulled it off and flung it away.

He must have been watching the doorway, for he stirred as soon as I walked in. His one dark eye blinked at the light, then glowered at me with disturbing intensity.

I approached the bed, keeping the phone's camera directed away from Grey. His position was all the more undignified because he refused to wear clothes to bed. "Are you stuck? What were you trying to do? You should have called me." I set the phone down on the table and picked up Grey's call button. "You can reach this, right?"

Apparently unconcerned about being caught in the bed rail, Grey lunged toward my phone and snatched it up. "Who?" His voice had a strange whistling quality.

"I'm talking to Bark. Let's get you into a more comfortable position, and then we can talk to him together."

Grey looked at the screen. "Hey. Brudder." He turned it so I could see. "Look. Bark."

I tugged at his leg but couldn't budge it. "Yes, I was just talking to him. You want to help me here?"

He looked at me. Though his reconstructed face didn't allow for much expression, I'd learned to interpret the subtle cues, and he seemed to be puzzled.

"Help me get you untangled. I want to move this bed rail down. Then we can sit here and talk to Bark together." I reached toward the phone but didn't try to take it. If I did, he may have misinterpreted my intent and tried to keep it from me. "Let me set that down for a sec until we can get you straightened around."

"He won' go 'way?"

I shook my head. "He won't go anywhere. I'll just set the phone down for a minute."

Bark said, "Don't worry, big brudder. I'll wait."

Grey relinquished the phone, and I set it on the table. After getting Grey arranged and decently covered, I sat beside him and picked up the phone. "Okay, we're back."

Bark grinned. "So you are." Pearl and Bark sat together on their bed too.

Pearl waved. "Hi, Ashgrey. Nice to see you."

Grey lifted one hand in an aimless wave. "Hi."

I leaned against him so we'd both show up on the screen. "Bark and Pearl want to give you a little birthday party at their place in Drevadell. Would you like that?"

He stared at the screen. "When'd he say that?"

"That's what he and I were talking about before I came into your room. What do you think? Would you like to visit Bark and Pearl?"

He ran his finger across the screen, maybe wondering if he could feel their faces as well as see them. "Birthday? How old?"

Bark chuckled. "*Really*, old, man. That's why we want to throw you a party. You're coming up to the half century mark."

Grey turned to me for confirmation.

If I looked him in the eye, I could stand it, though the rest of his face still made me want to cry. "It's true. Your fiftieth birthday is next week."

Something like a smile played at the corners of his lips, and he looked at the screen again. "You gonna gi' me a party?"

"That's right, brudder. You slept through your last birthday, so you can eat twice as much cake this year."

The lower half of Grey's mask-like face grinned. "I like to eat."

The rest of us chuckled, because it was so true.

For months, Grey had been sustained with only a feeding tube. After his mouth was successfully reassembled, he could take liquids, and once he mastered that, pureed foods. He'd progressed to solids a few weeks ago, provided everything was in small pieces and easily chewed. Since then, he couldn't seem to get enough of eating.

The four of us talked—Bark, mostly, with occasional comments from Pearl or me, and a whistling mumble from Grey now and then—for several minutes. The longer the conversation went on, the more animated Grey became, until it was obvious he'd had enough.

Bark took the initiative to bring the conversation to a close. "It's past your bedtime, isn't it? You're going to need your rest if you're going to come visit us."

Grey shook his head.

"He's right," I said. "We all need our sleep."

Grey shook his head harder and clasped the phone to his chest. "Not tired."

I pointed to his death grip on the phone. "You can't talk to Bark if you're smothering him."

Grey pulled the screen back to where he could see it, and I thought his face showed concern. "Y' okay?"

"Sure, we're fine." Bark yawned in a natural, believable way—he was an actor, after all. "But I need to hit the sack. I've got to get up early tomorrow. We'll talk to you later, brudder."

"Bye, Ashgrey! Love you!" Pearl blew him a kiss and Bark waved.

Grey waved back, and a moment later the word "Disconnected" flashed across the screen.

My heart welled with love for Bark and Pearl. I wished they were nearer. I wished I didn't want to lean on them so much.

Grey stared at the dark screen, then gave it a little shake.

"We'll talk to them again another day. And we'll see them face-to-face soon. That will be even better."

With an attitude of disgust, he dropped the phone onto the bed.

"Let's try to get some sleep now, okay?"

Sleep. I needed it desperately. But Grey was wound up. I knew the signs. If I didn't give him something to relax him, he'd be awake all night, demanding to eat, to play a game, to eat again, to talk, to exercise, to eat. All those things were good for him, but he couldn't do any of them alone, and I'd already been up for eighteen hours after only three hours' sleep the night before.

I got off the bed and slipped the phone into my pocket. "How do you feel? Does your head hurt?"

He stared at me with that one eye. I wished I knew how much he understood.

No one had expected him to make it the first twenty-four hours. Even the most hopeful prognoses had him in a semi-vegetative state the rest of his life. For him to have recovered so many functions and continue to make improvement defied explanation. I was fed up with hearing the word "miracle," but there was no medical term to describe what was happening.

If it was a true miracle—whatever that was—it was an exhausting one. An emotional roller coaster that had me clinging to the sides of the car to keep from flying out.

As he stared at me now, I wondered if he knew what I was thinking. Which was, "One way or another, you have to give me some peace."

A moment later, he tore his gaze away and struggled to move his legs off the side of the bed. "Gotta go."

"To the bathroom? Sounds like a good idea." I helped him sit on the edge of the bed, then got his walker. "Here you go. Do you need me to come with you?"

He grasped the walker and heaved himself up to stand. "Notta baby."

"I know that." I bit my lip. "You most certainly are not a baby. But I'd be happy to help if you need it."

He didn't answer. Just made his shuffling way across the room. After a dramatic weight loss followed by a rapid gain, everything on that naked, aging body wobbled and sagged.

I resisted the urge to go with him as he got himself through the doorway then shut the door behind him. Should I listen to make sure he was all right? Or would he be offended at my lack of confidence? His emotions were unpredictable.

I tidied the room and straightened the bed. What was that flat box-like thing tucked into the covers at the foot of the bed? I had to pull off everything but the bottom sheet to get at it, but when I saw what it was, my eyes filled.

It was our betrothal commemorative. The young Grey and even younger Jemma gazing into one another's eyes. I ran my finger along the glass that covered Grey's chiseled, perfect face, remembering the day. My naiveté. My eager willingness to exchange all hope of returning to Freedom for the privilege of knowing this man's love.

This man who was no more.

I set the frame on the dresser and remade the bed. He was making progress every day. Who was to say how much more he would recover? It was as much a guessing game for the doctors as it was for me. All anyone could do was wait and see.

And hope.

I picked up the photo again. Without daring to hope.

WITH AN EAR toward the bathroom, I sat on the bed and stared at the photo. Grey had been so desirable then. Even when I still feared intimacy, his physicality attracted me. His love, his patience, his gentle concern, conquered my fears, and my desire for him only grew stronger over the years.

In the mirror across the room, I critiqued my image. My observant gaze darted back and forth between the old photo and the present me. I had nothing to be ashamed of in the looks department. I was older, yes, but I wore the maturity gracefully. Any fifty-year-old man would be delighted to call me his wife.

Anyone but Grey. As far as he was concerned, my sole function was to wait on him hand and foot. To entertain him. To care for him like a mother cares for a child. Except this toddler was a giant.

In the bathroom, the toilet flushed. A moment later, water ran in the sink.

One of the neurologists had told me Grey would never be capable of experiencing arousal. As the doctor told me this, I got the impression he was open to the possibility of helping fulfill this need for me, should I ask. I didn't. I didn't even acknowledge that I picked up on the suggestion.

The same doctor told me Grey would never come out of his coma. And if he did, he would be unable to use any of his limbs, nor be able to swallow, eat, or talk. Yet he was doing all these things now, and more. Might not his libido also return?

I was in the prime of my life. This wasn't fair. It simply was not fair.

The bathroom door opened, and Grey shuffled out behind the walker. From the smell that wafted out with him, I had no doubt what he'd been doing in there.

He'd flushed, though. And washed up. Difficult as his condition was, he was truly making remarkable progress. But I couldn't help asking, "Are you clean?"

By way of answer, he maneuvered the walker in a half circle so that he faced the bathroom again and bent over to show me.

I suppressed a smile. "I see you are. I shouldn't have worried."

He turned back and moved toward me. When he saw the betrothal commemorative in my hand, his forward movement stopped, his expression puzzled. "Where'd y' find?"

"It was stuck at the end of the bed, under the sheets. What was it doing there?"

He didn't answer but moved toward me with greater animation. When I set the photo on the bedside table, he headed for it. Resting his forearms on the walker, he picked up the commemorative with both hands and ran his fingers over the faces behind the glass.

"Who these?"

"That's you and me, when we were betrothed. Remember when we had this photo taken in Alosmtak?"

He narrowed his eye as if the effort to remember pained him. He shuffled sidewise to sit on the bed, where he stared at the photo. "'S not me." He reached up to his face and touched it gingerly.

I moved the walker out of the way and sat beside him. "Of course it is. That's what you looked like when the photo was taken. But that was quite a few years ago. See, I don't look the same anymore either. We were both younger then."

He looked at the photo and then at me. "You still... pretty." He pointed back at the photo. "Not me."

Had he been looking at himself in the bathroom mirror? Did he understand why his face was so altered? "But you're still my husband, no matter what you look like. You're my husband forever. Remember?"

He hung his head.

When I reached for the photo, he let me take it and put it on the table.

"Do you remember what husbands do?"

I was sure he didn't, but it was worth a try.

He didn't merely shake his head. His whole upper body twisted in a negative response.

"Maybe we can figure it out together."

He allowed me to help him into the bed, though he didn't lie down.

"That's okay, that's good. How about I get in with you?"

He didn't answer. Didn't look at me. Didn't glance up when I removed my clothes. Grunted when I sat close beside him.

When I pointed out the differences between the male and female torso, he did turn his head to observe the features as I described them. When I touched him, he flinched.

"You can touch me back," I suggested.

He did, in a hesitant, exploratory sort of way. When I suggested we lie down instead of sitting, he made no objection.

"Remember when we used to do this?" I demonstrated.

He didn't answer, but neither did he push me away.

Nor did he respond. Until he finally said, "Feels funny."

I nuzzled his neck. "Funny good?"

He grabbed my hand. "No." His face twisted. Then he put his hands to his head. "Make it go 'way."

Make what go away? Physical pain? Ghosts of memory? Comprehension of his incapacity?

Still taut with desire but also tender with compassion, I kissed his scarred cheek. "You know I love you, don't you?"

Head in his hands, he curled away from me. "Make it go 'way."

I rose from the bed and slipped on my outer garments. "I'll do what I can."

I crossed the room and removed a vial and a syringe from a cabinet. All the while, he whimpered, "Go 'way."

When I returned to the bed, he was still curled up, the port behind his left ear readily accessible.

I sat on the bed and kissed him again. "I wish I could, Grey. I wish I could make all this go away."

Even as I spoke, I stiff-armed the thought that often crept up on me when I did this. A little stronger dose, a little too frequently administered, could make all this go away forever.

He lay still while I inserted the needle into the port and injected the drug. The tension in his body eased.

I set the needle on the bedside table. "Let's get you in a more comfortable position." I tugged at him to encourage him to unfurl and roll over while he was still conscious enough to cooperate.

I helped him lie on his back, head slightly elevated to assist his breathing. Then I affixed his airflow mask and turned on the machine. As I pulled the sheet up over his naked body, I tried to pretend I didn't resent his impairment.

But I did resent it. This shouldn't have happened. I was the one with brain worms. He was supposed to take care of me, not the other way around. And I needed someone to care for me. What would I do when my time came?

It would happen. And probably soon. But for now, my mind was still intact in spite of the stress, and so was my body. And the latter screamed for attention.

With a last look at my grotesque, worse-than-useless husband whom I loved and hated with almost equal intensity, I turned down the light and left the room.

I hadn't forgotten what I'd learned from the Kentans, that a woman can find satisfaction without a man.

It was an act of desperation, not of worship.

❧ Chapter 8 ❧

HAPPY BIRTHDAY

THE NEXT MORNING, Grey discovered reading.

Though he had, in theory, been capable of reading the past few months, he'd shown no interest in it. It may have been too fatiguing with only one eye. On this day, though, he went into the media room after breakfast and asked for his tablet.

Problem was, he couldn't think of what to call it, and he grew frustrated when I didn't bring him what he wanted. I figured it out when he held the palm of his hand up to his face and roared, "Read! I. Want. To. READ."

I found his tablet in the office and brought it to him. "It's been so long since anyone's used it, I'm sure there's no charge left. Let me plug it in first. You want to read something else while it's—"

He snatched it out of my hands. "Plug. I read."

His insistence flustered me. "I suppose, sure. You can use it while it's charging." I set it up for him, and as soon as it was on, he was lost in it.

I didn't hear a peep out of him for hours, and it made me nervous. I looked in on him from time to time, but he didn't budge until I suggested he take a break for lunch. He was so absorbed that he jumped when I came in.

"You've been at it a long time. What have you been reading?"

He exited the screen and laid the tablet on the seat beside his. "Stuff."

"Doesn't it give you a headache?"

He rose with effort. "Always have one. Whassa difference?"

I was glad he'd kept occupied, because I'd been busy preparing for our trip to Drevadell. Part of that involved speaking with Grey's doctors to let them know we were going to be away and to get some practical advice about traveling. Though I feared how Grey would handle the trip, I grew eager for a change in scenery.

We left the following morning. Though having access to private transportation made the trip less stressful, my fears about Grey's reaction were justified. He didn't want to stay in his seat during the flight. As soon as we disembarked, he loudly demanded something to eat even though we'd had a meal on the plane.

We'd only been at Bark's house for about three minutes when he declared, "Wanna go home." Trying to reason with him only made him more adamant.

"We can go home tomorrow," I said. "It's too late in the day to start now."

"Home!" He beat on the arms of his chair with his fists.

"All right, then." I rose and brought him his walker. "Let's get ready for bed. We'll head for home in the morning." It wasn't even dinnertime yet, but I had to do something.

He allowed me to lead him into the bedroom, where I got him bedded down and sedated. Bark and Pearl assisted in order to learn the routine, and I was embarrassed—at his behavior, at his humiliating condition, and at my resorting to sedation to deal with him. I wished they hadn't offered to give me a break.

He was lethargic the whole next day. He never mentioned going home, and I didn't bring up the subject. But the following morning—his birthday—he awoke bouncing with excitement and ready to celebrate.

"The party doesn't start until this afternoon," I told him. "I'm glad you're looking forward to it, but you'll have to wait."

He was more verbal than he'd been since the shooting, his mood expansive. When he demanded to help with the preparations, Pearl put him to work making the music playlist. It took him all morning, and he was pleased with the result. No one else was, but that day, it didn't matter. Especially since the party was outdoors.

It wasn't much of a party, really, but it was enough. We had decorations, plenty of food (all easily chewed), too-loud music, and a few guests.

Bark and Pearl's younger two, Tanstal and Droplet, still lived with their parents, so they were already at the party when the others arrived. Grey's sister, Silver, brought her son, Spenn, but Colaret was unable—or unwilling—to be there. She'd grown attached to her father since her parents' break-up and seldom attended Standtall family functions anymore. All the kids were polite to their uncle and wished him a happy birthday, but they were clearly uncomfortable around him.

The only guest who was not a relation was Grey's former partner, Kerby, who arrived about an hour into the party.

She and I had developed an unusual friendship. I can't say we were close, but we had a great mutual respect. Her relationship with Grey had never been romantic—turns out she was already with someone, and it wasn't a man—but she cared deeply about him. She'd intervened in the attack, and I felt I owed her for that. At the very least, she'd earned a place in our lives, and I was glad to give her one.

But the gift she brought him didn't please me.

"Happy birthday, Ash!" She flashed her pixie grin as she crossed the lawn and shouted above the blaring music.

He turned his head toward the voice. "Kerby. Hi." It was a bright day, and his sunglasses hid his eye. But his gaze must have shifted from her to the long-legged gray goshond beside her, because next moment, he sat up straighter. "What's that?"

"Your birthday present. His name is Tough-to-Snuff. I've trained him for you."

When she'd asked me about it a couple of months before, my first inclination was to say no. But her arguments were persuasive. "The kyukur I have in mind is well behaved and clean in the house. It will be good for Ash. I know he's been wanting a kyukur for a long time."

I still had my reservations. "I have no idea what to do with one."

"I'll show you, but there's not a lot to it, since he'll be already trained. I picked him out special for Ash, and I'm pretty sure it will be a good fit."

Trusting Kerby's judgment, I reluctantly agreed—and immediately wished I hadn't.

Until, that is, I saw Grey's face light up when Kerby introduced them.

Grey ruffled the animal's ears. "Tough-to-Snuff. Good name. Good kyukie."

Kerby squatted beside the animal and looked up at Grey. "I named him after you, you know."

"Ashgrey?"

"No, you big goof. You're not easily snuffed out, and neither is he."

As if it knew they were talking about it, the kyukur waggled at Kerby with an expectant look.

She petted him, then stood. "He likes you. You'll be best friends before you know it."

Grey seemed puzzled. "But—he's yours."

"No, he's your birthday present."

Grey turned to me with an expectant expression much like the kyukur's. "He's mine?"

Trying not to envision that big beast galumphing about our lovely apartment, I put my arm around Grey and kissed his cheek. "He sure is."

"When we get home?"

"We'll take him with us. He's yours."

Grey rubbed the goshond's neck and made a hiccupping sound, almost like he was about to cry. But his voice was steady, albeit whistly. "Thanks. Thanks." His misshapen mouth attempted a grin. "I can't believe it. Thanks!"

He looked back and forth between Kerby and me, and both of us responded with teary smiles. "Happy birthday."

☀

WHILE THE FAMILY ate and talked a short distance away, Kerby sat near Grey, and I pulled up a chair on the other side of her so I could listen to her instructions about handling the kyukur. She demonstrated the various commands we'd need to know, and I was impressed with the way he responded promptly to everything.

"He almost seems human," I said. "A strange-looking person, but human-like all the same."

She chuckled. "He'd like to think so. Ashgrey, want me to show you some of his favorite games?"

"Games?"

"Yeah." She rummaged in her bag, and the kyukur turned to her eagerly. What she pulled out surprised me: a bag of carrot chunks.

She smiled. "He loves these things." She pulled one out of the bag and showed it to the kyukur briefly before enclosing it in her fist. She put her hands behind her back, then put them out in front of her, closed. "Which hand, Toughie?"

He nudged one of her fists with his nose.

She opened the hand he'd indicated and gave him the carrot.

Grey's mouth twisted. "He smelled it."

"Sure he did. You can do it with other things too. Just make sure you show him what he's going to be looking for first, and reward him with a carrot when he identifies the hand it's in."

She removed an earring, showed it to the kyukur, then hid both hands behind her back. When she brought her closed hands in front of her again, Tough chose the correct one and eagerly chomped up the carrot she gave him.

She gave the bag to Grey. "Want to play with him?"

That kept them both entertained for a while, with Grey creating variations on the game and the kyukur adapting to each change. It was hard to say which of the two enjoyed it more.

Kerby and I watched them while we chatted. Our first topic of conversation, as usual, was the lack of progress by Ministry Security in figuring out who was behind the shooting. The trigger man was a common criminal with no known ties to any person or entity that made sense. Unfortunately, he'd died of his head injuries without regaining consciousness, so no one had been able to question him.

Although Kerby was no longer with Ministry Security, she still had friends there, and she was confident she'd hear about developments in the case. "No news on that front," she concluded, "but I do have some big news personally."

My stomach plummeted. I guessed what she was about to say, and it shouldn't have upset me. But it did. I feigned excitement. "No! Did it take? Really?"

She grinned and nodded hard. "Yes! I'm almost twelve weeks along."

"Oh, this is exciting! I'm so happy for you!" I hugged her, clothing my distress in a disguise of delight. "How are you feeling? You look great."

She beamed. "I feel good. Really good. And I've never been sick. As long as I keep a little food in my stomach but never too much, I'm not even queasy."

"This is huge. I hardly know what to say!" That much was the honest truth.

After Kerby left Ministry Security, she and Hannel wanted to start a family using Kerby's ova fertilized by sperm from Hannel's brother. After two failures at embryo implantation, they'd become discouraged.

Kerby grinned. "Third time proved lucky."

I hadn't thought Grey was listening, but he turned to Kerby, face alight. "A baby? That'sh wunna—" He ran his hand over his mouth as if to clear the muddle from it. "That is won-der-ful." He turned back to the kyukur and told it, "Babies are won-der-ful. I wish I had one."

⁂

ABOUT AN HOUR later, Bark came over and sat beside me in a patch of sunlight not far from where Grey and Tough-to-Snuff dozed in the shade of a tundurun tree. Holding a glass of wine, he nodded at the tumbler in my hand. "Nimrelade? We have better stuff here than that, you know." He had to speak up to be heard above the pounding music.

"I know." I made a face. "But with the meds he's on, Ashgrey can't drink alcohol, so I'm keeping him company." I was keeping him company with a headache, too, thanks to that obnoxious playlist he'd created.

Bark took a sip from his glass. "That's too bad. If I recall correctly, you always enjoyed a good wine."

"Your recollection is correct. But I like nimrelade too. I don't mind." I let out a long sigh.

Bark leaned toward me. "Your words say one thing, your body language another." He reached for my glass. "Let me put something in this to liven it up a bit."

His close proximity made me warm all over. He was so like Grey—but not incapacitated. I switched the tumbler to my other hand, out of his reach. "That's sweet of you, but I'll pass."

He raised his heavy brows. "You sure?"

"If I get started, I'm afraid I'll never stop." I was tempted to take him up on his offer, but when my mind followed that act to its inevitable conclusion, I went cold. "No, that's not true. I *know* I'll never stop. The only reason I wasn't living in a bottle when—" I waved toward Grey. "When this happened, was because Grey pulled me out. Gave me a reason to be sober. And now, I have all the more reason." I took a sip of the nimrelade, imagining myself handing it to Bark for an additional splash of something. "One of us has to keep our wits about us."

"You're a good woman, Jemma."

He wouldn't have said that if he knew what I'd just been thinking about him. Drinking wasn't the only thing I imagined. "No. I'm not." I shook my head, suddenly weary. "I try, but it doesn't work." A wave of sorrow rolled over me, and I wanted that drink. Badly.

No. I am a rock. "I'm not sure I want to leave him here with you and Pearl. It's a lot to ask of you." *And if I'm home alone, I'll succumb to temptation.*

"Oh, come on. You're not asking, we are. We want to do it. And didn't you say something about having a deadline to meet?"

"That's true." I pursed my lips. "When he was in the hospital having all those surgeries and things, he was often unconscious. I had nothing to do, lots of time to write. I was sure I'd have this latest book done long before the deadline. But since he came home, my writing's been at a standstill. The end is in sight, but I can't seem to get there."

"Then do it. Or—" He shifted in his seat, exuding manly strength. Slime, but he was even more attractive off-camera than on. "Tell you what. If you're not comfortable leaving him, you can stay here, but leave the babysitting to us. This is a big place. Go off by yourself and write until you're caught up. Take as much time as you need. We'll be fine."

My eyes widened. "Really? That's an idea. I just might do that, if you're sure you don't mind."

"We don't. Ask Pearl. She'll say the same thing."

Our conversation was interrupted as Willow made her entrance, bubbling with apologies for her tardiness. "I had to finish up a lab at school, and it took longer than I expected. My lab partner got there late, and she is *so* disorganized—" She spied Tough-to-Snuff. "Oh, what a sweet goshond! Whose is he?" She turned a hopeful face toward her mom. "Is he ours? Is he?"

"Glad you could join us." Pearl hugged her. "He's a birthday present to your Uncle Ashgrey from his former partner, Ms. Kerb."

Dancing to the beat of the loud music, Willow bounced over to Grey, who awakened and lifted his head at her squeal, "A kyukie! He's adorable!"

She kissed Grey on the cheek. "Happy birthday, Unca Ashy! Remember when I was little and I used to call you that?" She gave him a quick hug. "It's so good to see you doing so well! And I love your kyukie! What's his name?" She bent and fussed over the Goshond.

Grey watched her with an expression I didn't recognize on his re-arranged face. "Name's Tough-to-Snuff. I call him Toughie." As if he'd had the beast for weeks.

I could see the creature made him happy, but as far as I was concerned, having the smelly thing around was going to take a lot of getting used to. I took a deep breath. *I am a rock.*

Grey continued to stare at Willow. "You just get here? Didn' see y' before."

She squatted, petting the kyukur, and looked up at Grey. "Yes, I'm sorry I'm late. I got held up at school."

"Tha's good. School's good."

She continued to fuss over Tough-to-Snuff. "Such a sweet wittle kyukie. Unca Ashy is so lucky! I wish I could have a fuzzy wittle kyukie wike you."

Fuzzy, yes. But little? That beast had to be twenty-four or twenty-five kilos.

Grey leaned back in his chair, still gazing at Willow. "You're pretty, y'know that?"

Willow slowly rose. "Um, thank you?"

"Y' have nice breasts."

Willow flushed deeply. Bark hopped up with a, "Wait just a minute there." I was too shocked to move. Pearl stood still, gaping.

Grey didn't seem to notice. "I don' have any." He clapped his big hands to his own chest. "'Cause I'm a man, and men don't have breasts. You know why? 'Cause we don't have babies."

The kids, with the exception of Willow, suppressed laughter. But I found my feet. "Grey, stop it."

If he heard, he ignored me. "Breasts 'r amazing, y'know? They make milk. So you can feed your baby. I was jus' readin' t'other day about how they work."

Bark and I hurried toward Grey, saying, "Ashgrey, enough." Pearl went to the mortified Willow and put her arms around her.

Grey smiled when he saw me. "Breasts are pretty." He grabbed one of mine. "If you had a baby, I could—"

I yanked away his hand. "Grey!" I had never wanted to slap someone as much as I did that moment.

I'm pretty sure I'd have actually done it if Bark hadn't been there too, squeezing Grey's shoulder. "Enough of that, brudder. This is not an appropriate topic of conversation."

Grey looked up at Bark, then at me. I couldn't tell from his expression if he was hurt or merely confused. "I wish y' could a' had a baby."

Something in me snapped like a strained rubber band, and the sharp sting brought tears to my eyes.

My indecision vaporized. Taking a slow breath (*I am a rock... I am a rock*), I turned and spoke to Bark and Pearl. "I accept your offer to keep him here for a while, with thanks. But I won't wait for morning. I'm leaving now."

The music blared as I crossed the lawn to the house, Gray calling after me, "Freeman? Go where? Freeman!"

It sounded like Bark tried to calm him, but I couldn't hear what he said. Nor did I care. Whatever happened was up to him and Pearl now.

I was done.

❧ Chapter 9 ❧

———❧———

FACES FROM THE PAST,
FACING THE FUTURE

———❧———

IT WAS NEAR midnight when the autocab pulled up in front of the apartment.

Raig came out and opened the car door. "Good evening, ma'am." The doorman bent lower and peered inside the cab. "You're alone?"

"Mr. Standtall will be staying at his brother's for a few days. I have just one bag this evening."

"Very good, ma'am."

I'd ordered the baggage door open as soon as the car stopped, and Raig lifted my suitcase from the bin. "Please allow me to carry this to the elevator."

"Of course."

After he set it down, I handed him my tip card. The CFC habits came naturally now.

"Thank you, ma'am." He ran his scanner over the card. "I hope you'll give Mr. Standtall my regards next time you speak with him."

"I would be happy to. He'll appreciate hearing it."

I had a similar conversation with the elevator operator, who carried my bag into the apartment.

And then I was alone.

It should have been a relief to be unburdened, but I remained tightly strung. What would Grey do without me? Would Bark and Pearl be able to handle him?

I pulled out my phone and activated the new, updated app Kerby had given me for scanning for electronic devices. This latest technology showed a schematic image of every source of energy in the vicinity. If I found something unusual, I could take a closer look at it.

While I scanned the house, my mind whirred.

I shouldn't have left Grey. My first priority should be caring for my husband.

I can't care for him properly. I should put him in a rehab facility.

No, the doctors all said he makes faster progress at home. I should keep him here.

Grey needs me. I shouldn't have left him with Bark and Pearl.

I should leave him with Bark and Pearl forever. After all, he was Bark's brother before he was my husband.

While my thoughts chased their tails—and speaking of tails, what in the world was I going to do with a stinking kyukur when Grey brought it home?—I completed the scan, ending in the bedroom. Grey's room. Which we no longer shared. The cleaning crew had come yesterday, but unless it was my imagination, the room still smelled like Grey. His medications gave him a lingering body odor.

The betrothal commemorative was still on the bedside table.

I lay on the fresh bed and gazed at the happy faces in the photo. They didn't gaze back, for they only had eyes for each other.

Grey had been in his mid-thirties then, and the fresh flush of youth had left him, but I looked like a bright spring day.

I lifted my hand to ponder my bracelet, its beauty and luster enhanced by wear over the past fifteen years. Marital bracelets were designed to do that. To get better with age, like a good marriage. Like fine wine.

The thought of wine made my mouth water, and I wanted some. Badly. There was no alcohol in the house, but it could be obtained easily enough.

My phone was still in my hand.

I activated the calling app and spoke into the device.

"Call Bark. Video."

It was nearly midnight, but Drevadell was three hours behind. It wasn't too late to call.

Bark picked it up on the third ring. "Hi, Jemma."

"I'm home. How's Grey?"

"Everything's fine. He fell asleep in front of a movie, and Pearl and I were just trying to figure out the best way to get him up and ready for bed."

"I usually start by kissing him awake—"

"No, thank you."

I chuckled. "Is the chair protected?"

"Pearl talked about putting down a waterproof sheet before he sat. I think she did."

"Did he get his PM meds?"

Bark nodded. "Yes."

"Then maybe you should let him sleep right where he is. But stay close, because when he wakes up, he'll be disoriented. He'll need you to reassure him."

"And what if Pearl tells me the chair isn't protected?"

I shrugged. "I'll leave that up to you. He's getting a lot better about going to the bathroom, so it might be okay. But when he's sound asleep, anything can happen. How much do you like that chair?"

AFTER TALKING WITH Bark, I lay on Grey's bed looking at the photo in the commemorative.

I wanted that Grey back. The one in the picture.

I didn't care that we were older. I just wanted him whole again.

Maybe he would be someday. Probably not, though. He'd certainly never be handsome again. But, broken or not, I'd keep him. He promised to take care of me, and I'd do the same for him. It's what Standtalls do.

I AWOKE A couple hours later. The light had shut off, as it was programmed to do when it detected no motion for thirty minutes.

I lifted my head and squinted at the clock. Two thirty.

I was cold. I should get under the covers. But my mind prodded me to get up and get to work on my manuscript. The deadline loomed near, and I was never one to wait until the last minute.

The light came on when I sat up. I wouldn't waste the opportunity Bark and Pearl had given me.

First, I went for a swim to clear my mind. An hour and a half later, I was in my favorite writing spot, with a view of the aquarium across the room and the twinkling city lights outside the window. As my hair drip-dried and a cup of crim steamed on the table beside me, I opened my manuscript.

This was not the story I'd started earlier, the one that celebrated Mimma and her love for her husband. I still didn't feel capable of writing that one.

The story I started when Grey was in the hospital was a suspense loosely based on our mission to spy on the rebels meeting at Bowl Rock in Obicon Timbers. Loosely. I changed the location and created additional difficulties for the characters, because our own mission went too smoothly to keep things interesting. In this version, the female protagonist was captured, and the male had to rescue her.

I re-read the last couple of scenes to refresh my memory. It was a good story. Energized, I began dictating.

I COULD SLEEP when I wanted, eat fish every meal, go shopping on a whim, write until the wee hours, all without interruption or obligation to anyone.

Problem was, I couldn't stand being away from Grey. Whether I swam or ate or worked or shopped, I thought about him. Worried about him.

I called Bark and Pearl so often that after two days, Bark asked me to stop. "I don't think you've quite grasped the 'relax' part of 'get away and relax'. We'll give you a call in the evening so you can say goodnight to Ashgrey, but otherwise, put it out of your mind. Everything's fine."

Tears sprang to my eyes. "If he was a problem, you wouldn't tell me, would you?"

Bark chuckled. "No. Not unless it was a big problem. But he's been no trouble at all. How long has he been such a voracious reader?"

"What do you mean?"

"All he wants to do is eat and read. And play with Toughie. He gets a kick out of that kyukie. I make him do his therapy and get a little exercise now and then, but he always acts like he's in a hurry to get back to what he was reading."

"I hope he's not straining his eye."

Pearl's face came into view. "He's got the font pretty big, and it doesn't seem to be bothering him. But really, Jemma, Bark's right. You worry too much. He's a grown man. No need to mother him."

I don't know the first thing about mothering. And I never will.

I squelched those thoughts. "Thanks, you two. I appreciate your help. But I've got to go. Call me tonight."

I disconnected before Bark and Pearl could see the tears leave my eyes and begin a journey down my cheek.

Grey was supposed to take care of *me*. I didn't know how to take care of anyone—which was obvious, as much a mess as I was making of this, my one attempt at caregiving.

It was a good thing I never had children.

I finished my manuscript the following week and sent it to two of my writer friends for their critiques. They promised to get it back to me as soon as possible, but I still had to review their suggestions and make revisions.

I could do all that, though, with Grey around. With the finish line in sight, I went back to Drevadell to fetch him.

☀

AS SOON AS our autocab pulled up in front of our building, the night doorman came out.

"Good evening, ma'am." Raig bent lower and peered inside the cab. "Mr. Standtall, sir! Welcome home."

After I got out, I went with the doorman to the other side of the car to help with Grey. Raig opened the door, and I pulled out the walker and had it unfolded by the time Grey was ready to heave himself out of the vehicle with Raig's assistance.

"Thank you," I told the doorman. "We'll be fine now, if you could just get the bags."

"Very good, ma'am." Then he saw the kyukur on the seat waiting for permission to leave the vehicle, and his face lit up. "What do we have here?"

Hanging onto his walker, Grey bent and looked in. "Come on out, Toughie."

I took the leash. Grey's kyukur, but my responsibility. "One of Mr. Standtall's birthday presents. He's big, but quite the gentleman."

While at Bark's for a couple of days before bringing Grey home, I'd learned the basics of kyukur management. I'd also developed an appreciation for Kerby's skill as a trainer. The beast knew his manners, he seemed to understand everything I told him, and he usually obeyed cheerfully.

"He's beautiful." Raig grinned. "May I pet him?"

Grey nodded. "'Course."

"You two will be seeing quite a bit of one another," I told the doorman. "I've arranged for a walker to take him twice during the day, but I'll have him out mornings and evenings."

Raig scratched behind the kyukur's ears. "It will be a pleasure to see you each time, my hairy sir." He straightened. "I'll get those bags now. Mr. Standtall, I'm happy you're home."

Grey shuffled toward the building. "Thanks." He glanced at me. "Tip card?"

"Right here." I already had it in my hand.

"Multiply by five. F' my five bags."

I caught Raig's eye. He'd heard, of course, and seemed pleased.

"I'll tell him." I was pleased, too. Not because of the generous multiplier, but because it was the first time since the shooting that he'd mentioned tipping.

A welcome glimpse of the old Grey. Would he really come back to me?

GREY'S CONDITION HAD been improving steadily before, but the gains seemed to accelerate after he got that glishing kyukur.

A week after his return, a stressful afternoon therapy session left him with no energy for reading in the evening. I did some paperwork in the office, then went into the media room to check on him. He and the kyukur were on the couch watching a movie. Toughie's head was in Grey's lap, and Grey stroked the kyukur's back.

I frowned. "No animals on the furniture."

Toughie lifted his head as if startled at my voice—which maybe was a bit sharp—then jumped down with what I'd have to describe as a guilty expression, if a kyukur can have one.

I brushed off the cushion. "Look at that. It's covered with hair. You both know he's not supposed to be up there."

Grey patted the couch. "Up, Toughie. It's okay, boy."

Ears flattened and watching me out of the corner of his eye, the kyukur crept back up and laid his head on Grey's lap again.

Grey rubbed his ears. "Good boy. Don't listen to her. You're allowed here with me."

Toughie gazed up at Grey in adoration. Grey couldn't pucker and kiss, but he brushed the beast's nose with his lips, and Toughie licked his face.

I shuddered. "What the glish, Ashgrey, he's not supposed to do that. It's disgusting."

Three sad eyes gazed up at me, one glaffcrim-black and a pair like milk chocolate.

"I think you love him more than you love me." I left the room, stomped to the janitor's closet, and returned with the small vacuum. I frowned at the skulking kyukur. "You, Toughie." I pointed to floor. "Get down. And stay down."

He did, reluctantly, looking back and forth between Grey and me.

I pointed toward the doorway. "Go to your place."

His "place" was his bed in a corner of the office where he stayed when he was home alone, or where we sent him to keep him from being underfoot. I had to admit he was good about going there when told and staying until one of us gave him permission to leave.

I turned on the vacuum and spoke above the hum as I scrubbed the couch cushion with the wand. "You're confusing him, Grey. Telling him to do something he's trained not to do."

Grey didn't look at me. Just turned up the volume on what he'd been watching.

"I'm surprised at you. You of all people should know better."

He paused the movie and pointed at himself. "Why me of all?"

"As a Standtall, you understand about doing what's right. And you were in the military for twenty years, so you should respect order and rules."

Those fuzzy little hairs stuck to the upholstery with determination, and I went at them with a vengeance. "Keep this up, and that animal is going to ruin everything we own. And you'll ruin him."

His pant leg had hair on it, and I vacuumed it too.

"Ruined? Like me?"

I stopped in mid-swipe. How could I answer that? After a moment's pause, I resumed my cleaning of the sofa. "No, Grey. Not like you. Like a pampered, spoiled child."

"We don't have a child."

I shut off the vacuum. "I know."

He unpaused the movie and turned his attention to the screen.

"You can turn the volume down again. I'm through making noise."

After I put the vacuum away, I went into the office where the kyukur lay on his bed looking glum.

"Okay, Toughie, you can go sit with Grey again."

The animal hopped up, eyes wide and ears twitching.

"But stay on the floor, do you hear me? No more getting on the furniture."

I could have sworn he grinned as he trotted out.

When I looked in a short time later, the beast lay on the floor, and Grey was asleep.

☀

THAT EVENING, I took Toughie out for his nighttime walk in the park across the street from our building. As I cleaned up after him, I wondered if Grey would ever be well enough to take care of the animal himself, or if I'd be condemned to doing it forever.

We crossed the road toward home, and the doorman smiled as we approached. "Good night, Mrs. Standtall." He petted the Goshond. "Good night, Toughie."

I handed him the tip card, and he thanked me. "Good night to Mr. Standtall as well."

"Thank you," I said.

After sending the hairy child to bed, I went into the media room, where I sat beside Grey on the sofa and woke him with kisses.

He shook me off. "Don' do that."

"Don't do what?"

"Kiss." He yawned, a grotesque and no doubt painful procedure.

"What?"

After the yawn, he rubbed his jaw, frowning.

"Since when do you not want me to kiss you?"

He didn't look at me. "Since—since, y'know. Now." He let out a deep sigh. "I s'pose you want me t'go t'bed."

"I think you'd sleep better there than on the sofa." I put my hand on his arm. "But why don't you want me to kiss you?"

I'd attributed his gruffness to sleepiness. His answer, enunciated clearly, came like a punch to the gut.

"You irritate me."

I don't know what my expression revealed, but it didn't matter, because he never looked my way. "I what?"

He reached for his walker, pulled it over, and heaved himself up to stand. "Y'r always pest'rin' me."

I made no move to help him. "Well, excuse me for loving you."

"Yeah." He shuffled out of the room. "Maybe you shouldn'."

❧ Chapter 10 ❧

TIRED OF THIS

THIRTEEN MONTHS AND four surgeries later, Grey's mouth was fully reconstructed, his ear looked almost normal, and he had two eyes. One of them was artificial, but unless you looked at it closely, you might not notice.

The mouth reconstruction meant he no longer whistled when he talked, and as a consequence, he was a great deal more verbal. Though his speech was slow and careful, every word was clear.

And therapy had made a dramatic improvement in his strength and balance. His movements were still a little ungainly, but he walked without assistance.

One morning, I went into the media room where he sat. "I'm making travel arrangements for my book tour. Instead of having the in-home care people stay with you while I'm gone, why don't you come with me?"

He glared over the top of his reading glasses. "Toughie and I will be fine. You can leave us."

I frowned. "That's okay for a few hours, but I'll be gone for ten days. Would you rather go visit your brother? Or how about Silver and Spenn? You haven't seen them for a while."

"When will you figure out I don't need 'round the clock nagging?"

I gasped. "I do not nag."

His brows rose in their new, uneven way, but he offered no rebuttal. "Toughie and I have plans too. We're going hiking at Ogenchuck Park later this morning. Do we have anything around here to pack for a lunch, or should I buy something?"

"It rained last night. You'll both get muddy."

"We're washable."

I sighed. "I have some of that chipped beef you like." I headed for the kitchen, then had a sudden thought and turned back. "Do you mind if I come?" I was out of oilfish, but I could make myself a fried egg sandwich.

"I'd rather you didn't."

I can't say his answer surprised me, but it did hurt, and I wasn't sure how to take it. I stormed into the kitchen, contemplating the best response. There was no good one.

After getting the meat from the fridge, I called to him, "If that's what you want, I won't go."

He came to the kitchen while I made his sandwich. "It's not that I don't want your company."

I couldn't look up. "There's enough meat here. Do you want two sandwiches?"

"Yes. Please. But you walk too fast. You always want to hike and hike like you're on a mission or something. You don't stop and play along the way like Toughie and I do."

I glanced at the beast in the doorway beside him. I didn't allow the kyukur in the kitchen, and Grey stayed at the boundary line with him. "I guess I never did learn how to play."

Something like distress flashed across Grey's face, and he took a step into the room. "No, never mind. Come with us. I don't want to shut you out."

A lump in my throat prevented me from answering. These days, all he did was shut me out.

"I still like you, you know." The corners of his eyes crinkled, reminding me of the old Grey. "Even if you are a nag."

I snatched a sponge from the sink top and threw it at him. He tried to bat it away, but it hit him on the bicep. The old Grey would never have missed.

He came the rest of the way into the room, and in a once-familiar but now-forgotten gesture, gently pulled me into an embrace.

I didn't fit like I once did. His thick arms didn't wrap around me properly, and his protruding belly got in the way. The doctors said his steady weight gain was a side effect of his medications.

"You're good to me, Freeman." His embrace seemed hesitant, as if he didn't remember how to do it. "I wish I could love you the way I used to."

I caressed the portion of his back I could reach. "I know, hon." If this hug was as good as it got, I didn't want it to end. "I understand."

"I want you to come with us. I want to be with you while I can. Because when you go on your trip, I'm going away too."

I pulled back and stared up at him. His face, round and distorted but no longer revolting—or was I just used to it now?—revealed nothing.

"What do you mean, going away?"

"I've been wanting to tell you, but I couldn't figure out how. Now that I'm able to get around better, I have some traveling to do."

"Traveling?" I stepped out of his arms. "Where? What do you mean?"

His mouth twisted in what I guessed was regret. "I have unfinished work. I need to get back to it."

"Work?" I stared at him, uncomprehending. "You're on disability. You don't work anymore."

He put the sandwiches into a container. "I'm not talking about official business. What are you going to eat? We should take something to drink, too."

"Grey, what are you talking about?"

Something like a frown creased his scarred, puffy brow. "See? This is why I hesitated to say anything. I knew you'd ask too many questions." He pulled two water bottles from the cabinet. "I have work to finish. That's all you need to know. For now, though, we need to pack you some lunch." He opened another cabinet with a fat-fingered hand. "I don't see any of those stinky little fish you like."

⁂

MY FIRST NOVEL for adults didn't create the stir my publisher and I had hoped.

After a good start, sales dropped at an alarming rate, and my publicist arranged a tour of talk shows and speaking engagements to help rally interest.

When I returned home, Grey was gone. He'd messaged me when he left, and I hadn't heard much from him since.

The day doorman, Dez, helped me out of the autocab. "Good afternoon, Mrs. Standtall. You are alone?"

"Yes." I didn't understand the question at first, then realized he'd expected to see Grey with me. "Mr. Standtall is traveling separately." I immediately regretted the wording, for I didn't want to give the wrong impression. "He will be returning later."

But as I entered the empty apartment, I wondered if *separately* might not be more accurate than I wanted to admit.

I used to think the distance between Grey and me was temporary. That as he recovered, so would our relationship. I was desperate to regain what we used to have, but every time I tried to draw closer, he pulled away. Even our hike in Ogenchuck Park had felt like Grey with his Goshond and me their unwelcome guest.

I unpacked my bags and stuffed my clothes down the chute whether they were dirty or not. The laundry service hadn't had any work from us for almost two weeks, so let them make up for it now. While I was at it, I stripped Grey's bed and tossed the sheets down the chute. He no longer used a hospital bed and had bought a whole new suite of furniture for what used to be our room, as if trying to erase the memory of the times we'd shared in it.

I didn't put clean sheets on, though. Let him make it himself when he got home. Whenever he got home. From wherever he was. And whatever he was doing. Work? What work could he possibly have?

A memory flashed through my mind. Grey standing in this very room, his hand and arm heavily bandaged, his heart still bleeding from the loss of his father. "I will fix it," he'd sworn. "I swear on the death beads around my mother's neck. I will fix it."

He never had, because he couldn't. The situation was beyond repair. But I suspected, and Kerby had reluctantly verified, that he'd been conducting some sort of personal investigation before he was shot. And that investigation had, possibly, been the reason someone tried to kill him.

The official reports said the shooter had no real motive but was merely deranged. After a few months, the City Fathers ordered Ministry Security to discontinue their investigation. Not that it had been going anywhere anyway. Both Kerby and Brose N'Lee—before Brose had been transferred to Saltcreek Point and subsequently lost touch with us—had told me the leads all ended, in his words, at freshly built brick walls. As if someone didn't want Ministry Security learning the truth.

Was that what Grey was doing? Trying to continue the investigation that had nearly gotten him killed? What could he possibly find now, in his condition, that he hadn't been able to uncover before?

Especially if Father Hold and Minister Janren Stock, two of the most powerful men in the world, barred his path?

⁂

WHEN HE AND Toughie returned home, Grey told me as he unpacked, after setting his bag on the unmade bed without comment on its nakedness, "I want you to leave me."

He was matter-of-fact. Almost casual. Just plopped the bag down. "I want you to leave me." Then opened the bag.

"What?" I rubbed one of my ears, hoping it and its partner were playing a trick on me. "You say hello, yes, thanks, we had a good trip, I want you to leave me, all in the same breath?"

He removed his grooming kit. "It was more than one breath. You are not usually prone to that sort of exaggeration."

I pulled the mesh sack of soiled laundry from his bag and wrinkled my nose. "Did you not shower the whole time you were gone? And okay, it was three breaths. But what in the world has gotten into you?"

He snatched the sack out of my hands. "If you don't like the way it smells, keep your hands off it." He lumbered across the room, opened the laundry chute, and shoved the clothes into it, sack and all. "The way I disgust you, you should be eager to leave me."

I followed him across the room and blocked his way when he turned around. "I don't want to hear you say such a thing again." I put my hands on his fleshy shoulders. "Grey, I—"

As soon as I touched him, the goshond drew near, growling.

Grey spoke to him sharply. "Toughie! Easy. Sit."

The beast obeyed, but didn't take its eyes off me.

Grey removed my hands from his shoulders. "I apologize. My request was abrupt."

Remembering the day, so long ago, when he'd blurted out an equally abrupt proposal of marriage, my eyes filled. "Yes, it was." I couldn't fathom where it came from. "What do you mean, leave you?"

"I see it when you look at me. You find me repulsive."

"How can you say that?" I searched his face for a clue as to what he might be thinking. "I married you for life, and I'll love you for life. No matter what you look like, no matter how bad you smell."

He almost smiled.

"We both knew we wouldn't be young and healthy forever, but we promised to stand by one another no matter what. You meant it when you promised me that, didn't you?"

"I did."

"And I meant it too. If I didn't abandon you when the doctors said you'd never get out of bed again, why should I now?"

His twisted mouth grew more misshapen. "You promised to obey me, didn't you?"

"No." I narrowed my eyes. "I promised to give you the honor, defense, nurture, and affection that is due you as my husband. I don't remember anything about blind obedience to stupid commands."

"If I tell you to leave me, it's not stupid. It's for a reason." He turned back to his suitcase. "And if you love me, you'll do what I say."

I shook my head. "You can't ask me to do that. I will never do that. You want me to quit harping at you, I can do that. Or at least, I'll try. I won't pressure you. I won't ask you to—" My voice caught in my throat. "To show me affection like you used to. And I will be faithful to you in every way. But I will never." I took a breath to steady myself. "I will never leave you."

He nodded but didn't look at me. "Stay then. For now. But when I tell you to leave, you have to. You must."

I put my hands on my hips. "I won't. I'm telling you right now, I won't leave you, Grey, so just get that thought out of your head." I headed for the door, almost afraid to go near Toughie for fear he might bite me, but he let me pass. "And if there's anything clean in there, you might as well throw it down the chute too. It's bound to smell as bad as the rest."

"You're harping," he called as I left the room.

"Just making a suggestion." I turned around and stuck my head in again. "And I'm not leaving."

In the kitchen, my hands shook as I poured water into the reservoir of the glaffcrim maker. Leave him? Surely he didn't mean that.

THAT EVENING, I let Grey think I was hard at work, writing—as in fact, I had been doing a little while before. Now, though, I reviewed our accounts. By tracking Grey's recent spending, I should be able to ascertain where he had been and, maybe, what he'd been doing.

I quickly learned he was as good at cyber stealth as I was at the physical version. I found where he used his tip card when he came home, and when he paid for the autocab that delivered him from the airport. I also found the cab fare from the week before, when he'd left. Between those two dates, he had charged nothing to any of our accounts. No airfare, no hotel accommodations, no restaurants. How had he traveled? How had he lived? I checked everything. Found nothing.

He must have set up another account under a fictitious name. When had he done that? And why?

The why, I could guess. But he had to have secured those funds before the shooting, because since then, he'd never had the opportunity.

Or had he been using his tablet to do that some of the times I thought he was reading?

For a man who had been shot three times in the face, he sure had his wits about him.

One thing he was not, though, was physically subtle. I heard him rise from the sofa in the media room though it was half a house away. By the time he'd lumbered all the way to the office, I'd long since exited the accounting pages and brought up my manuscript.

His bulk filled the doorway and filled me with something like fear. He'd always been tall, but the extra weight made him enormous. His hair was unkempt, his clothes rumpled, and his face—what I could see of it through his overgrown whiskers—was scarred and unreadable.

I looked up, pretending I was surprised at his not-so-sudden appearance. "Hey, hon."

"I fell asleep."

"You usually do. You going to bed?"

"I just woke up. How can I go to bed now?"

I studied the hulk before me. "I don't know, Grey. I don't know what you can do these days. I just—" I closed my computer. "I don't know you at all anymore." I rose and moved toward him. "Want to take a walk?" Maybe out of the apartment, he'd speak more freely.

One of his eyebrows frowned. "It's thunderstorming."

I hadn't been aware, as the house was well soundproofed and my office had no windows. "We've got umbrellas."

"And I hope we also have more sense than to walk in a storm carrying lightning rods."

"So what do you want to do?" *You might try cleaning yourself up like a civilized person.* I clenched my jaw to keep from speaking my thoughts. He used to be meticulous about his appearance. Now I had to badger him to change his underwear.

Something resembling uncertainty crossed his face, but he didn't answer. Behind him, the kyukur yawned.

A wave of weariness rolled over me. I was tired of living like this. Maybe I could deal with it better in the morning. "Well, if you don't want to walk with me, I'm going to bed."

His mass blocked the doorway. "Don't. I mean, not yet."

"What do you want?" Did that sound a little sharp? I sighed. "What can I do for you, Grey?"

I reached my hand toward him, and he took a step back. He must have put his foot on the kyukur, because Toughie yelped.

Grey grabbed either side of the doorframe to steady himself. "I'm sorry, Toughie, I didn't mean to step on you." He turned and bent to comfort the beast.

Still blocking the doorway.

"You wouldn't have stepped on him if you hadn't—" I felt a scream coming on but paused to compose myself. "Why do you hate me so?"

From his expression, you'd think I spoke a foreign language.

My last thread of patience wore through. "If you're not going to talk to me, then get out of my way so I can go to bed. Once the storm's past, you can take the kyukur out yourself."

He moved out of the doorway. "I always do."

"Yes, when the two of you are away." I passed him on my way out of the office and turned my back on him as I walked toward my room. "When you're home, you fall asleep in the chair and let me do it."

"I don't *let* you do it. You just do it. You take it upon yourself. I don't ask you to."

I shut myself in my room.

He thudded after me. "I don't ask you to do anything. But you try to do everything." He stood in the hall, speaking through the door. "You'd—you'd still be taking me to the bathroom if I'd let you."

I opened the door and glared up at him. "Maybe I should still do that. Maybe I should bathe you and shave you and dress you, because you can't seem to figure out how to do it yourself. Or better yet, I'll have Kerby come and teach Toughie to do it for you."

I tried to slam the door, but he grabbed it. "Don't—"

Seeing that big hand gripping the door, I was suddenly a little girl again, helpless against Ibro's advances. My heart raced and I backed away, speechless with fear.

"What are you doing?" He stepped toward me.

I shrank further, feeling my eyes widening but unable to hold back the terror.

"Freeman—" He stopped and stared, as if seeing me for the first time. "What? You're not afraid of me, are you?"

I couldn't speak. I couldn't nod. I could only tremble.

The kyukur sensed something going on and whined, but Grey ordered him to go out into the hall and lie down.

I was terrified Grey would shut and lock the door. Lock me in with him, with no escape. No one to help me. The room seemed to close in and spin.

"Freeman." I heard the voice but didn't know where it came from.

I felt hands on me—but they were gentle ones. Arms around me—my husband's arms. My husband's smell, my face on his chest.

"Freeman."

I trembled in his arms, weightless, sinking together with him onto the bed, his whiskers brushing my hair.

"I'm sorry I made you cry."

Was I crying? Yes, I was, wasn't I? I couldn't stop.

"It's true what you said. You don't know me anymore. How can you? I don't know myself anymore."

I shuddered and sobbed.

"I look in the mirror and don't know myself. I look into my thoughts, and don't know myself. I remember who I used be and I wonder who I am now. And I don't know."

I couldn't stop weeping.

"I do remember, though, how I loved you." His voice broke. "How very much I loved you."

My tears, apparently, were contagious.

"I would have done anything for you." He caressed my hair. "I would have died for you."

He took in a long sniff. "And now I can't. I can't love you. I can't do anything for you. I can only—" He choked on a sob. "I want to love you, Jemma." He rocked me in his arms. "I want to love you. I want to love you. But I can't."

❧ Chapter 11 ❧

UNTHINKABLE

GREY'S WORDS EMBEDDED themselves in my brain like a worm. *I would have died for you.*

It was true. He'd almost done that very thing. When I lay buried in rubble, he was ready to travel across the rocket-seared plain of Arkentak to reach me in Suthfan—and would have likely died in the effort, if Jeriah hadn't stopped him.

Jeriah. An empty hole yawned in my mind, in my heart—in my soul, if there were such a thing—the part of me he once inhabited. But after what he'd done to Seena and his kids? And what he'd said about Grey and his family?

No, he was dead to me. I had no brother.

I WORRIED ABOUT Grey when he was away. When he was home, I could hardly wait for him to leave again. And I berated myself for both.

Not knowing how to deal with it, I immersed myself in work. How could I be a good wife to a man who kept shutting me out? I did all I could for him, but he only pulled farther away.

Now, whenever he returned from one of his mysterious escapades, he greeted me the same way. "I want you to leave me." It didn't matter how often I told him I wouldn't.

Other than that inevitable opening argument, we didn't speak much. We weren't even usually in the same room.

The only thing I did that seemed to make him happy was cook. Problem was, he now insisted on praying before eating. He didn't wash his head, like the Sonmanists did on Freemansland—too bad, because it wouldn't have hurt him to bathe more often—but he always thanked that god of his for the food. Even though it was I who had made it. What, did he think it miraculously appeared in front of him? If I pointed that out, he'd launch into a convoluted explanation about how our very lives were from God, as well as our health and the ability to eat and digest the food God provided. About the time he got to, "Every good and perfect gift is from above," I'd pick up my plate and go eat in the office. I couldn't listen to that nonsense.

Then one time, he was only home long enough for the laundry service to clean and deliver his travel clothes. As soon as they were returned, he carried the package into the bedroom and shoved it into his bag.

I couldn't help but comment. "Leaving again so soon?"

"I'm nearing the end. Gotta finish while I can."

I stood in the doorway frowning. "Finish what? And what do you mean, *while I can?*"

He closed the suitcase and turned to me, his expression plaintive. "I would do anything for you, Freeman. You know that, right?"

Perhaps it was true. He was probably doing the best he could. After a brief hesitation, I nodded. "I know that."

He gazed at me. "That book. You promise to read it?"

"Book?" I tried to think. "Oh. *That* book. The one about the space aliens?"

It irked me no end the way he acted like that crazy religion was the most important thing in the world. He seemed to love it even more than he loved the kyukur.

"It's a book from God."

I put my hands on my hips. "I sure hope that's not what all this traveling is about, searching the world for some mythical book."

"It's not mythical. And I don't need to search for it. I know where it is." Bag in hand, he strode toward where I stood in the doorway.

I stepped aside so he could leave the room. "So it exists."

"Of course it does. Despite what you think, I'm not delusional." He headed for the front door. Toughie followed, tail waving with kyukur delight at another trip.

When Grey reached the door, he turned to me. "So if I give it to you, you'll read it?"

"Yes." I sighed. "I promised I would."

Was that hope that flashed across his face? "I'll get it for you soon."

Then he and Toughie were gone.

I got my computer and settled across from the aquarium with my own book. The one I was writing. With the drapes open to the sunshiny city on one side and the fish swimming through the underwater Freemansland in front of me, and a gnawing ache within that threatened to drown me, I dove in.

Jeriah, my true other half, was dead to me. The old Grey was gone, and the new one was dead to me in a different way. And so I immersed myself in Mimma's story. The kind, noble woman who lost the love of her life at the hand of a traitorous colleague. I could almost feel her pain. Almost.

I worked on the plot, the intrigue, the surrounding details. I wove in a subplot. But I wasn't ready to delve into the pain. Not yet.

※

THREE DAYS LATER, I was at an impasse in my story. Hoping to clear my mind, I worked on our accounts. I chatted with the girl who came to clean the aquarium. I went to the grocery store and made myself enough fish stew to last me a week. I cleaned out my closet and set aside five dresses, eight blouses, and six pairs of shoes to go to Next Tier, an organization that offered used CFC clothes for sale at a drastic discount to lesser citizens who didn't care if the fashions were a little outdated.

Before the errand service came to pick up my cast-offs, I decided to go through Grey's closet as well. I could probably fill half a dozen boxes with useless things from there.

As usual, when I entered his room, the scent of him filled me with sorrow and longing. But the closet just smelled like clothes, as if he hadn't entered it for a long time. Sliding through one hanger after another, I realized he'd never wear any of these again. He'd put on too much weight, and he cared too little about fashion. The new Grey refused to wear anything but casual clothes. The looser and shabbier, the better.

"I might as well give away every one of these," I said to the wardrobe. My voice sounded strange, as if it didn't belong there.

I stiffened. What did I just hear? I left the closet and was halfway through the bedroom to the hall when Grey lumbered toward me from the front of the house.

Seeing me, he turned to the kyukur behind him and pointed. "Toughie. Go to your place."

The beast slunk away as ordered, though he seemed to wonder why he was banished.

I wondered too, with a back corner of my mind. The forefront was busy absorbing the shock of what I was seeing.

Both Grey and the animal were covered with mud. Grey had neither shaved nor changed his clothes since he'd left home, and he didn't carry a bag. With his bloodshot eye, filthy beard and matted hair, he made me think of a mad stellasede.

My own worm-imbedded mind grappled to make sense of the vision before me. "What are you doing? You're tracking mud all over the house. You rode in a *cab* like that? Transportation is going to sock us with a huge cleaning bill. What must the doorman and the operator think? And our tenants? Ashgrey Standtall, you—"

"Shut up." His voice carried a threat I'd never heard before.

My jaw dropped. "What did you say to—"

"We haven't got time for this. You need to leave."

This was all too familiar. "That again? No. Grey, I told you—"

"And I told you to shut up!"

The kyukur yelped from the office, and Grey swiveled his head and barked, "Toughie! Down!" He turned to me again. "You need to leave. Now. The cab's waiting."

"Send it away. We've been through this before. I'm not going anywhere."

"You *are* going, and you are going *now*."

"Grey—"

"I am through arguing with you." His expression was unreadable, but his tone was firm. "Pack a bag."

"Send the cab away. I'm not leaving you."

"You promised."

"No." I shook my head. "I never promised to obey you, remember? I promised to—"

A backhanded blow like an explosion inside my head knocked me off my feet. My ears rang as the ground flew up at me. I couldn't breathe. I sat on the floor, stunned.

Grey's voice coming through the ringing helped me remain conscious. "You promised to leave me if I ever struck you."

I didn't want to believe this was happening, but the pain assured me it was very real. How could it be?

I put my hand to my face. It felt like he'd broken my cheekbone. And what was that sound? It might have been the kyukur yelping.

"Now you have to keep your promise."

How could he be so matter-of-fact? My breath came in huge gasps.

"Go to your brother. He's still in the same house in Saltcreek Point."

How did he know that? Squinting against the pain, I lifted my gaze to look at the monster before me. His expression was easy to read now.

Utter agony. "I didn't want to do that. You should have gone when I first told you."

Yes, it was Toughie I heard, whining and carrying on in the other room. Clearly distraught, but obeying his master, staying in his place as ordered.

"I'm going out now, but I'll be back in fifteen minutes. If you want to live until morning, you'll be gone before I get back." Tears poured down his face, but his voice only wavered a little. He turned and lurched from the room. "Toughie. Come."

Before they went out the door, he called to me, "I'll send the car around back."

☀

THE AGING CAB pulled away and rattled off as I climbed the steps to Jeriah's house. It was dark, and I shivered as I rang the bell. There was nothing else for me to do. Nowhere else to go. Deny it as I might, Jeriah was my other half. And I needed that completion.

Since I'd slipped out the back door of the apartment eleven long hours before, I'd failed at Stealth. Though I'd taken the stairs and used the back exit to avoid seeing the elevator operator and the doorman, everywhere else I went, people stared at me. It was as if I had a flashing sign on my head. "Thrown out by husband."

I had to take a commercial flight to Saltcreek Point because one Standtall jet was in use and the other was in for repairs. That required a humiliating security check, a long delay before boarding, and a layover in Zapad. It was the first time I'd been in Arkentak since they'd pulled me out of the rubble.

Grey would have died for me then. How had he gone from that to threatening me with death? *If you want to live until morning, you'll be gone before I get back.*

And now, here I was. Jeriah's stoop was small and shabby. Looked like it hadn't been swept in a year except by the ocean breeze. The headlamps of passing vehicles cast moving shadows across the front of the house. From the flickering lights and sounds coming from the front room, I knew the video screen was on. He must be home.

I'd pulled myself together during my travels. Dug up my inner Freeman. Grey had slapped me back into the cold, rock-hard Jem I'd been before I'd met him.

Footsteps approached from the inside.

The inner door opened, and Jeriah peered through the smeary glass, hand on the outer door's latch. "Jem?"

His hair was graying and his face lined, but his eyes were still a clear blue. A surprised smile lit them and pulled his mouth up at one corner. "Jem? What are you doing out there?" He opened the door. "Get in here!"

"Riah, I—"

He took my bags from me. "Put those down." He dropped them on the floor.

I set my purse beside them. "Riah, I—"

"Never mind." He took me into his strong, familiar arms. "Doesn't matter."

That empty place within me soaked up his love. No, it didn't matter. Jeriah was still Jeriah, and I was still me. The Papevine Twins against the world.

⁂

WE TALKED AND drank and drank and talked until after three in the morning.

"I'm sorry," he said, "But I need to catch a little sleep before I leave for work in a couple hours."

"I understand." I poured myself another shot of whisky. "I'm sorry to keep you up so late. I s'pose I could use some sleep too."

"I'd say. You look like slime, y'know that?"

"O' course I do. 'Cause we look alike." I downed the shot.

"You're not used to drinking, are you?"

I shook my head, then held it with both hands to keep it from falling off. "It's like swimmin'. Throw me in, an' I remember how, no matter how long it's been."

He stood and offered me his hand. "Come on. Let's hit the mat."

I rose without his help, but not without hanging onto the table. "You shouldn'ta let me drink so much."

"How could I know you can't hold it anymore?"

Lucky the kitchen sink was near, because the next moment I demonstrated how right he was about not being able to hold it.

Eventually my stomach calmed and I went into the guest room he'd prepared for me. Formerly Kylee Jem's room, it now contained a table, which held my things, and a mat with a blanket. I carried my overnight bag into the bathroom. But when I came out, I took one look at the empty spare room and went into Riah's room. "What's this? You've got a real bed?"

He'd just finished turning down the covers, and he looked sheepish. "Seena insisted on it." He sat on its edge. "And I kept hoping she'd come back." Realization stole across his face. "You're not used to a mat anymore either, are you?"

I shuffled around the bed and eased myself onto the other side. "I've gone soft. Lying on a restroom floor with a building on top of you for five days and nights tends to make you appreciate a mattress."

He stood. "You can sleep here and I'll take the mat."

"No." I grabbed his hand. "Lie here with me. Like you used to do. I need to know you're with me."

He didn't disengage his hand. After the briefest of pauses, he shut off the light and lay beside me. "I'm here, Jem. I'll always be here."

⁂

WHEN I AWOKE, sunbeams squinted through the dirty window and fingered the rumpled bedclothes. I was alone.

Lifting my pounding head, my bleary eyes sought a clock. After seven. Riah had gone to work. I'd never heard him leave.

I let my head drop onto the pillow and replayed the last twenty-four hours in my mind.

A tentative feel of my tender cheekbone confirmed that my memories were true. Every unthinkable one of them.

I hadn't cried when Grey struck me. I'd been too stunned. And then, when traveling, too mortified. And by the time I'd arrived on Jeriah's doorstep, too stubborn.

I didn't cry now, either. I dragged myself off the bed and out of the room, found the whisky on the table where we'd left it, took another chug or two, and went back to bed.

Sometime after that, a voice woke me. A woman's voice. "Hello?" It came from the front of the house. Who the slotting slime could that be? But who cared? I didn't stir.

"Ms. Freeman?" The voice came closer. "Your brother sent me. He asked me to stay with you. He didn't want you to be alone."

I lay on my side with my back to the doorway and pretended not to hear her when she reached the room.

"I won't bother you. Just wanted to let you know I am here. If you need me."

It sounded like she waited for an answer, but I wasn't about to give her one. I didn't care if she was there or not.

"I see you'd rather be left alone. He said that would likely be the case. No matter. I am here nevertheless, as he requested."

Her footsteps moved quietly away.

I drifted in and out of sleep. She cooked herself some breakfast—the smell turned my stomach—then did some much-needed cleaning.

Seena would have been appalled at the condition of the house. But no matter. Riah had done worse things for her to be appalled at.

He'd told me the night before that she was living on Coldclime. KJ was studying biology in Centre City and Jeo was in his last year at Freemansland Academy West. Neither of the kids had anything to do with their father. From what he told me, I couldn't blame them.

Who this woman was, I had no idea. Nor did I care. But at least she was leaving me alone.

Over the course of the morning, my phone rang in my purse in the spare room, but I let it ring. This happened three times. The fourth time, the strange woman came to the doorway. "Your phone is ringing. Would you like me to answer it for you?"

I covered my head with the pillow.

The fifth time it rang, the woman went and got the phone. "It says the call is from someone named Kerby. This Kerby has called before times now and will likely call again. I believe you should see what Kerby wants, or Kerby will not leave you alone."

I threw the pillow off my head and reached toward the doorway. The woman placed the phone in my hand and left the room.

I took the call. "Kerby."

"Oh, Jemma. Finally! I've been calling Ashgrey, calling you, leaving you both messages. What's going on?"

I tried to make my voice sound like I hadn't been sleeping off a drunk, but without success. "Whadda you mean?"

"Are you all right? You sound terrible."

"No, I'm fine." I slowly sat up, as if trying to convince her. "What do you mean? What makes you think something's wrong?"

"What am I supposed to think? We took the baby to visit Hannel's parents in Finador, and when we got home, Toughie met us at the door."

"Who?"

"Tough-to-Snuff. The goshond? Ashgrey's kyukur? How did he get in my house? And where's Ashgrey? What's going on?"

I moved the phone away from my face to yawn, struggling to understand what she was saying. "Grey's kyukur is in your house? How did he get there? You sure it's him?"

"Of course I'm sure. I raised him from a cub. But where's Ashgrey? And what is his kyukur doing in my house?"

"He takes that creature with him everywhere. Are you sure he's not there too?"

Kerby sounded exasperated. "A man of that size would be hard to miss. What the glish is going on?"

"I don't know, Kerby. Why don't you call and ask him yourself?"

"I've been trying all morning. He doesn't pick up. You didn't pick up. I've been going nuts. I take it he's not with you?"

Tears sprang to my eyes. "No, he's not with me. I can't tell you what's going on because I don't know. Maybe he got tired of the kyukur like he got tired of me."

But I knew that wasn't the case. He would have never tired of Toughie. A cold stab of fear plunged like an icicle into my heart.

❧ Chapter 12 ❧

SINKING SAND

I CONVINCED KERBY I had no idea how Grey's kyukur got in her house, nor why, nor where Grey was now. Beyond that, I told her as little as possible. When she said she was coming to see me, I told her I wasn't at home and abruptly ended the call.

I shut off my phone, but my plan to sleep the day away was already spoiled. Head pounding, I rose and shuffled across the room. I found some clean gym pants and a shirt of Riah's to put on. My suitcase was in the other bedroom, and besides, the clothes in it were too fashionable. The sort of thing a CFC wears. And I wasn't in the mood.

I combed my hair with my fingers and tried to avoid my reflection in the mirror. Even without looking, I could see the bruise darkening the left side of my face.

How in Umban had this happened? Nothing made sense. Nothing.

The whisky was in the kitchen, so that's where I headed. Too bad I had to pass through the front room, where the woman sat. She looked up from the tablet in her hands and gave me the sort of attention-to-every-detail scan I would have given her if our roles had been reversed.

She put down her device. "Would you like some lunch?"

"No. Who are you, anyway?"

She was in her early thirties, casually dressed. Her clothes were tasteful in a Next Tier kind of way. Her face was pretty, but something in her expression said she was not one to be taken advantage of.

"A fair question. I am Pettyne Salid. I work with your brother. Would you like to see my ID?"

"Yes, please." I extended my hand for it.

Her eyes widened for an instant, showing surprise at my answer, but she readily complied. "Very well." She rose and pulled an ID folder out of a culottes pocket. She opened it before handing it to me.

It looked legit enough. My guess as to her age was spot-on. I handed it back. "You are from Kenta City."

She slipped the ID back into her pocket. "I am."

I went toward the kitchen. "Not much left of that place anymore."

She followed me. "They are rebuilding."

They, not *we*. "So I hear."

She'd cleared the table earlier in the day, but I knew where Riah kept the whisky. I didn't bother with a glass. "So tell me again, why are you here?"

"Your brother sent me. He did not want you to be alone."

I gasped at the whisky's burn. Whew. "Does he think I need a nursemaid?"

"I believe he is concerned that whoever did *that* to you—" She gestured toward my face "—may try to do more. He seems to think your life may be in danger."

"He worries too much."

Her dark gaze slid to the object in my hand, suggesting the more imminent danger was in the bottle.

Her dark gaze, the color of glaffcrim... I gripped the table, weak-kneed at the memory of Grey's face, taut with concern, dark eyes glimmering with tears. *When I come home and smell alcohol on you, night after night, it's like a lash tearing skin from my back.*

"Perhaps you should sit."

I saw Grey in the hospital bed, head covered with bandages, breathing tube in his throat.

I set my jaw, stoppered the bottle, and put it in the cabinet.

The room did a little spin, and I opened the next cabinet door, more to give me something to hold onto than to see what was in it.

Crackers. That's what was in it. I grabbed the box, then went to the refrigerator. Found some oilfish paste, a small spatula in a drawer, a plate from another cabinet—I found each item the first place I looked, because Jeriah's mind worked like mine. I started a pot of crim. Only then did I sit.

In the meantime, Pettyne went to first the window, then the back door, looking out intently. She had a sturdy, shapely figure. I could see why Riah liked her.

I scooped up a generous dab of fish paste and smeared it on a cracker. "Do you really think he's coming to get me? If he wanted to kill me, he'd have done it yesterday."

"I am merely doing my job."

"Oh?"

"I am a security agent, and this is my assignment."

The crackers were stale, but I was hungry enough that it didn't bother me. "Which doesn't mean you don't slot with my brother."

"That would be unprofessional."

"That it would."

She poured a cup of crim before the machine finished humming—I hated it when people did that—then set the cup on the table in front of me. "Milk and sugar?"

"I could have gotten that."

"But I got it for you. Milk? Sugar?"

I glared at her. "Neither. I'm a Freeman, remember?"

"You make that difficult to forget."

I spread another cracker with the fish paste. "Don't you have something to do?"

"No. I'm rather bored." She pulled out another chair and sat. "Besides, I am an investigator. And this case intrigues me."

I ignored her.

She rested her arms on the table and clasped her hands. She wore no jewelry on finger or wrist. "I read one of your books."

I chewed, swallowed, then took a sip of crim. "Congratulations."

"I did not care for it."

"So don't read another."

"I do not intend to."

I wasn't hungry enough to stay in the room with her. I rose and picked up my glaffcrim cup. "Nice chatting with you," I said, and left, leaving the food for her to put away.

Her answer followed me. "It has been my pleasure."

≈

THIS BUSINESS OF not knowing was more than I could stand.

Why did Grey want rid of me? Why had he given the kyukur back to Kerby? Where was he? Should I look for him and try to help him? Or should I fear for my life?

I'd thought myself at a standstill with my manuscript, but the impasse in my life was far worse. I moved to the room where I'd left my computer, and for the rest of the afternoon, I sought comfort in my fiction—something I could understand and control.

No one interrupted me until Riah came home. Pettyne opened the door for him.

The sound of his voice as he entered reassured me. The smell of Flocking Dock, my favorite carry-out chain, made its way to the mat where I sat cross-legged on the floor, reminding me how hungry I was. But I didn't get up.

Riah and Pettyne spoke in low tones, almost in an intimate way, and I felt like an intruder. I didn't belong in my own home anymore, and I was an outsider in Riah's.

I didn't look up when manly footsteps came toward the room, then entered.

Riah's quiet, "Hey," didn't induce me to lift my gaze from the computer screen nor my hands from the keys.

He sat beside me on the mat. "Nice outfit."

I leaned against him. "Hey."

"Save that."

I tipped my face toward him, brows lifted.

"The document." He pointed at my computer. "Save it. Come eat."

I laid the computer aside, then followed him out into the kitchen, where Pettyne had set the table with disposable plates—three place settings.

Riah guessed my thoughts as I looked from the table to Pettyne. "Yes, Pettyne is eating with us. I figure she earned a free meal after putting up with you all day." He gestured to a chair. "Sit."

"I need to wash up."

When I returned a short time later, Riah had poured white wine into three glasses. Still standing, I took a sip. It was cheap stuff, but if I didn't leave it in my mouth long enough to savor the flavor, it wouldn't be too bad. I took a few swallows then refilled the glass. Then I pulled out the chair and sat.

Pettyne and Riah made casual conversation while we ate. I believe the only contribution I made was to ask him to pass the repkava sauce. He'd brought quite a bit of food, but once I started eating, I couldn't seem to stop until everything was gone.

Pettyne stood. "I should be going."

She started picking up the mess, but Riah stopped her. "I'll get it. Thanks. I'll call you in the morning."

"Very well." She turned to me. "Good evening, Ms. Freeman."

I replied with a somber, wordless wave and drained my wineglass.

Riah accompanied her to the door and bolted it behind her while I cleared the table. Then he came back into the kitchen.

He said nothing, but he didn't have to. All I needed was for him to hold me. And he did. For a long time.

All the things he could have said, he didn't. Like, *You are such an idiot.* And, *Why have you been a stranger all these years?* And, *I told you he'd hurt you.*

He didn't have to say those things. He knew I knew them.

I didn't have to say anything either. Like, *I know.* And, *I'm sorry.* And, *I should have listened to you.*

No one and nothing would ever come between us again. We didn't have to say that either. We both knew it.

⁓⧾⁓

JERIAH FELL ASLEEP in front of the video screen. Did all men do that after a certain age? Perhaps, but more likely in this case it was because I'd kept him up late the night before.

I stared at the screen as if drugged. I had no desire to see the movie, but I didn't have the will to get up and do something else.

We sat that way until nearly midnight—he snoring, me staring—when a shrill beeping jarred me.

Riah jerked upright and was on his feet before I knew what was happening. "The back door alarm." He opened the coat closet, reached above the doorjamb, and pulled out a handgun. "Go into the bathroom and shut the door." He moved toward the kitchen.

Hide in the bathroom? Not likely. I followed him to the back of the house. The alarm had only sounded a few seconds, but now someone pounded on the door. The exterior light revealed a big hulk of a someone.

The beeping started again. It was an intermittent alarm, apparently. The pounding stopped, and I knew the husky voice that replaced it. "I need to speak with my wife."

Jeriah spoke through the door. "She's not here."

"Yes, she is. I don't need to see her. Just let me talk to her."

"Get away from the door. You've already set off the alarm. Do you hear the siren?"

I heard it. Were the constables really coming in response to Riah's alarm, or was the siren a coincidence?

"I just need to talk to her." He pounded again.

I wanted to open the door and pull Grey into my arms. He wasn't well. He needed help. But Jeriah stood between us.

As well he should.

"I'm warning you, Standtall. Get away from that door. Touch it again, and I'll shoot you right through it."

The image those words evoked made my knees buckle, and I sank to the floor, helpless to do anything but listen to the exchange.

"I have something to give her. I must give it to her, you understand? She has to have this."

The urgency in his voice was genuine. I wanted to go to him.

"I'm not opening the door. Get away from my house."

The sirens didn't seem to be getting any closer. Maybe they were a coincidence.

"I'm leaving it here on the stoop. She has to have this. Make sure she gets it. I'm putting it down now."

There was a shuffling sound outside the door, and the bulky shape bent out of sight, then reappeared. "I'll be gone by the time the constables get here. But please, make sure your sister gets this!"

And then, nothing. No shadow. No shuffle. No voice.

Gun in hand, Riah peeked through the curtain. "Looks like a marsh bear lumbering away."

I wanted to look too, but couldn't move. What had Grey put on the step?

The sirens were getting closer after all. Riah's phone rang. He answered it as he went from window to window, looking out. "Yeah? Yeah, he was here. Tripped the back door alarm." While he talked, Riah reset the alarm. "He's gone now, he can't have gone far. He headed south."

I found my legs but stayed in the kitchen. When Riah's window-checking took him out of the room, I peered around the curtain of the back door into the gloom. My husband was out there somewhere, stumbling in the dark. The motion light above the door went out as I stared, but not before I'd seen a tiny box lying on the stoop.

Jeriah hurried in and pulled me into the middle of the room. "What are you doing? Get away from there."

"It's not a bomb, Riah. It's a little box, like for a piece of jewelry."

"Leave it where it is." He took me by the hand and led me into the front room. "We'll let the constables see what it is."

"No, Riah, this is a personal matter. I don't need City officials sticking their noses into this."

He pulled me down beside him on the sofa and took my other hand. "You're glishing right, it's personal. I take it personally when a man belts my sister in the face. But when he comes to my house demanding to do it again, it's *real* personal."

"That's not what—" I tried to get up, but he held tight to both my hands.

"Okay, so that's not what he said. But he hit you, and that's assault, and he was trespassing at my house. That alarm doesn't go off unless someone tries to get in. Attempted break-in makes it a criminal matter."

My heart raced and I flushed hot. A criminal matter. Ashgrey Standtall? This couldn't be. "No! He's not a criminal, he's got brain damage. He's probably stopped taking his medication. He needs a doctor, not handcuffs."

Riah pulled me close. "I know. I know. If he's sick, they'll see that he gets help. He's a Standtall. They won't treat him like a common criminal."

I pulled away and hopped up. "Oh, like they didn't mow down his father? Like they didn't try to kill him already? Being a Standtall doesn't mean a thing."

Riah stood too. "Being a Standtall won't stop bullets, but it does mean the local law enforcement will handle him with care."

I doubted it. I doubted everything in that moment. Everything I'd ever considered firm as rock had turned to sand beneath me. Everything level had tipped. Everything safe sprouted poisoned barbs.

I stared, eyes wide, mouth open, mind searching for something to say, something that made sense, something that could put this crumbling mess back together.

Only one thing was sure anymore. Jeriah.

I nodded. "Okay."

☼

THE CONSTABLES CAME. Two men. They asked questions. They investigated. They took pictures—including shots of my bruises.

They were polite, respectful, and sympathetic in a distant, professional kind of way. They took the box with them in order to check it out in a quarantined environment. "If it's harmless, we'll bring it back to you along with whatever is in it."

Riah thanked them.

Beyond answers to direct questions, I didn't say much.

When they left, I got out the whisky.

THE NEXT MORNING began as a replay of the previous. Pettyne came, Riah went, I stayed in bed in my alcohol-soaked misery.

At first. Then at mid-morning, everything changed.

Everything. Forever.

❧ Chapter 13 ❧

THE KEY

IN MY STUPOR, I heard a knock at the front door, but I didn't get up. That's what Pettyne was for.

Then I heard Riah's voice. "Where's Jem?"

"Still in bed."

Footsteps coming.

"Jem." His voice husky. "You need to come."

I groaned and rolled over to face him. "Come where?"

"Into the front room."

Pettyne was talking to someone else. Riah had not been alone. I had no desire to see anyone, but his urgent manner discouraged argument.

I'd slept in his clothes, so I didn't have to dress. I merely ran a hand through my hair as I shuffled behind him.

Two constables stood in the front room with Pettyne. I'd met Tannlid last night, and the other was a woman I'd never seen before. Cold as a NaHorian winter, she introduced herself as Detective Nossred.

I asked the first question. "What was in the box?"

Tannlid pulled it out of his pocket and handed it to me. "Nothing dangerous, ma'am. You can see for yourself."

Riah took my arm and guided me to the sofa, then sat beside me. Before I had a chance to open the box, he said, "That's not why they're here."

I looked at them standing in front of me. They seemed uncomfortable. I cast a glance at Pettyne, but she didn't meet my eye.

I lifted my gaze to them again. "What... are you here for, then?" Did I really need to be sitting down? Riah took my hand. Apparently he thought so.

Tannlid spoke. "We found your husband, Mrs. Standtall."

This felt all too familiar. "Where?" *Do not tell me he's been shot. Do not tell me that.*

"In Salton Heights."

I didn't know Saltcreek Point very well, but I did know Salton Heights was the seediest part of town. I couldn't answer.

"He was stabbed to death." Detective Nossred wielded words like a blunt weapon, and I fell beneath the blows. "He was disemboweled, and his organs examined. It appears the killer was looking for something."

My head buzzed. Only Riah's grip on my hand kept me from passing out.

"We think," said Tannlid, "they might have been looking for what's in that box."

The detective nodded toward it. "We recommend you guard it very carefully."

I sat frozen, disbelieving, unthinking when Riah asked the constables, "You didn't put anything in your report about the box, did you?"

Tannlid shook his head. "No. The report now states that we merely answered a call from a home alarm. We checked it out and found it to be a malfunction. No mention is made about your houseguest, nor the item found on the back stoop. The statements we took last night and the photographs have been permanently deleted."

Riah nodded. "Thank you."

"Least we could do. We owe you."

Owed him for what? I didn't ask. I wanted to throw up. I stared at the box in my hand but couldn't bring myself to open it. Grey had given this to me.

He would never give me anything again.

The detective added, "We have no reason to believe Mr. Standtall's attackers know he was here last night, but you should take serious precautions anyway. Especially in view of what we learned from the constabulary at River Park. I understand that is where your home is, Mrs. Standtall?"

In a fog, I roused enough to nod. "Yes."

"We called them after we found the body to see if there were any reports of trouble there. It seems there was an incident two days ago at your building. Your property manager was notified, but they haven't been able to get a hold of you."

I lifted my head. "What?"

"They've been trying to notify you that someone broke into your penthouse. Slashed open all the furniture, tore into walls. One of the neighbors and the elevator operator heard the commotion and went to see what was going on, and both of them were killed by whoever was up there. The perpetrators got away. No one even got a look at them. No one who's alive to give us a report, anyway."

I visualized it as she described it—the wreckage in the apartment, the slashing, the smashing, the elevator operator, the blood—but through the horror I caught the dimmest ray of light. "Two days ago?"

"Yes, ma'am. The local authorities believe the invasion began some time in the middle of the afternoon. Broad daylight. Pretty unbelievable."

"He saved my life."

All four of them said, "What?"

"Grey saved my life."

Riah scowled. "He tried to kill you."

"No. He told me I had to leave. I wouldn't. I told him I would never leave him. He only hit me so I would go. That happened late in the morning, two days ago. Somehow he knew they were coming. He only hit me to get me out of there."

They stood—or in Riah's case, sat—in silence at that.

I slipped my hand from Riah's and opened the box. It held a key on a chain. Considerably larger and heavier than the key to my marital bracelet.

With a trembling hand I picked it up, trying to think what it opened. I'd never seen a key like it before. "This? You think this is what they were after?" I tried, unsuccessfully, to block out the image of someone cutting open Grey's gut.

The detective spoke. "They were obviously looking for something. Something small enough to swallow. They didn't find it at your house, so they looked for it on his person."

"Maybe they were after something else. Maybe they found it on him. Maybe this isn't it."

Jeriah reached for the key. "Or maybe we should assume this is what they're willing to kill for."

"THIS IS YOURS now." In the back of the limo, Riah held my hand as we traveled up the lane toward Sentinel Pines. "Will you move here?"

"It's beautiful in the spring, isn't it?" In the clear sunlight, the lawn gleamed a rich, healthy green. Blossoming trees competed with the flowerbeds in a coloring contest in which all were winners.

"It's beyond beautiful. Is that a yes?"

I shook my head. "I'm surrendering my one-third ownership to Grey's brother and sister. Their children will end up with it all eventually anyway. After the mourning protocol is ended, I'll have no use for the place."

Though the ritual was traditionally carried out in the home of the deceased, our apartment was uninhabitable. Even if it had not been destroyed, it couldn't have held the number of guests I expected. The family estate was a better venue altogether.

I've already explained the CFC mourning process, and I don't care to relive that nightmare with you now. I'll just say that from the moment I stepped out of the limo at the coach door, I was First Survivor. Temporary ruler of the realm.

Though some of the mourners seemed to begrudge me that honor, I didn't care. It wasn't as if I wanted to do this. I'd have far rather been home with Grey in our little apartment, arguing about how he dressed or what he ate or how he babied the kyukur. I'd even have rather been at his bedside in a hospital, stroking his scarred hand as he lay in a coma, a trache tube in his throat and his face hidden in bandages. At least then, I had some form of my Ashgrey. Now, I had nothing but ashes.

And Jeriah. One of Grey's last acts was to give me my brother back. We both cherished that gift.

When the vigil was ended, the financial and legal matters sorted out, Grey's beads placed around my neck, and the insane dance performed on the grounds in the sunlight, allowing his alleged spirit to rise from the box and ascend into the sky—when all that agony had been endured, Riah took me home. That is, to his house in Saltcreek Point. It was our house now.

But Grey had a brother too. And before we left—at dinner after the Presentation ceremony—Bark asked me, "Would you like to take a little walk before dark? The gardens are spectacular this time of year."

His manner was casual, but I sensed an undercurrent of urgency. A glance at Riah told me his interest was also piqued. I patted clam sauce from the corner of my mouth with a Nionese silk napkin. "I'd like that."

Bark had evidently noticed my wordless consultation with Riah, for he added, "Just the two of us, if you don't mind."

Riah nodded his assent, and I said, "The gardens are lovely indeed. I look forward to seeing them with you."

So after our dessert of peach ice cream, Riah retired to our suite while I took a stroll with Bark.

Though we didn't speak at first—not even small talk—I'd become almost as comfortable with Bark as I was with my own brother. We had a history. A different history from mine and Jeriah's, but no less meaningful.

He broke the silence when we were at the farthest reaches of the formal gardens, a walk of eight or ten minutes. "You needn't have turned so many of your assets over to us, you know."

We passed through the gate and into the green beyond the garden. The woods loomed ahead, darkening in the dusk.

"I know. But neither did I need to keep them. I have more than enough of my own, and no heirs to pass them on to. I'd rather keep the Standtall fortune in the family."

By unspoken agreement, we followed the garden's immaculately trimmed hedge boundary. "I understand your thinking. But you didn't have to do that."

"So you said."

Several deer browsed under the trees a short distance away. One lifted its head to watch us. When it flipped its tail and snorted, the others looked up as well. Next moment, they bounded into the woods.

Bark chuckled. "Why don't they come out and show themselves like that when I'm hunting?"

"Perhaps they prefer to stay alive."

He didn't answer for a few somber moments. Then he said, "Before we get back to the house, we need to talk."

"About what?"

"I've got to know. Did you ever get—" He took a deep breath. "Grey wanted you to have a key. But I don't know if he was able to get it to you. Everything happened so fast."

I almost stopped breathing. I did stop walking, and grabbed his arm. "Bark! Do you know—" I paused to calm my voice. "Do you know what all this is about? Who did this to him? Why didn't you say something?"

He frowned. "I am saying something. Or I'm trying to, anyway. Did you get the key?"

I gaped at him. In the twilight, he looked so much like the old Grey, and yet was not. My heart cried for the real one, whom I'd never see again. "I have it. But what is it? What do you know?"

His gaze wandered over my face. "I know he loved you."

"He did once."

"He did always. Even when he didn't know what he was feeling, you were the thing he cherished most." He must have read my mind, because a sad grin made a brief appearance. "Even more than that kyukur."

I steeled my jaw against another flood of tears. I was sick of crying. "The key, Bark." I lowered my voice. "What do you know about that?"

He took my hand, placed it on his bent arm, and put his other hand on it as he resumed walking, leaving me no choice but to move with him. "Not much, but I'll tell you what I know."

As we neared the next gate into the garden, he slowed and spoke so low, I had to lean close to hear. "Almost a year ago, he asked me to help him with something. All he needed me to do was pretend to be him. To be a decoy."

I said, "What?" more through my expression than by audible word.

"He said I wasn't in danger. But he thought someone was tracking him, and he wanted to throw them off. So sometimes we'd arrange to both go to the same public place, like a tram station or an airport or a shopping complex. We'd meet at a restroom and switch clothes. I'd wear layers to make me look heavier, and I imitated his walk. I'd leave first and go one way, and then later, he'd go another. I followed whatever itinerary he'd laid out for me. I never had any problems, and I don't know if I was ever followed."

"So what was he doing?"

Bark shrugged. "He never said, exactly." He paused. "I didn't want to ask, but I got the impression—" He glanced around. "Ever since Papa was murdered, he's been trying to find the truth about what happened."

"Do you think the people who killed your father had Grey killed too?"

"I don't know." He shook his head. "I don't know." We'd stopped at the gate without re-entering the garden. "But a couple weeks ago, he contacted me to say it was getting too dangerous. He didn't want me to help anymore, and I was not to mention any of it to anyone. Of course he'd sworn me to secrecy at the beginning, and I assured him I'd never breathe a hint of it."

"So why are you telling me now?"

In the deepening dusk, it was hard to say, but I think he blushed. "Because I need to know if you ever got that key. That last time he contacted me, he told me he'd try to give it to you, and if he succeeded, I should give you a message." Bark started walking again.

"I couldn't figure what he was talking about. If he was going to give you a key, wouldn't he also tell you whatever he wanted you to know? But he said I'd have to tell you something, and I had to do it in person. And in private."

As he led me through the gate into the garden, I removed my hand from his arm. The house lights in the distance drew us toward the mansion and made me worry someone might see us and think us too cozy. "So what is the message?"

"I'll quote it exactly, but I have no idea what it means." He took a breath and recited softly, 'Exxie's gentle auntie makes five buys in Little Nion.'"

I repeated it to make sure I'd heard him right.

"That's what he said."

"And you were supposed to deliver that message if Grey gave me a key?"

Bark nodded. "Does it make any sense to you?"

"Not a bit." The rising song of the spring tingino-tinginas was beginning to make quiet conversation difficult, so I spoke a little louder. "Thank you for the lovely walk. It helped me unwind a bit. Perhaps now I'll be able to get a good night's sleep before we leave in the morning."

"The pleasure was all mine. You're going to your brother's house in Saltcreek Point?"

"At least until I get the mess at the apartment straightened out. Everything needs to be replaced. Especially in the sitting room where the aquarium used to be. I'm told that when the thugs smashed it, the water not only ruined the floor, but it damaged the suites two stories below."

"What happened to the fish?"

"They all died, of course. Which is sad, but nothing to compare with the deaths of the men who came to see what was going on." I heaved a long sigh. "This garden is beautiful, Bark, but it's a very small bright spot in this dark, horrible world. I almost envy Grey for being able to leave it. I hope to be able to follow before long."

I was thinking, of course, about the brain worms long overdue to awaken. No one had ever been known to co-exist with stelli as long as I had.

Bark didn't know I was a stellasede—or at least, I didn't think he did. He must have thought I considered ending my own life. "Now, Jemima, don't talk like that! Your life is far from over. Give yourself time to heal, and then you should have no trouble finding a good husband, if that's what you want."

I started to argue, but he kept going. "But he's got to meet with my approval. Promise you won't marry anyone without clearing it with me first."

"I'll never marry again. My heart's been torn out of my chest and squeezed dry. There's nothing left for anyone else."

"Well, promise me anyway. No marrying without my blessing." He held up his palm for me to pledge to it.

I raised my hand and pressed it into his. "All right, I promise." I remembered Mimma's declaration, *When we truly love our husbands, that love endures beyond death.* "In fact, I'll give you the key to my bracelet. If I ever want to marry again, you'll have to release me. But you can throw away the key for all I care, because I'll wear Grey's bracelet until I die."

Mimma had been on my mind since our arrival at Sentinel Pines. Her story had become my story. It was written in my life.

Now I was ready to complete it on the page.

❧ Chapter 14 ❧

REMEDIATION

A WEEK AFTER we returned from Sentinel Pines, Riah and I sat on the sofa watching the first Stillwater movie.

He wanted to watch them all end to end, but with my limited interest in films, I doubted I could finish watching the first before I went stir crazy. Especially since I'd already seen them.

I laid my head against his shoulder. "Now I know how a balloon feels when the air has leaked out. There's nothing left in me."

"I know." Riah gave me a sympathetic kiss on the forehead. "I deserved to lose Seena, but none of this is your fault. You were a good wife to him."

Now that Grey was gone, Riah seemed to feel more charitable toward him. I hated that this was what it took to heal the rift between my brother and me. "I'm really sorry I said all those things to you—"

"Hey." He pushed my head off his shoulder. "I told you, we're not going to talk about that. We're past it."

"Yeah." I nodded. "I'm still sorry, though."

"So am I. Now shut up and watch the movie."

I leaned against him again and tried to pay attention to what was on the screen.

The moviemakers had done a great job. Though the Freemansland they depicted was more fantastical than real, that didn't bother me the way it had Grey and Dr. Simelum. With the real world so harsh, the fantasy made for a nice escape.

But there was no escape from my sorrow. Within the darkness of my still-sharp grief, my mind darted about faster than a swarm of arrowflies. Everything reminded me of Grey—something in the story he'd commented on, a piece of dialog I'd taken from his mouth to put in a character's, the memory of our seeing this movie together at its debut screening—and every time my mind ricocheted against an image from the past, my heart tightened in my chest.

My mind drifted from the story before me and went back to my work in progress, and Grey's prediction. *You're going to finish that novel. Maybe not right away, but when you're ready, you'll finish it. And Brick House will publish it. And it will win a Centre.* It was as if Grey was telling me to quit wasting time and finish that manuscript.

I rose from the sofa. "I'm sorry, but I've got to get back to work."

Riah turned his blue eyes away from the screen and up to me. "You've been working on that book day and night. You need a break."

"I'll take a break when I'm finished. A couple more days yet. Then I'll do this movie marathon with you."

JERIAH WAS RIGHT when he said I needed a break, because for the first week after we returned to Saltcreek Point, I did nothing but work. And so did he, until I persuaded him to put in his notice and quit his job.

"You don't need to earn a living anymore," I told him. "I've got enough for the two of us."

"I'm supposed to live off my sister?"

I shrugged. "Think of it as my payment for room and board."

One of his brows rose in a dubious arch.

"And for your investigative expertise. I'm going to need your help finding out what that gift is." After years of being careful of what I said even in my own home, I was afraid to be more specific.

But he knew what I meant, and he seemed to relax. "Oh. Yes. There is that. And that could take some time."

"More than you can devote to it if you keep working a real job."

Concerning that "gift," he'd already been a big help. Shortly after the detective put it in my hands, Jeriah had taken the key, left me with Pettyne—whether for protection against possible intruders, or against self-destruction, I wasn't sure—and disappeared for the rest of the day. When he returned, he assured me it was safe. I didn't ask where it was, and he offered no hints.

※

RIAH GAVE NOTICE to his employer but spent the next two weeks helping install his replacement. After that, we took a trip to Kerby's house not far from River Park.

She and Hannel had a humble place in a suburban area, brightened by the presence of their daughter, Haribel, and made chaotic by a kennel of noisy kyukurs. One of the latter was on the front porch when we arrived and bounced with delight at seeing me.

I greeted him as we approached. "Well, hello there, Toughie."

After giving Riah a cautious sniff, he apparently judged him unworthy of further note and had eyes only for me. If those eyes could speak, they'd have asked, "Where's Ashgrey? Why'd he leave me here? When will he come back?"

I petted the creature's head, trying not to think about the answers to its unvoiced questions. "Good to see you, boy." I told myself that was a lie, that I couldn't stand the sight of him. The truth was, though, I was happy he was well, that Grey had taken him to safety. I was fond of the beast. "Is Kerby at home?"

She came to the door then, looking a little bedraggled and hollow-eyed. "Yes, she is. Please, come in."

She and Riah had already met, during the mourning. Now, she introduced him to Hannel and the child.

Hannel shook his hand. "Very glad to meet you." After an unsuccessful attempt to get Haribel to smile at him, she went on, "But we can't stay. We're on our way out to give Toughie a little exercise."

They departed, leaving us alone with Kerby.

She brought us Allocks to drink, and after taking a seat with us in the sitting room, her chin jutted with resolve. "I want to help. Tell me what I can do."

We hadn't asked for her help—had merely asked if we could come to visit. But she was sharp enough to read between the lines.

Her gaze went back and forth between Jeriah and me, and he allowed me to answer. "As we said at Sentinel Pines, we have a lot of unanswered questions."

She nodded, her mouth a thin grim line.

"You worked closely with Ashgrey in the past, and you're in a better position than anyone to know what he was working on. With that and your investigative connections, we hope you'll be able to help Riah sort out some of the clues Grey left." I shook my head. "I'm afraid this sort of thing is beyond me these days."

Kerby's eyes filled. "I know. I don't know how you stand it. After Ashgrey was shot, I couldn't think in a straight line to save me. I kept thinking, 'I killed a man. I took a man's life.' It was like— I don't know, like I had to do something to make up for it. For not stopping the shooting to begin with, and for killing Ashgrey's attacker besides. I should have just apprehended him, not killed him. He could have told us something. Maybe we could have put a stop to this before—" She took a breath. "Before it got this far."

I started to say, "You did the only thing you could, under the circumstances," but before I got past the second word, she interrupted me.

"Even today, I see that first shot into Grey's face. I see him go down, and the next two shots. I feel the impact of my body against the shooter's under me when we fell to the ground, hear the crack of his head against the pavement." She shuddered. "I don't see what I could've done differently. But if I hadn't fractured his skull—"

Jeriah leaned forward and spoke gently. "You had only two choices at that moment: do nothing and let the shooter kill Standtall and get away. Or do what you did, and stop him. You saved Standtall's life. The shooter died because of his own actions, not yours."

She shook her head. "That's what everybody tells me. Counselors and therapists, Hannel, everyone. But—" She turned her mournful eyes to me. "I can't help but think that if I'd done something differently, Ashgrey would still be alive."

I gave her my most severe frown. "That is absolutely not true. How can you—"

Jeriah put one hand on my knee and raised the other like a traffic control officer. "Might-have-been's get us nowhere. We need to look at the what-now's. Let's lay out what we've got, see where it points, then go in that direction. We'll move forward until we can't go any farther, then find a way around whatever lies in our path. But we're not going to let regret knock us out from behind. Agreed?"

How had my brother grown so wise? Kerby and I both gave him appreciative glances.

A wan smile creased the corners of her pinched mouth. "Thank you. But you need to give me something to do. I mean, something useful. I can't bear sitting around out here in the middle of nowhere, doing nothing."

Middle of nowhere? But of course, she'd lived most of her life in the heart of Centre City. The River region would seem remote in comparison.

"I'm pretty sure we'll be able to satisfy you." The warm smile Riah gave her seemed calculated to make her melt.

He was playing with her. Didn't he realize she wasn't interested in men? Maybe it was just a habit with him. Maybe he couldn't help himself. Either way, I didn't care. As long as we solved these mysteries, he could play the slotter all he wanted. I was the one committed to standing tall, not him.

His smile may not have melted her, but she did seem to relax. After that, the three of us spoke comfortably. We were united by our common love for Grey—or in Jeriah's case, his love of me—and our outrage at the injustice of all this. We sympathized with one another's pain. We knew how to follow leads.

And that's what we did. Then we made our plans.

From Kerby's house, Riah and I went to my apartment building in River Park. I had authorized repairs to the other damaged units but had made no decision as to renovating our penthouse. Now, with the insurers hounding me to begin the process, I couldn't put it off any longer. I arranged to meet the remediation rep at the building at eleven the day after we visited Kerby.

When our cab pulled up, he stood outside waiting for us.

Dez opened the car door, his expression sorrowful. "Mrs. Standtall. It is good to see you. I cannot tell you how sorry I am."

Tears were always just below the surface in those days, and I cleared some from my throat before I answered. "Thank you, Dez. I am sorry too. And for the two men who died. It never should have happened. But I'm glad you're still here and keeping things going. You're a good man."

Riah exited and walked around the car toward me.

"This is my brother, Jeriah Freeman. Jeriah, this is Dez, one of our faithful doormen."

Dez gave a respectful nod. "A pleasure to serve you, sir."

"We have no luggage. I'm here to meet with Mr. Hooner over there." I bobbed my head toward the insurance man standing by the building's entrance. "We won't be long."

Dez bowed. "Very well, ma'am." He went ahead toward the building and waited for us to complete the introductions with Hooner before opening the door for us.

The lobby looked the same as ever, but a pang of grief rolled over me when the elevator door slid open to reveal an operator I had never met before. His nameplate identified him as Tomasor.

We stepped inside, and as we rode up, Hooner shifted from small talk and pulled out his tablet. "I'm not sure what sort of restoration you have in mind for the penthouse unit, Mrs. Standtall, but your insistence on following certain specifications for the lower floors caused us to use a grossly uneven ratio of the renovations allocation. If you wish to restore the suite to its original condition, you'll have to dip into your own funds. We can restore the rooms, but there will be nothing left for furnishings, household goods, or personal items."

Numbers people always made me impatient. "Why would I want to replace everything? I understand the upholstered furniture was slashed, but it's my understanding that not everything was ruined, and we ought to be able to salvage household goods and personal things."

Hooner's brows rose high. "Do you really want to use them after this?"

"If I don't come back here, I can at least keep my things and move them to wherever I decide to relocate."

The elevator stopped, the door opened, and I tipped Tomasor before leaving the car. "Let's just see what needs to be done, and then we'll figure the cost. If my coverage isn't enough, I can afford to make up the difference."

"There's no 'if' about it, ma'am. This has been a very expensive incident."

The broken door lock had been replaced by a temporary mechanism, which I unfastened as I spoke. "Extremely. But the loss of property is incidental. The real cost is the loss of life. It's senseless. I don't understand any of this."

The door swung open, and we all three gaped at the sight before us.

To say the apartment was empty would be an understatement. Not only was there no furniture, but no floor to support it. No artwork was left on walls, and no walls to which to affix it. All that remained were bare studs and joists, with a few loose boards laid down to step on.

I walked the planks into the sitting room, where everything was in the same state. Stripped to white bone. My skin prickled. "I thought the renovators hadn't touched this suite yet."

Hooner remained in the foyer, staring about with wide eyes. "No one has. We authorized no one. No one has been here."

"I was told the place was ransacked, not that it had been gutted."

Hooner took careful steps along the planking, gazing about. "I was here the day after the incident. It was not like this then."

Jeriah had been silent but spoke up now. "Obviously *someone* has been here. And they couldn't have done this quickly or quietly." He strode into the hall and called for the elevator. "Somebody had to have known they were here."

I followed Jeriah, leaving Hooner to puzzle things out in his own way.

When the elevator returned, Jeriah accosted the operator. "Who's been up here?"

Tomasor looked back and forth between Riah and me. "I don't know what you mean, sir—"

I took a step forward. "How long have you worked here?"

"Four weeks, ma'am."

"Did you take anyone up to this floor before today?"

Jeriah's initial question had caused Tomasor's eyes to widen with alarm, but now they narrowed, and he drew himself up. "I am paid to work the elevator. When three citizens get on and ask to go to the top floor, I don't question it. But I am not paid to be interrogated like this."

"You are when I'm the one paying you."

His eyes widened more than before. "Are you Mrs. Standtall? I'm sorry, ma'am. I haven't seen you here before."

Jeriah frowned. "You knew who she was. You heard the conversation on the elevator, and you took her tip card. Now answer the question. Who else was up here?"

Tomasor wet his lips. "My apologies, sir, but I was hired to replace a man who was murdered on the job. Right there in that doorway." He pointed to the one we'd just walked through. "Some funny things are going on around here, but I don't care to know what they are. I'd like to stay alive, if you don't mind."

"No one's going to kill you," I said. "But ten minutes from now, you will not be employed. And before that happens, I'd like you to tell us what *funny things* you've seen."

Sweat broke out on the man's forehead. "I'm sorry, ma'am, but I surely don't know. That is, some men were here, yes. It was my second day in your generous employ. They came in the back door, dressed like the laborers who did the work on the other floors. They said they were to clear everything out of the penthouse after the incident, and who was I to say no?"

Jeriah's voice was hard. "Did you ask them for authorization? Did you see their IDs?"

Tomasor shook his head. "No, sir, but they looked—"

"They *looked?* I don't care how they *looked.* They were—"

I put my hand on Jeriah's arm. "He was afraid for his life, and for good reason." I turned to the elevator man. "Tomasor, did you see or hear anything that would tell you who they were or who they worked for?"

Jeriah added, "Where did they take the stuff? Did you see a truck?"

"I didn't see or hear anything, sir. They came up on my car the first time in order to tell me what they were doing. After that, they used the freight elevator. I heard noises up here sometimes, but I never saw them again."

I got out my phone. "The security cameras behind the building might tell us something." My first call was to Dez, asking him to summon the constables. Next, I called the building manager. "I'm firing Tomasor, the new elevator operator here. Please send someone to replace him for the rest of the day. I'll be over to see you this afternoon to discuss your hiring practices."

Jeriah escorted Tomasor onto the elevator. "Until the constables come, I'll keep you company."

Once the door closed behind them, I went back into the apartment to see what Hooner was up to.

Wandering around with a blank expression on his face and a tablet in his hand, was the answer to that question.

Every room was the same. Empty.

As I gazed about at the bare studs, the shock of the sight ebbed and relief took its place. The intruders had taken everything I owned, everything Grey and I had shared. But in doing so, they took everything that tied me to this place. It made my decision easier.

"Mr. Hooner."

Hearing his name seemed to snap him out of his daze. He blinked and turned toward me. "Yes, Mrs. Standtall?"

"We can go. I'll put the place up for sale just as it is."

⁂

MEANWHILE, KERBY CONTACTED a number of rehab clinics in Cararre that used pets in therapy. She informed them she had a trained kyukur available and asked if they had need for one.

While waiting for answers, she searched for the restaurant owned by Jano in Little Nion. Information wasn't difficult to find, but the listings she came across indicated that the famous mirtositi artist had retired and closed her establishment. After considerable effort, she found Jano's personal contact information. Kerby tried to get in touch with her, but if Jano got the messages, she chose not to respond.

One of the clinic administrators called back and indicated an interest in a mature therapy kyukur, so Kerby made arrangements to take Tough-to-Snuff to Cararre. If the therapy coordinator decided Toughie would be a good fit, the clinic would buy him and have Kerby train a handler.

Before she left, Kerby apprised me of the situation, messaging me through a secure channel she had set up with her cyber expertise. "I think I've found Jano, but she isn't responding to my messages. Do you think you can get through to her?"

Using the contact information Kerby provided, I reached out to Jano. I told her an associate of mine was interested in interviewing her for a magazine article. After a wary exchange, she told me about a shop where she served mirtositi by appointment only. "If your friend wishes to see me, he must have lunch. My price for citizens is now five hundred urexi."

I made the reservation, paid for the meal, and told Kerby where and when to show up. "Make sure you're hungry," I said. "Jano won't be satisfied until she's stretched your stomach to near bursting."

Kerby's reply was resolute. "I hate mirtositi, but if that's what it takes, I'll choke it down."

I smiled when I read Riah the message. "I wish I could take her place. Jano's mirtositi is pure delight."

Jeriah shook his head, jaw set. "Keep your distance. If that chef has something to do with whatever your husband died for, I don't want you anywhere near her. We can't have you drawing anyone's notice to her."

I agreed. If someone was tracking my whereabouts, I didn't want to lead them to the prize.

Whatever it was.

The thought that we might be close to finding it made my stomach flutter. I didn't know what we were looking for, but if it was worth killing for, it must be important.

IN PART TO direct attention away from our surreptitious task, I came out of mourning to embark on a new book publicity campaign.

The Stillwater series continued to be a steady seller, a fact I could never quite understand. But after Grey's death, sales on the two books I'd released for adults made a sudden spike upward. Though evidence photographs of his torn-open body in a dark alley had never leaked out, the public could envision it well enough from the news reports, and the image seemed emblazoned on people's minds. Public and social media were awash with talk about it, making me more famous than ever and creating curiosity about my books.

While I didn't exactly want to capitalize on that, my agent and Jeriah both convinced me that, for different reasons, it would be smart to keep myself in the pubic eye for a while. All the reasons made sense. Not only did I want to keep the attention of the enemy—whoever that was—on me and off Kerby's activities, but the publicity frenzy would set the stage for massive sales when my next release came out.

The new book was, of course, *Mimma's Song.*

It had only been available for a month before I had to quit scheduling personal appearances, because as soon as I entered a room, people would literally fall on me, weeping. The story itself was sad, but my personal situation made it all the more poignant. Everyone who'd ever suffered a loss felt a kinship with both me and the story's protagonist.

The following year, the book was nominated for a Centre Award, as Grey had predicted. But the drama surrounding the award must wait for another chapter. First, let me tell you about Kerby's visit to Cararre.

✷ Chapter 15 ✷

FIVE BUYS IN LITTLE NION

I WASN'T INVOLVED in the next part of the story, but I'll tell you what Kerby reported.

At Cararre, she got Toughie settled into his new job and home. The rehab facility paid her travel expenses as well as a nice fee for her training services. She wasn't really foolish enough to squander five hundred urexi on one meal, but if anyone were watching her activities, that income would explain how she could afford an exclusive lunch at Jano's private mirtositi bar.

As far as Jano knew, Kerby was a food writer researching an article. I had a casual friend who ran a magazine conglomerate, and I persuaded him to do me a favor. In exchange for an exclusive personal interview with me—and I rarely did interviews—to be published in *Regional Treasures*, he would print an article about Jano's shop in *Food Treasures Across the Globe*, written by me but under a pseudonym. To explain why I'd ask such a thing, I made up a story about how I wanted to do a favor for Jano. I think he would have agreed to anything to get that interview, and he didn't even seem suspicious when I swore him to secrecy about the true authorship of the feature I'd submit on Jano's shop.

So, after Kerby had completed her duties at the rehab facility, off she went to Little Nion. The directions Jano had provided took her deep into the region. Because she was small like the Nionese and familiar enough with the dialect to get by, she didn't attract undue attention. But anyone who looked closely could see she was an outsider. Little Nion did not welcome citizens, and the farther she traveled into the heart of it, the darker the glares the residents leveled at her.

Kerby found the shop and entered three minutes before the appointed time. Five other people—all native Nionese—sat at the counter. They ignored her as she took one of the four empty stools— the one nearest the door. Though I'd warned her not to expect a warm reception, her skin prickled at the disdain projected by the others.

Three more men came in and took the remaining stools, giving her no more than a dismissive glance.

Right on schedule, the assistants filed in from the kitchen and prepared the stage for Jano's performance. Then they retreated, and the mirtositi artist herself emerged with a fierce frown and formidable bearing. Starting on the far end of the bar, she accosted each customer with an insult, a demand for payment, or a sharp command to sit up straight and stop smirking. Kerby watched with trepidation as the little tyrant drew near.

When the man beside her objected to having to sit beside an outsider, Jano poked her cleaver at his chest. "Each person is here by my invitation, just as you. You not like my guests, I not like you." She flourished the knife. "You pay six hundred." She gestured toward one of the assistants who stood by. "Give Tremo another hundred urexi."

The customer grimaced but pulled out his wallet without argument. The others at the counter chuckled. Kerby didn't get the joke and wondered how anyone could find any of this amusing.

Jano turned her fiery gaze upon her. "You! Little citizen! No poking that one." She bobbed her head toward the man who'd objected to sitting beside her. "He not like you because you pinch him. So keep your hands to yourself."

Her steely glare seemed to demand a response, so Kerby nodded. "Yes, ma'am, I promise. No more poking or pinching."

From the way the artist's mouth twitched with a wisp of a smile, she must have appreciated Kerby's reply. "You lucky my mood is jovial today." She made a jabbing gesture with the knife. "Otherwise I poke you back."

Jano turned and addressed the whole group. "You hungry?"

Everyone nodded. "Yes, Chef Jano." Kerby also answered in the affirmative, though she dreaded what was coming and wasn't sure she'd be able to get through the meal without vomiting. The very thought of eating raw fish was almost enough to make her get up and flee the shop.

Jano repeated, "You hungry? I not hear you."

Everyone said some version of, "Yes, I'm hungry."

Jano nodded. "That's good. But you will not be hungry when you leave. Prepare yourselves. I am an artist."

While Grey and I had found the experience a gastronomic delight, Kerby said she barely survived it. She'd hoped mirtositi would grow on her, but it only grew more disgusting as the meal dragged on.

"I think it was worse seeing what went into it," she told me. "When the assistant brought out that bowl with the live gel eel, I almost let out a scream. Fortunately the sauce on that one was spicy enough to peel the skin off the roof of my mouth, and the pain distracted me from the slimy sensation."

I tried not to laugh. "I admire your fortitude. And I mean that. If I had to eat something I hated that much, I wouldn't have been able to keep it down."

Kerby wondered how she'd be able to talk to Jano about the things she wanted to discuss. Even if the food hadn't come too fast for speaking, the woman's manner discouraged conversation. Kerby looked for opportunities, but none ever came. She could only watch the show and shovel in the food. Fortunately, just when she'd reach the limit of her endurance for raw seafood, Jano would serve something seared or deep-fried.

Finally it was over, and Jano slipped back into the kitchen. Not only did Kerby feel very full and very ill, but it seemed it was all for nothing. As the customers rose from the counter—still ignoring Kerby, but among themselves praising the food and replaying some of the action—one of the assistants approached Kerby. "Please, madam. Jano is not satisfied with your method of payment. She wishes to discuss it with you."

Kerby's heart raced. Was she going to have to actually *pay* for this torture? She couldn't afford five hundred urexi. She asked the assistant, "What's the problem? I thought the charge was already taken care of."

"I don't know." The assistant shrugged. "You must discuss it with Jano. Please wait, she will be with you."

Kerby breathed slowly, trying to calm her mind and her stomach as she resumed her seat on the stool and the assistants cleared the counter and prep table.

After she'd sat alone for several agonizing minutes, Jano came out with two bottles of Allock. She set one on the bar in front of Kerby. "This will settle your stomach." She then opened the other and drank from it.

Kerby's brows rose. "Pardon me?"

"You are green. I not want you getting sick in my mirtositi bar."

"I didn't know it was so obvious." Kerby opened the bottle and took a sip. "I apologize. I'm just not used to mirtositi. And that was a lot of it."

"You must be a poor food writer if you not like mirtositi." Jano took a seat on the stool beside her. "You will not pinch me if I sit here, will you?"

Kerby smiled despite her queasiness. "I will not. Not after you were thoughtful enough to give me an Allock. But is there a problem with my payment?"

Jano scowled. "No, you foolish little citizen. That was just a ruse to get you to stay so I can speak with you. Your friend, J. S. Freeman. Terrible thing about her husband. He not a bad person, for a big City man. I just cook for him a few months ago. You ever meet him?"

Kerby took another sip of the Allock and swallowed a lump of tears along with it. Then she nodded. "We'd met, yes. And I agree, it was a terrible thing. In fact, I find the whole thing very difficult to speak of. Would it be all right if we talk about you instead?" She pulled a notebook from her bag, planning to start with the obscure clue *five buys*. "I'd like to know where you get such wonderful fresh ingredients."

Jano nodded. "I am glad you noticed. They are very fresh, yes. When I have guests scheduled, I go to the wharf before the sun come up. I meet the fishermen when they come in."

"Are there certain vendors you prefer?"

"Oh, yes. I go first to Hastao Fleet. Sometimes I know what I want, sometimes I just see what looks good that day. Hastao goes out to the reefs where they catch the pink suba. In season, of course. No suba now, when they are breeding. Later, I like their suba."

Kerby took notes. "What else do you get from Hastao?"

"This is the season for anutti, and they have the very best. But for gel eel, I go to Hinama." Jano described with animation the fish sellers she visited, what she liked at each one, and which she avoided for certain items. She mentioned more than five vendors.

Kerby tried not to think about the nasty things she'd just eaten as she listened for clues as to how to unravel the puzzle. "About how many stops do you usually make in the mornings when you shop for fish?"

Jano shrugged. "Three or four. Maybe more. It depends on how quickly I find what I want. But I have different routine on other days, when I purchase ingredients that do not have to be fresh-caught. Like nionarz or greenroot."

"Oh? Where do you get those things?"

Jano launched into another long explanation.

Taking notes, Kerby sifted through the details of what she was hearing, but nothing took shape. "Do you order these things to be delivered? Or do you carry them with you?"

Jano chuckled. "I strong, but not so that I can carry a fifty kilo sack of nionarz. What do you think? I have them delivered. Except the fish, of course. It must be fresh from the sea, and it must be the very piece I pick out. I do not trust the delivery girls."

"What if you have to visit several stalls in order to get everything you need? Do you carry it all with you?"

"No. Especially not in warm weather. The fish would not stay cold on a hot morning. If I go to more than four vendors, I take it to the chill locker."

"If you have to make, say, five buys, you put the first things you purchased in a locker to keep them cold? Do you do that often?"

"I have cut back on my work. Do not cook the quantity I used to. Have not used the locker for couple years."

Kerby rubbed her nose, trying not to show her excitement. "You call it a locker. You keep it locked, then? Or is that just a figure of speech?"

"Of course I keep it locked." Jano's familiar scowl returned. "This is important work. Each fish must be perfect. Competitor might try to take them, substitute for something inferior. It would ruin me. And you know what?" She leaned toward Kerby as if to tell her a secret.

Kerby leaned in and lowered her voice. "What?"

"It opens with special metal key. Not electronic thing someone can hack. Must have key. You know what else?"

"I can't imagine. What else?"

"You know I tell you competitors want to ruin me?" Jano spoke in a husky whisper. "You may think I crazy, but I have proof. My key, the key to my locker, is missing. Someone stole it. Wants to ruin me."

Kerby widened her eyes. "No! Where did you last see it?"

"I help my son, Lodo, at his shop at the Zavazda." Jano nodded as if confirming the truth of her own story. "I had it that day, in the pocket of my chef's robe. Not loose, but pinned inside so it not fall out. I spill broth all over, soak my robe. Put on a clean one. When I pick up the soiled one to take to wash? The key is gone."

"How can that be?" Kerby tried to sound incredulous, but she knew the answer. Somehow, her former partner had picked the poor woman's pocket.

"Competitor trying to ruin me. But I not ruined!" Jano flashed a grin. "That was six, seven months ago. I have another key, but I not use locker. No one going to steal my fish."

"A locker that requires a key. That's very unusual. Where did you manage to find such a thing?" It took self-control, but Kerby continued chatting with Jano calmly, sipping her Allock and taking notes while Jano told her everything she wanted to know.

MY PROMISED INTERVIEW with *Regional Treasures* went off as scheduled. They asked insightful questions, I answered with enough specificity to be interesting but not enough to bare my soul, and I managed to get through it without losing my composure. It went so well, in fact, that I gave them permission to broadcast the video on their television network.

The whole process took the better part of the day, and afterward I was glad to retreat to the emotional safety of Riah's house. I'd just walked in the door and said hello to my brother when I got a text.

So did he, at the same time.

Both from Kerby, saying, "Call me."

Riah stood. "I'll get it." I followed him into the back bedroom, which he had, at my expense, made safe from electronic eavesdropping. He dialed the secure line while I closed the door, then stood with my ear close to the phone so I could hear both sides of the conversation.

She picked up on the second ring. "Riah. I found what the key goes to. It's a cold-storage locker."

We grabbed each other's hands and he said, "Are you sure?"

"As sure as I can be, without trying the key. Do you want to bring it?"

Riah and I exchanged glances. We both knew he'd have to go without me, but the thought of being left alone filled me with cold terror.

He squeezed my hand. "No. I think it's time you went home. On the off chance someone's watching you, they'll wonder why you're hanging around. After a week or two, you can come here and visit Jem, and I'll go see what's in that locker."

So that's what happened. Except it was more than a week or two.

Before Kerby was able to get away again, Haribel was hospitalized with an infection. About the time she recovered, Kerby and Hannel had to straighten out some complicated tax matters. It was over a month before Kerby finally arrived.

A month of intense wondering what could possibly be in that locker. If it had to be kept cold, how would Riah transport it all the way from Cararre? It wasn't something dead, was it? Or worse yet, some*one?* Kerby had said the locker was fairly small—not big enough for a body. But it was a cold-storage locker, and I found that unsettling. I could tell Riah did too, though he pretended there was nothing to be concerned about.

❧ Chapter 16 ☙

NOTHING MAKES SENSE

WHY DID JERIAH think I needed Kerby to keep an eye on me? If I couldn't be with him, I'd rather have been alone. Every time I looked at her, I thought of Grey. To avoid her, I spent most of my time in the bedroom and let her fend for herself.

When Jeriah had been gone two days, I sat on the bed working at my computer. A sleepy spell overtook me, and I lay down. Just as I drifted off, my phone rang. I groaned, rolled over, and grabbed it.

It was from Riah, so I answered. But my greeting came out more like a grunt.

"Sorry, did I wake you?"

"I was working on book publicity stuff and fell asleep." I yawned. "So what's happening?"

"It's a book."

"Yeah, I know. I'm overwhelmed with fan mail."

"No, not that book. Another book. It's handwritten on banroo skin."

"What are you talk—" I sat up straighter. "Oh!" I slid off the bed and shut the door. Even though the room was now secure, I spoke low. "That's what was in the locker? A book written on banroo skin?"

"Yeah. It's in an ordinary plastic box, like what you'd put cookies in or something. And that's all that was in the locker."

"You sure?"

He sounded exasperated. "Yes, I'm sure."

I sat back on the bed, frowning. "Handwritten. And on banroo skin. What's the book say?"

"Like I've had time to read it? I don't know what it is. There's no title on the front. Inside, there's a letter to you, from Standtall. The handwriting's really terrible. And then there's pages and pages of book that's written neater, but I didn't have the chance to really look at it."

A tingling started in my extremities and traveled to my core. "A book. He told me he was going to get me a copy of some crazy book from some god."

"A book from what? Never mind. Look, I've got to go. I'll be home in a couple of days. Tell Kerby." He disconnected.

I sat on the bed, stunned. Grey had promised me that book, and I had promised to read it.

But that couldn't be what he'd been killed for. It couldn't be what someone had torn up our home to find. No one would kill and destroy for a science fiction story.

I put my head in my hands, trying to force my brain to make sense of this.

It didn't work. Nothing made sense. Nothing at all made sense anymore.

JERIAH RETURNED AS promised, but without the book. He told me he'd put it in a safe place.

I didn't blame him for not wanting it in his house, and I honestly didn't want it anywhere near me, either. If it was that book

Grey used to talk about, I wasn't sure I wanted to read it. Yes, I'd promised to, but I only told him that to shut him up. Besides, he was dead now. Was the promise still binding?

Riah, Kerby, and I sat in the kitchen eating Nionese take-out. Not mirtositi, for Kerby's sake.

"What did you do with the key?" she asked Riah. "Do you still have it?"

He shook his head as he sucked in a noodle. "I put it in a padded envelope and mailed it to Jano's shop."

Envisioning Jano's probable reaction, I chuckled. But Kerby said, "I hope you cleaned off your fingerprints. And you did wear gloves while handling the envelope, right?"

Riah shrugged. "I doubt those precautions were necessary, but I took them anyway. I guess all us folks in the security business tend to get paranoid after a while."

"Paranoid?" Kerby's eyes widened. "Somebody out there has been murdering people. You think they wouldn't do the same to you, or to me, or to Jemma? If anybody finds out the key came from you, they'll guess you've got the contents of that locker, and then they'll—"

Riah put his hand on her arm. "Kerby. I understand all that. I'm a professional, okay?"

"I know you are. I'm sorry for doubting you. But I don't mind telling you, I'm scared. I don't understand any of this, and that's what scares me. I just know it's a dangerous business. And I have a family to think about." She turned her wide-eyed gaze to me. As if I should explain it and put her mind at ease.

I shook my head. "It makes no sense to me, either, though I've been thinking about little else. But honestly, Kerby, I don't think you and your family are in any danger."

From her expression, she wasn't reassured.

"Why would you be?"

"That's what I mean," she said. "We don't know the 'why' about any of this. And not knowing is what's getting to me." She laid her fork across her empty plate. "That's why I'm anxious to get home. I hate the thought of Hannel and little Haribel out there in the country without me."

My brows rose. "I thought you were staying the rest of the week?"

"Now that your brother's home, I changed my plans. A cab's coming to take me to the airport in about an hour, so I'll help you clean up, and then I'm on my way."

Perhaps she was right to be concerned. Or maybe what happened was a coincidence. But at airport security, her bag never emerged from the screening booth. When it didn't come through, a search was conducted, but it had vanished. The security personnel were at a loss to explain it.

AND NOW I expect you're itching for me to tell you the whole story about the drama surrounding *Mimma's Song* and the Centre Awards.

The book was popular with critics and readers alike. I became highly selective of the newsfeeds I'd listen to, because I couldn't stand hearing constant references to the book and accolades of its author. I rarely left the house for fear of being recognized. The only thing that kept me sane was the City's protection order forbidding reporters or photographers from coming within three hundred meters of my home.

Or rather, Jeriah's home, which was now my permanent hideaway. Unlike me, though, he seemed to enjoy the attention, provided it came from pretty women.

Because *Mimma's Song* was on everyone's mind, no one was surprised when it won the Centre Award for Literature. I think if another book had been named instead, every member of the awards committee would have been stoned by angry mobs.

In the days leading up to the official announcement of that quadrennial awards' recipients, however, the newsfeed buzz was dominated by another story. A number of Kentans, recently escaped from the so-called resettlement communities where they had spent more than a decade, had contacted various City and news agencies to tell their stories and plead for relief for their people.

"Our children are starving," one gray-haired man reported, his eyes hollow and cheeks sunken. "We have a school, but few books and no computers. The children learn their letters by writing with a stick in the dirt. Much of the time, we have no electricity. We have running water, but it is not safe to drink."

A one-eyed woman whose face bore a diagonal scar from forehead to chin told a similar story. "What little we have is taken by the gangs who control the streets. No one is safe from their violence and extortion. Rape is a way of life."

Another woman corroborated the report, adding, "We are behind electronic barriers so we cannot get out. Somehow there is always power for those, even when we have no light in our homes. The constabulary makes no effort to control crime. Their only concern is keeping us captive."

A young man just beginning to grow whiskers spoke in a hushed voice. "We were sometimes visited by our priestesses' arms. They always brought supplies, but never enough, never the necessities. They brought statues of Our Lady, not seeds for our gardens. Candy and Laffcrim, not meat, grain, or clean water. These men were always well fed, well dressed. They walked with confidence, not in fear. 'We plead with the City Fathers for help,' they tell us. 'We tell them of the terrible conditions under which our people labor. But they tell us we get what we deserve.'"

Through a series of video reports, more than a dozen told a similar tale. Each one's flight from their community was accomplished as if it were a break from prison. Each knew others who tried to leave earlier but were caught and severely punished.

I felt a kinship with those Kentans, partly because I had lived among them for so long, and partly because, apparently, they really were my kin. It made me livid to think that those innocent people were forced to live like that while I, a Standtall, with enormous wealth and influence, was unable to do anything about it.

"I wish I were a sniper," Jeriah said after we'd watched one of the reports.

I relaxed my set, angry jaw enough to say, "Huh? Why?"

"I'd love to get Diag Lar in my crosshairs."

I nodded. We both remembered Lar, the suave, slippery arm of the High Priestess, from when we served in Arkentak. He was not only her arm, but her fist as well. He was the hand that delivered gifts to those in favor and a savage blow to anyone who stood in her way.

Or in his way. By the end of the war, it seemed it was Lar who was in charge, not the Priestess. She, it appeared, was merely the figurehead. The flag around which to rally his troops. The battle cry that made Stridentan hearts sing.

The High Priestess had made no personal appearances since the war. But Lar made frequent reference to her, and she—or someone posing as her—appeared in video messages exhorting the faithful to demonstrate their devotion by donating to the cause. Definition of that cause was a little nebulous, but it often involved relief to the unfortunates who had been injured or displaced by the City's attacks.

Donations poured in from all over the world. Estimates were in the billions of urexi. Populations in the resettlement communities endured desperate squalor, their photos tugging at heartstrings and loosening purse strings, while the Kentan elite built magnificent homes in clean, modern cities. They traveled the world in private jets and purchased vacation islands in Omaseen. They met with the City Fathers, sent their children to the most exclusive City schools, and received praise from the Fathers for their efforts on their people's behalf.

Their people who now spoke to the world, their faces scarred, cheeks sunken, and stories desperate.

"I don't blame you for wanting to kill him," I told Jeriah, though I wouldn't allow myself to visualize what a head looked like after a bullet had entered it. "I wouldn't mourn his loss. But that wouldn't fix what's wrong with this world."

Janren Stock came to mind, Father Hold standing beside him as they paid their respects at Grey's mourning. Those were two heads I might appreciate seeing explode. But there had been too much of that going on already. I shuddered. "No. There's more evil involved than anyone can know. Killing people won't put a stop to it."

Riah finished his beer. "So we just accept it when the City takes our tax money and gives it to the traitors? We say nothing when the sliming Stridentans who killed our people are granted citizenship? We bend over and smile when they come at us with—"

"No," I said. "We don't accept it. There are still honest people in the world. Even honest pigeonheads. The fact that these videos are being broadcast is proof of that. It's just so hard to know who you can trust. What you can believe. I wish I knew what to do."

My voice broke. I'd scarcely gone a day without tears since Grey had died. "He was going to fix it. That's what he said after his father was murdered. He was going to fix it. And he died trying. If Grey couldn't reverse what's happening, how can I?"

Riah frowned. "With that book he hid? What use could that have been? I think he was off his rocker. I'm sure he *thought* he knew what he was doing, but he was brain damaged. He wasn't thinking straight."

"Well, you can't deny *somebody* thought he was onto something." I rose and took the bottle from his hand. "Want another?"

"You're encouraging me to drink?"

"You're a Freeman." I headed for the kitchen. "It comes naturally."

He chuckled. "All right then, sure. I'll have another."

A few days later, the Centre City Awards Commission sent me a hand-delivered envelope. When the bell rang, Jeriah accepted it from the messenger and signed for it. He carried it to me in the kitchen where I mixed up a sauce to go with the rappu cakes I'd just put in the oven.

"I believe you've been expecting this." He pulled out a chair at the table. "But maybe you should sit down to open it."

It was a good suggestion. My legs went weak at the sight of what he held out to me. Hands shaking, I opened the envelope.

Jeriah took a seat across from me as I read the letter aloud.

In formal pigeonhead language, it informed me that my novel, *Mimma's Song*, was chosen to receive the Centre City Award for Excellence in Literature Exceeding the Expected. I was invited to attend the entire three-day Quadrennial Awards Conference where the various winners would receive their awards at the conclusion of a series of dinners, panel discussions, and related events. Or, if I preferred, I could limit my attendance to the Awards Banquet and Presentation only. I would be allowed to bring a maximum of three guests with me to the banquet, but I should respond within five days so arrangements could be made.

I laid the letter on the table.

"Well? Are you going?"

I saw Grey sitting in my room at Crater Lake. Heard him say, *You're going to finish that novel. And Brick House will publish it. And it will win a Centre.* "Of course I'm going. How could I not?"

Jeriah rubbed the back of his neck. "You haven't been wanting to go out in public lately."

"I can make an exception in this case." I paused. "That is, if you'll go with me."

He smiled. "Just try to keep me away."

"It says I can bring three people. Would you mind if I asked Bark and Pearl to come too? Can you stand going to something like this with a couple of pigeonheads?"

"Invite whoever you want. It's your party."

I breathed slowly, trying to still my racing heart. "I guess it is, isn't it?"

Although I knew Pearl had other plans for that date, I called her anyway. She didn't hesitate. "Must you ask? Of course! We'd *love* to go!"

Once the initial shock wore off—though why should it have been a shock? We all knew it was coming—I realized I looked forward to getting out of the house. The prospect made me feel alive again for the first time since Grey's death.

It almost seemed as if he would be with me too. I only became a writer because of him, and my story was only possible because of him. I couldn't help but feel this whole thing was his doing.

I would bring him with me—I'd wear his death beads around my neck.

⁂

MY EUPHORIA LASTED until the end of the week, when the Awards Commission publicly released the names of the recipients.

Jeriah and I watched the newsfeed at breakfast. The announcer read the list of Centre Award winners, showing the photo of each: "In Medicine, Stelhan Leron, for his promising research in stimulating the regrowth of severed limbs. In Ecological Science, to Bina Rav for her breakthrough in utilizing algae to grow useable fuels. In Literature, to J. S. Freeman for the novel *Mimma's Song.*"

Jeriah grinned.

But his glee faded instantly, and I choked on my crim, when the announcer continued, "The Humanitarianism award goes to Diag Lar, for his tireless efforts on behalf of his people displaced by war."

❧ Chapter 17 ❧

INDECISION

MY SPILLED CRIM spread across the table and dripped onto the floor, but neither Riah nor I reacted. We stared at each other, silently questioning what we'd just heard.

The Humanitarianism award goes to Diag Lar...

Riah roused himself first and shut off the newsfeed. Then I cleaned up the crim. We exclaimed and ranted and tried to figure out how a man who was so publicly and consistently and obviously-to-anyone-with-a-brain *not* a humanitarian, could win a prestigious Centre Award for being an exemplary one.

My breakfast had gone cold. I covered the bowl with storage wrap and put it in the refrigerator. Riah attacked his with fury, shoveling in the tepid goo with angry motions.

The sight made me queasy. I turned my back and rinsed out the pan. "You're going to make yourself sick."

"I already am sick. The world is sick. What kind of a sick world do we live in, anyway?"

I had no answer.

He sucked up the last of his porridge, then leaned back in his chair, crossed his arms, and glared at me. As if it this was my fault. "So what are you going to do?"

I picked up his empty bowl and spoon and took it to the sink. "What am *I* going to do?"

"Are you going to accept the award? Or will you boycott?"

The running water hit the spoon and splashed up at me. "I don't know." I wiped the water from my cheek with the back of my hand. "I just don't know."

Conflicting thoughts chased one another through my mind:

Grey had wanted this for me. I should accept the award for his sake.

The award was a farce.

Mimma's Song was about integrity. Faithfulness. Lasting love. The book's popularity told me people wanted to confirm those values.

The award was a sliming farce.

This was the greatest honor an author could receive.

The award was a dripping, slotting farce.

The world equated integrity and faithful love with my story. With Ashgrey Standtall. With me. They would be watching me. I couldn't let them down.

I couldn't have anything to do with this. Couldn't accept recognition from any committee that could reward Diag Lar for his atrocities.

"I don't know," I repeated. "I just don't know what to do."

"Well." Riah rose and came to me at the sink, putting his hands on my shoulders. "Whatever you decide, I'll support you. That's one thing you can count on."

☆

I BOUGHT A DRESS for the banquet, and Riah got a tuxedo. We booked transportation and lodgings. I wrote and rehearsed my acceptance speech.

But still couldn't make up my mind about what to do.

Riah didn't seem concerned. "Whatever you decide, I've got it covered."

"What do you mean, got it covered?"

He shrugged. "Don't worry about it. We'll go with whatever you decide."

The most public decision of my life, and he says don't worry about it? I couldn't eat, couldn't sleep, couldn't think straight. Went through the preparations in a trance.

Grey would know what I should do, but he couldn't tell me.

What would Mimma do? She couldn't answer either.

I remembered a past conversation with the now-silent Grey: *If your god is such a great and powerful person-like thing, don't you think he'd communicate like a person?*

He did. His book is amazing. Once you read it, all this will make sense to you.

Was it possible that alien god of Grey's could answer me? No, of course not. My ancestors had fallen into that delusion centuries before, and then Grey's damaged mind was sucked in as well.

Once you read it, all this will make sense to you.

I had the book now. Or at least, Riah had it. Knew where it was. But I'd never seen it.

Grey said his god would make things make sense. And I needed that. Above all else, I needed things to make sense.

The night before we were to leave for the awards presentation, I lay awake, exhausted. Desperate for sleep. Desperate to understand. Desperate to escape my mounting desperation.

What should I do? What *could* I do?

I rose and went into the bathroom. I knew nothing about that god of Grey's but what he had told me—and since I'd refused to listen, he hadn't told me much.

Remembering that silly Sonmanism ritual I'd seen performed back on Freemansland, I turned on the faucet, scooped up a handful of water, and wet my bowed head. "Thanks be to thee, O Good Giver, for thy generous provision."

This was ridiculous. I might as well talk to Grey, for all the answer I'd get. Besides, that was a pre-meal prayer, not one for direction. How did this prayer stuff work?

Should I re-wet my head? Did that make for a better connection? Feeling like I needed all the help I could get, I doused myself again. As water dripped from my hair into the sink, I fumbled for words. "Grey's god, whoever or whatever you are... I don't know what I'm supposed to say. But this world needs help. If you care about us, which Grey said you do, though I can't figure why, show me what to do, would you please? We're a mess down here."

※

BY MORNING, I HAD slept a fitful two hours. I'd heard nothing from Grey's god, either—no surprise there.

But Riah and I were prepared for the trip. Bark and Pearl were too. And so my decision was made: I would go and accept the award.

※

ON THE DAY of the awards presentation, the recipients and their guests attend a mid-day banquet at Ottava Xenio Hall. Following that, everyone goes into the auditorium, where the recipients have places of honor on the stage. Their guests get front-row seats in an audience made up of academics, peers of the Award recipients, City bigwigs, and anyone the City Fathers want to impress.

I'd been through some stressful situations before, but I had never been strung so tight as when Bark, Pearl, Riah, and I entered that hall.

Earlier, while we made our plans, Bark told me he'd performed there and knew of an obscure side door we could use without attracting much attention. But I told him the Award recipients and their guests were expected to make a grand entrance. "The public will not be allowed anywhere near," I said. "Just three camera crews approved by the Committee, and they have instructions to keep their distance."

And so we entered grandly and safely. No fans of Bark calling out for an autograph. No devoted readers of mine trying to weep on my shoulder. Just the ornate immensity of the Ottava Xenio Hall, with a purple carpet, uniformed ushers, banners flying, flowers everywhere, and a brass choir erupting in a fanfare when we entered. I was accustomed to CFC formality, but this ratcheted the pomp up several notches.

I won't waste time with all that we saw, all we were served, the music and entertainment, nor the thoughts that went through my mind. I was there, but I wasn't really present. I felt disconnected, as if I were elsewhere watching it onscreen. I projected an image for people to see, but the real me, the me that observed and processed, was hidden from view.

My projection ate and drank, smiled and chatted, applauded and approved. The hidden observer reserved judgment, watching everyone and everything.

After the meal, we moved to the auditorium, where a row of seats for the recipients was on the left of the stage. Facing them, the City Fathers sat stage right. The Awards Committee sat upstage, facing the audience. Center stage, a thin rug bearing the Centre Awards crest covered the floor. A podium stood just behind the symbol.

Riah and I had to part. I hadn't realized until that moment how very much I'd been relying on him. He and Bark both were so strong, so confident, and so was Pearl. How could I walk away from them—from my brother especially, but also Bark, with his reassuring Grey-like presence, and Pearl's comforting warmth—and mount that intimidating stage alone? And sit up there with the cold and brutal Diag Lar, and the lying and manipulative Father Hold and the people he held in his power?

Before we went our separate ways, Bark and Pearl each gave me a quick hug. Riah squeezed my hand and whispered in my ear. "We've got it covered."

There it was again, that inexplicable assurance. Who's we? What are we covering? For a moment I was the wild child Jem, wanting to flee. But the memory of Bark's embrace reminded me I was no longer a Freeman, and the tickle in my ear from Riah's words gave me the strength to stand tall as I crossed the stage and took my seat. They had it covered.

Grey's death beads felt heavy on my neck as I sat between ecologist Bina Rav and the humanitarian, Lar. I listened to the music. Then to the welcome, the introductions, the accolades.

I watched and applauded as Dr. Leron accepted his award. I smiled and nodded at his acceptance speech. I applauded again when he left the podium, and shook his hand as he returned to his seat.

I repeated the process for Bina Rav.

All the while, Lar's presence loomed beside me. I smelled his expensive cologne. I was aware of his every shuffle, twitch, shift, and ahem. Occasional side glances reminded me of his smug expression. He brushed against me when he rose to shake hands with the other recipients.

It all came back to me in that cologne. The stench, the pain and the terror, the interminable darkness of my burial in the rubble in Arkentak.

The sounds on the newsfeed of the destruction of war. The harrowing stories told by the escaped refugees. I heard those in his self-satisfied throat clearing.

The hopeless sorrow of a mother holding her dying child, the terror of a child missing his mother, the agony of a man searching the rubble for his family. I saw that in Lar's benevolent nod.

Knowledge of what I must do. I felt that when he brushed against me.

The Committee Chairman took the podium to talk about me. He rambled on and on.

Grey's remains around my neck reassured me. I scanned the audience, and my eye found my brother. He met my gaze and nodded. I noted vaguely that the seat between him and Pearl was empty, but I didn't have the presence of mind to wonder where Bark was.

As if from a distance, I heard my name. A wave of applause lifted me from my seat. The Chairman said something. I said something back. He shook my hand. I shook back.

He handed me a certificate and a velour box containing a medal.

"Thank you," I said.

More applause. I turned to the podium, where I set down the certificate and the box. The Chairman left my side, and the applause petered out.

Grey's beads massaging my collarbones, I spoke. "Thank you, Mr. Chairman, and all the esteemed Award Committee."

I gave a small bow to the three men to my right. "Honorable Father Hold, Father Ganns, Father Stern."

I nodded toward the other recipients. "My fellow laureates."

I faced the audience. "Ladies and gentlemen. It is an inexpressible honor and privilege to be here this evening. I have been amazed at the reception the world has given my novel, *Mimma's Song,* and I am deeply humbled by it."

Movement in the audience caught my eye, but I kept speaking as I saw Riah leave his seat and an usher hurry toward him. "I could never have imagined the world would be so moved by a simple story of a woman's love for her husband."

I departed from my prepared speech at this point and made up the rest as I went. "I would be gratified by this—I would be heartened to see how many others can relate to this devotion."

Two ushers were with Riah now, all three hurrying toward the foot of the stage. But I couldn't spend the mental energy wondering about it. I had to compose my words. "I would be gratified by this, but I cannot be. Instead, I am grieved. I do not know what to think when the same eminent people who would honor a story about gentle strength and undying faithfulness—" My voice broke.

I swallowed and continued. "When the same eminent people thus honor a story portraying the world's greatest good, and with another stroke of the same pen, reward a man who is responsible for the death and despair of tens of thousands—no, hundreds of thousands—"

Everyone in the room let out a loud gasp. A man to my left—probably Lar—uttered a loud, Kentan expletive.

Jeriah and the two ushers ran up on stage.

"I cannot participate in this tragic charade. I must decline this award. To accept it would be to condone this travesty. Diag Lar is a murderer and an extortionist." I had to raise my voice to be heard above the shouting in the crowd and on the stage. "He is not a humanitarian. And the whole world knows it."

Before I had finished, the crowd was on their feet. Whether they shouted in opposition or agreement, I couldn't tell. Guards rushed to the stage, but Riah had a head start—and apparently the two ushers were friends of his, because the three of them surrounded me.

"Duck!" Riah shouted above the din and pushed my head down. Something fell from above. A heavy tarp of some sort? Whatever it was, I was glad I'd ducked. The lights went out. Women screamed. Men shouted. There was jostling and shuffling all around. Beneath the tarp, Riah and the ushers took hold of me and directed me, all of us bent double, across the stage. One of the ushers scuttled ahead, lifted a corner of the floor's decorative overlay, and opened a trap door.

"Down, quick!" Riah ordered, and I scurried through the opening and down a ladder, with him so close behind that he stepped on my hand.

As soon as he was through the door, it closed. At the bottom of the ladder, someone held a light. "Hurry!"

My heart almost stopped. Grey!

"Wha—" I jumped off the last rung and grabbed hold of him. "How did—"

"No time. Hurry!" It wasn't Grey, it was Bark.

My heart thumped wildly. My head spun with confusion and rang from the clamor above us.

Riah grabbed my hand and pulled. "Come on!"

Bark gave me a push. "Move quickly!"

"Bark!" I tried to turn back.

Riah tugged me forward. "He's not coming. Come on!"

We ran.

I never saw Bark again until my fourth life.

❧ Chapter 18 ❧

PURIFICATION

THE SLOPE WASN'T as steep as a Freemansland sharpfall, but I could hardly catch my breath. "I thought we were in NaHora. This seems more like Thinair."

Jeriah snorted as he climbed. "How would you know? You've never been on Thinair."

"True." I was determined to keep up with him, but I sure wished he'd stop for a break. My heart pounded like it was trying to hammer its way through my breastbone. "But the air's thin. Like it must be. On Thinair." I took a deep breath. "And it's cold."

He trudged on ahead. "You're just out of shape."

I hadn't the breath to answer. It was just as well, because if I had, I'd have argued with him. And that would have been foolish, because he was right. I had been holed up in the house for months. Hadn't swum, worked out, nor so much as walked around the block in all that time. I was in no condition to hike in the wilds of mountainous NaHora.

Without a trail. Clambering over rocks and fallen trees, like we used to do every day on Freemansland.

We were used to it then. And considerably younger.

Grasping a sapling with one hand and an exposed root in the other, I hauled myself up a particularly steep part of the slope to where Riah stood on a flat rock above. "How much farther is this cabin, anyway? We've got to be near the top by now."

"Not sure." He breathed heavily too, I was gratified to note.

"You even sure we're on the right mountain?"

Riah bent, hands on his knees. "Absolutely. Whew. It's a climb, though, isn't it?"

"No kidding."

It was the eighth day since we'd fled Ottava Xenio Hall in the strangest escapade I'd ever had. Riah had trustworthy friends who didn't ask questions. Under the circumstances, I didn't either. I trusted my brother completely. But I was not happy with him at that moment.

Because he was Jeriah, he'd known I wouldn't accept the Centre Award. It took me weeks to decide, but he'd known it all along. That's how he'd been able to make a plan, enlisting Bark and a few dependable friends who were poised and ready when the time came.

Bark never ceased to amaze me. Publicly, he gave the impression of a big, happy-go-lucky guy who never took anything seriously. But he'd helped Grey with his sneaking about, and now, he not only told Jeriah about the Hall's secret passageways and exits, but he also provided disguises. Riah had somehow obtained fake ID papers, and by the time we left the Hall, we had donned new personas with our costumes.

In the Hall's underbelly, as we hastily changed, transforming ourselves into utility repairmen, my brother said, "Get rid of the necklace."

I pulled my head through the authentically stained and faded shirt. "It's not just a necklace. It's Grey's remains."

"I know. Leave it." He slipped on a boot.

"I can't—"

"You can't take it. Ditch it."

He was right, of course. But how could I?

I unfastened the clasp with unwilling hands, my mind searching for ways to take Grey with me. The beads were too bulky to carry without leaving a lump in a pocket or garment. I didn't know where we were going or what we were doing, but Jeriah did. And he knew it wasn't safe for me to keep them.

In an uncertain world, I knew only one thing for sure: I could trust my brother.

My heart wept, but my eyes didn't as I wrapped the beads in my discarded dress and shoved the bundle into the disposal chute. Riah stuffed his new tuxedo in after it, and we resumed our flight, with our old lives on their way to the incinerator.

It was necessary. I knew it was, but I mourned the loss. All that remained of Grey now were my memories.

Still experts at Stealth, Jeriah and I had no difficulty getting out of Centre City. We traveled north by rail to Indopso, then took a cargo ship to NaHora. We disembarked posing as stevedores and melted into the wharf's bustle.

I was tall enough to pass for a man. Gloves disguised my feminine hands, and layered clothing gave me bulk and kept me from shivering in NaHora's brisk autumn air. I let the deep-voiced Riah do the talking.

Using funds connected to a fake identity, he bought ziptrain tickets—economy class, as befitted a pair of dockworkers—and we spent our sixth night on the run in hard, cramped seats speeding through an impressive succession of tunnels to Woodbridge, eight hundred kilometers inland.

At Woodbridge Station, we bought water and a supply of Compact Foodsources. Newsfeeds playing in the lobby told of our disappearance—abduction, they called it. The City searched for us everywhere. I would have feared for Riah's friends who'd posed as ushers, and especially for Bark. But the reports said the authorities had no suspects. I hoped innocent people wouldn't be forced to pay for my actions.

We continued our journey on foot. My body and mind screamed for rest. When we lived with Aunt Lanie and Uncle Rhe, I'd wanted to disappear. Just my brother and me, on our own in the wilds. But that was a different time, place, and circumstances. I'd never envisioned a flight like this.

After we'd caught our breath on the flat rock, Riah consulted his GPS. "Looks like it's close. Ready to move on?"

I nodded. "The sooner we get there, the sooner we can rest."

IT WASN'T AS close as all that. We climbed another half hour before we found the cabin.

Tucked behind two massive fir trees and beneath a rocky overhang, it would have been easy to miss if Jeriah's friend who built it hadn't given him detailed instructions.

"There it is," Riah said about the same time I spied it.

It should have been a relief to finally reach our destination, but I was not comforted. "Doesn't look like much."

Truly, my broom closet was bigger. And more habitable.

"You and I have both slept in worse."

We passed between the two fir trunks—something inside me laughed at the observation that the hovel might be called Sentinel Pines—and up one step onto what might pass for a porch.

I saw nothing resembling a window. The door had a latch, but no lock. I supposed the only likely intruders were animals, and the latch was sufficient against their unwanted entry.

That, and the surprising thickness of the door. It looked like it could survive a battering ram. Riah unlatched it and pulled. It opened on its leather hinges with a creak.

The interior was musty, dark, and uninviting, and I let him go in first.

Did I say it was dark? It was like a cave. No windows. Riah turned on his electric torch and found a battery lamp.

Once we were inside, we could see that it actually was a cave, and it extended farther back than we could see in the lamplight.

Though primitive in the extreme, it seemed to contain everything we needed: a modern smokeless wood burning stove that vented outside. Cast iron cookware. A rustic but sturdy table and two chairs. Shelves and bins of all kinds of nonperishable foods. Two thick sleeping mats and a stack of blankets.

The sound of trickling water provided background music. Riah took his torch and moved toward the rear of the cave, scattering the gloom. I turned mine on and followed. A narrow opening to the left—Riah had to go through sideways to avoid scraping his shoulders—led to a low passage, the end of which was covered with a heavy curtain. Riah pulled back the curtain and shone his light in.

"Ablutions." We said together.

It was a classic Freemanslander version of what civilized people called a bathroom, and it appeared to have been a natural feature of the cave. To the right, water trickled out of the wall and onto a stone shelf. Someone had put a container beneath the slow but steady flow to collect it. An overflow spout near the top of the container emptied into a bowl on the floor.

The water overflowed the bowl and ran into an uneven stone trench, twenty-five centimeters or so wide, crossing the far side of the small room. Jeriah shone his light into the trench. It was deep, but the glittering reflection and the rushing sound told us there was running water down there.

A short-legged chair made of lashed-together sticks stood against the left wall. Or rather, it was the frame of a chair, but it had no seat. "Look at this." I picked it up and set it over the trench. It had obviously been made to fit the space.

Jeriah nodded. "All the comforts of home."

I was more hungry, thirsty, and exhausted than I'd ever been in my life, except when I was buried beneath the rubble in Arkentak. But this was a close second. I had no qualms about drinking the water that spouted from the top container into the bowl below.

It was cold. I was cold. Everything was cold. "I suppose there's wood for that stove somewhere?"

Jeriah shrugged. "I suppose there is." But he didn't make an effort to look until after I'd finished drinking.

While he took his turn at the water fountain, I left the ablutions room. As I emerged from the passage, my torch revealed a wall of cordwood toward the back of the cave. It was bound to be damp, but I was sure we could coax it to burn.

Riah came up behind me. "Pretty homey, don't you think?"

I stepped aside to let him out of the passage. "I'm too tired to think. And starved. We finished our last CF this morning, didn't we?"

"There's food out there." He nodded toward the front of the cave. "I'm going to grab some wood and make a fire."

Now that we were at the end of our long, grueling journey, I hardly had the strength to lift my feet. I shuffled into the main room and picked up one of the floor mats. "I'm too tired to eat." I unrolled the mat and grabbed a blanket. "I'll eat when I wake up."

I'd scarcely lain down and covered myself before I was asleep. I never even heard Riah make the fire.

The stove glowed with warmth, and a covered pot steamed on its flat top when I awoke to the smell of something delicious. Riah slept on the other mat beside me.

I rolled over and went back to sleep, dreaming of verlik stew.

WHOEVER RIAH'S FRIEND was who had built this place, he knew what he was doing. We had everything we could possibly need—by Freemanslander standards, at least—to survive for at least a year.

"How'd he get all this stuff up here?" I asked over my second bowl of stew—for that was what had been on the stove. Riah had gone out and killed a verlik while I slept, and those NaHoran rodents got huge up there in the mountains.

Riah sucked a bone clean. "I didn't ask."

"Did you tell him what we'd need?"

He shook his head. "He built this for himself, not for us. In case he ever needed it someday. I think he's been working on it for years, here and there."

"He doesn't mind us using it? Eating his food and burning his firewood?"

"He assured me he doesn't."

I slurped up the last of the broth in my bowl. "When we leave, I'd like to restock it for him. Or at least, pay him for what we used. How long do you figure we'll have to hide out, anyway?"

Riah sobered. "When I was out hunting, I turned on my phone."

I almost choked. "You brought your *phone?* They can track that!"

"No, another one. Unregistered. I'll keep it shut off except for emergencies, since there's no way to recharge it."

"So, who'd you call?"

"A friend of a friend of a friend. Who's been waiting for me to call to let him know we got here. And this friend told me the High Priestess has issued a Purification Order."

My heart lurched. "For... for me?"

"Afraid so."

When the High Priestess ordered a Purification, it meant the object of the order was to be removed. Permanently.

Everyone who bowed to the High Priestess was obligated to participate in the Purification any way they could. Most people were merely expected to contribute money to the cause, but some of the funds were used to pay informants—and when the person to be purified was located, skilled assassins.

Traditionally, a Purification Order was good for nine months. The idea was if a target stayed alive that long, it was a sign the Lady Striden had the person under her divine protection. In that case, the person to be purified was declared to have been "born anew" and could then emerge from hiding as if from her womb.

I happened to know of one case where the person in question experienced his blessed new birth only to die of "natural causes" a month later. Apparently, Our Lady could sometimes change her mind.

"Are you telling me—" The verlik chased its tail in my stomach. "I have to stay here for nine whole months? Through a whole NaHora winter?"

Riah's mouth narrowed into a hard, firm line. "After ten months, I'll turn on my phone again and see what the situation is. Don't even think about leaving here before that."

Too angry to speak, I set my bowl and spoon down, shoved away from the table and went outside.

And regretted it immediately. It was dark out there, and frigid. Far too cold for a Freemanslander to be outside without coat. I huffed in frustration, and my breath formed a cloud in front of me. In three seconds, I was shivering.

I dragged the door open and went back in. "I hate you sometimes. You know that, don't you?"

He had the stew pot in his hands. "There's just a little bit left. Do you want it?"

"Sure." I sat at the table and put my head in my hands. "I can't stand it here. How am I going to survive for ten months?"

"It'll probably be longer." He emptied the stewpot into my bowl.

"You shouldn't have brought me here. I'd rather die."

He set down the pot with a thud, then gripped my shoulders in both hands. "Listen to me, you spoiled brat."

"What—"

"Seena's gone, my kids won't talk to me, and thanks to you, I don't even have a job anymore. I'm stuck with you. Stuck out here, living in a cave on a freezing mountaintop for what may turn out to be the rest of my life. So get your precious little tush off that velvet CFC cushion you've been sitting on all these years and quit your whining."

I pulled away. "I haven't whined one bit since you dragged me off that stage. I've done everything you said. I even threw Grey's beads into the incinerator. How dare you say I'm—"

He wrapped me in a hug. "I won't let you die. Whatever happens, you're not going to die. You're all I have in the world, and I won't lose you again."

IT WASN'T UNTIL the next morning that we realized Riah's friend had neglected to provide either crim or crim maker.

"Okay," Riah said. "That's bad."

"It's worse than bad. We're going to go through withdrawal. Can you..." I tried to think of a way to avoid the certain calamity before us. "Can we walk back down the mountain and buy some crim and—"

"With a Purification Order on your head? Forget it. We'll just have to get through it."

We did. It was two weeks before the blinding headaches eased, and even after the pain was gone, we didn't feel well for several more. But that wasn't the worst of our problems.

For the first three days, we kept ourselves busy exploring the woods around the cabin, hunting for fresh meat, searching for edible roots, nuts, or anything else to supplement our dried, tinned, and otherwise not-fresh diets. The exercise and activity kept us from going mad with boredom and crim-deprivation.

And then winter hit.

We later learned it was NaHora's earliest, coldest, and snowiest winter in recorded history. At the time, we only knew it was cruel and unrelenting.

At least Riah had thought to bring in more firewood while we were still able. The stove was efficient and our living space was small, so it didn't take a big fire to keep it warm. Even so, we were a little alarmed to see how the pile dwindled.

In our explorations, we'd found where more was cut and stacked outside. Once we realized our indoor supply would not last indefinitely, we carried in as much as we could store, hauling it through the bitter cold and driving snow so it could dry in the warm cave before we needed it.

Then one morning, the snow was so packed against the door we couldn't open it. We were, for all practical purposes, imprisoned.

But we had food, water, firewood, and warm clothing. We even had an impressive supply of batteries for the lamps. We'd be okay.

What we didn't have was something to occupy ourselves. After one day of inactivity, we were ready to kill each other.

The next morning, as we took our time preparing and eating breakfast, knowing we'd have nothing to do once it was done, Riah rubbed his beard. "Do you suppose the light's good enough for reading?"

I snorted. "I guess we'll never know, will we?"

He got out a torch and shone it on the table. "Sure, that will work. Between this and the lamps over there, that's plenty of light."

"Good. Now all we need is something to read."

His face fought with a smile. "Oh, we have something. I'll show you after breakfast."

"What? A shopping list? The laundering instructions for the long underwear we don't have?"

"I'll show you after breakfast."

I couldn't get excited about it. If there was any reading material in that little half-cabin, half-cave, I hadn't seen it, and I'd investigated every nook. Besides, we were both fast readers. Even if there were a couple of books hidden somewhere, we'd finish them in a day or two.

After breakfast, he went to the door.

I frowned. "We're stuck in here, remember?"

But instead of trying to open the door, he felt along its rough-hewn surface, tapping here and there. Then he took his torch and examined something, did some more feeling, some exploratory pressing. "Ah." He slid a panel upward to reveal a large rectangular opening—a door within the door.

I sat at the table and watched. "What in the world is that?" It looked like there was a plastic box inside.

He pulled it out. From the way he handled it, it must have been heavy.

He set it on the table with a thud, then opened it and pulled out a book. A thick one. Made of banroo skin. No title on the front.

He dropped the plastic box to the floor and set the book on the table in front of me. "This is what your husband died for. I think it's time you took a look at it."

❧ Chapter 19 ❧

———❧———

MY THIRD LIFE ENDS

———❧———

I RAN MY HAND across the book's blank cover. This was no mass-produced volume. Grey had put it together. For me. When he said he'd get a copy for me, I had no idea he meant he'd *make* me a copy, writing it by hand.

The cover was dragonskin, the pages banroo, and it was bound with what looked like sinew, probably from a dragon. Where had Grey gotten the materials, let alone learned how to make a book like this? Probably from that strange Dr. Simelum at the Zavazda. When I opened the cover, I almost expected to see crumbs from the historian's beard.

Instead, I found a letter on ordinary paper written in the clumsy scrawl that was the best Grey could do after the shooting. The uneven scribbles covered three pages, front and back. As I smoothed the letter across the book's frontispiece, I envisioned Grey writing this for me, head tipped to see through his one eye, his scarred face pinched with concentration. I had to wipe my eyes before I could get them to focus on it.

Meanwhile, Riah had turned away as if to give me and Grey some privacy, busying himself with emptying the ashes from the wood stove.

My heart swelled with gratitude for his finding and giving me this book. For abandoning his whole life to be with me. For accepting that Grey and I had truly loved each other, that Grey had been faithful, that he was a good man.

"Thank you."

Riah grunted. "For what?"

"For this. For everything. For being my brother."

He closed the stove door. "I never exactly had a choice in that." He carried the bucket of coals to the ablutions area.

I called after him. "Did you read this letter?"

"Of course not. It's personal."

"It is."

He returned and set the empty bucket beside the stove.

"But I want to read it to you. I figure we're both going to be reading this book, out of boredom if nothing else. So we might as well both know what it's all about."

He sat at the table across me. "If you want to, go ahead."

And so I read aloud.

☀

"FREEMAN," THE LETTER began. "When I was a different man, loving you made me very happy. I remember the delight I once felt when merely thinking of you. Now, I think of you and feel sad because I have let you down. You look to me for something I can no longer give you. I am not even certain what it is.

"You think I love the kyukur more than you? I do not. I am comfortable with Toughie because he has no expectations. I cannot disappoint or offend him. He is always happy to be with me, and that eases my pain."

My voice didn't break while reading—I don't know how it didn't, but I remained steady.

"I suppose on some level I still love you, though I do not remember how that is done. I only know that a husband should provide his wife with all she needs. In that, I fail. But this one thing, I can give you.

"I once said you would understand if you could read this book. The book of God, or all that remains of it as far as I know. Dr. Simelum has allowed me to copy the text from the fragments his people have found.

"When your forebears were marooned on the island, they could take nothing with them. But they had memorized much of the book. They met together to remember and compare. They worshipped together. They figured out how to make banroo skin in order to record as much of the book as they recalled.

"They believed what they put together from memory was an accurate copy of what they had received from the glowing-eyed visitors, and I have little doubt that was true. When you read it, you will see. This is no ordinary book. It is a collection of many books. It is said they were written on another planet over the span of some two millennia by dozens of authors in different parts of that world. But it is cohesive. It tells one story with many facets, and with such depth that no person can plumb its extent. As a writer, you will see how unique this book is. You will know something like this could never come from human intellect.

"I know you will realize this, because you are a wise woman, and this book is wisdom. I know you will read it, because you promised you would. I pray that its truth will open the door to freedom for you, as it did for me, and for your forebears. For though they are dead, and I am too, we are alive. The God of this book has broken our chains and set us free.

"There is more here than you can see. I have written on one side of the page. If anyone asks, tell them this: There is more here than you can see."

I looked up at Jeriah. "What does that mean?"

"I have no idea. He wasn't in his right mind, though."

I frowned. "That's what I used to think too. But lately, I'm not so sure. Does anything else in this letter sound like a crazy man wrote it?"

"It seemed pretty lucid until where he said he and our forebears are dead but alive." He shook his head. "And that bit about what to say if anyone asks? Sounds like he was falling apart by that point. Does it end like that? Or is there more?"

I turned the pages over and looked for another. "It just ends. He didn't even sign it."

"I guess the rest of his message is the book."

"I suppose so." I laid down the letter and turned my attention to the volume.

The title page said simply, "The Book of God."

The next page, in flowery and archaic language, but in Grey's sprawling hand, was a brief history of how the book came to be compiled. It was much as the letter had explained it, but in more detail. It concluded a list of the names of the prisoners who participated in the project. There were nearly fifty names, and twelve of them were named Jeriah.

A table of contents followed.

I turned the next page, where the text began.

Unlike the front matter, this was written in Grey's old handwriting. That meant he'd started this before the shooting. The words were neat and precise, the lines straight as a ruler.

I pictured him in Dr. Simelum's big lab, working at one of those tables under the lights. Peering first at the recovered fragment, then transcribing it on the page, letter by careful letter.

Why do it by hand instead of a computer? Why on banroo skin instead of paper? Why only on one side of the page?

And who wanted this badly enough to kill for it?

I tried to imagine the other people who had given their lives for it. My ancestors. They had forsaken the Lady Striden to worship this alien god, and it had cost them everything. What in this book was worth that?

Jeriah's voice jarred me from my reverie. "So're you going to read it, or just stare at it?"

I caressed the page. The page Grey had handled. Written upon. With all his faculties intact. How many hours had he devoted to this—for me? "I almost feel as if it's holy," I said. "Hallowed with blood."

But Grey hadn't taken such pains so I could sit and admire it. I took a deep breath and began.

"In the beginning, God created the heavens and the earth."

☼

WE TOOK TURNS reading aloud. We stopped often and discussed what we read.

It was interesting, after a fashion. Bewildering at times. But not what I'd call enlightening, by any means. After a couple of hours, we took a break. It was hard on the eyes, hard on the mind.

I got up from the table and stretched. Riah shut off the torch he'd been using to help us see the small writing. "Want some lunch?"

I put Grey's letter in the book to mark our place and laid it back in the box. "Can't say as I'm hungry. I don't work up much of an appetite sitting around doing nothing."

"Agreed. And maybe we should take it easy on the food anyway. Who knows how long we'll be shut up here. I'd been counting on hunting to supplement the stored goods, but we can't do that if we can't get out."

I did some stretches. "How long do you figure it'll be before we can get that door open?"

"Hard to say. It's only autumn, though. There's bound to be a thaw soon. Soon as I can get out of here, I'm going to see if I can build some sort of a barrier to keep the snow away from the door."

"Yeah. I don't like being trapped in here. When I hid out in your house, there was plenty of room to move around. And I could leave whenever I wanted, I just didn't want to. This is different. It's almost like being buried alive."

Jeriah frowned. "I imagine it is a bit like that." He went to the door and tried again.

It unlatched just fine, but when he pushed against it, something pushed back, just like yesterday.

I helped throw my shoulder into it, but it didn't yield. I wanted to cry with frustration. "I hate snow."

The next morning—and we only knew it was morning because that's what Riah's watch said. With no window, we had no idea if it was day or night—we both woke up feeling ill. Body aches, fever, chills, and deathly exhaustion. For some time, it was all we could do to keep the fire going, chew a plug from a CF bar now and then, and wash it down with water. Hour after hour, for who knew how many days on end, we lingered in that state, speaking only enough to ascertain that the other was still alive.

Finally, after what Jeriah determined was the fourth day, we began to improve. We forced ourselves to move around, to eat and drink more, trying to regain our strength.

A couple weeks after falling ill, we tried the door again to find that the thaw we hoped for had come. We could force the door open enough to squeeze through, but there was no place to go. After fighting through the wet snow beyond the narrow opening, we found only drenching rain from above and a meter of slushy snow to soak us from below.

Even if the weather hadn't discouraged us, we couldn't have moved about the treacherous mountainside in those conditions.

We tried clearing the icy mess away from the door and building up walls of snow in the area surrounding it, but it was cold, miserable work, and we quickly ran out of steam. It all seemed pointless anyway.

We went back in and removed our wet clothes. Having nothing else to wear, we hung the things to dry on the backs of the chairs and sat huddled in blankets on the floor mats, chilled through and shivering. We were too cold to talk.

When my eyes grew heavy, I lay down and slept.

I awoke some time later to hear Riah snoring beside me. The fire had burned low. I got up, opened the stove, and jabbed at the coals with the poker but didn't add any wood. I felt my pants on the chair. They were still damp.

Riah woke up when I closed the stove door. He peered at me through half-closed eyes. "Oh. I guess I fell asleep."

"We'll never get out of here, will we? We're going to die here."

He yawned. "You didn't put any wood on that?"

"If we keep it going night and day, we'll run out."

"How will our clothes dry if the fire goes out?"

"Doesn't matter. We shouldn't wear them unless we go outside. They're all the clothes we have, and they have to last us the rest of our lives."

He gave me a quizzical look. "You think we should only wear clothes to go outside? But if we're stuck in here forever, we'll never have occasion to wear them."

I didn't answer. Just wrapped myself tighter in the blanket.

"I know," he said. "When we run out of firewood, we can keep warm by burning our clothes."

"Won't work. I'm pretty sure they're flame-retardant."

He got up and put a log on the fire. "Are we losing our minds?"

"Probably. If we haven't yet, we surely will."

"Being confined in a small space with you would drive any man crazy."

Remembering Grey's impatience with me the last year of his life, I collapsed onto the floor mat in tears.

"Oh, for—" Riah stood in front of me a moment, then squatted. "Look, I'm sorry. It's the confinement that's making me crazy, not you, okay? If it makes you feel any better, I can't think of anyone I'd rather be buried alive with. Does that help?"

I shook my head. The sound that came out of me was something like a cross between a chuckle and a sob.

"We were in the womb together, and that space was a lot tighter than this."

I wiped my eyes on the blanket.

"And we left the womb. We made it out alive. Together. And we're going to do the same this time. We're going to get out of this. Alive. Together. D'ya hear me?"

I nodded. "Don't know if I believe you. But I hear you."

He sat beside me. "We're Freemen. We like to run free, so it's hard being imprisoned. But I'm seeing it as kind of our heritage, you know? Our forefathers were imprisoned in the cold, and so are we."

I wiped my eyes again. "Yeah. And they died there."

"But they left us that book."

"Grey left us that book."

"He just copied it. They wrote it down for us. For the people that would come after them. And that's us. It meant a lot to them, obviously. I don't know why, but it did. So I think, while we're stuck here, we should read it. Try to figure out why it was so important to them."

We hadn't picked up that book since the day Riah pulled it out of the door. He'd put it back when we were through with it. We didn't have much storage space, after all, and it was safe there. We both felt it was important to keep it safe.

But now, we read it. Every day. Because we had nothing else to do, it took up a large part of our day.

Or maybe our nights. We lost track. Riah's watch quit working, and we had no way of knowing what time it was.

We opened the door on a regular basis, but after a little while, it only opened into a cave of ice. We weren't buried figuratively, but literally. On a sunny day, the walls of the ice cave were a little brighter. At night, it was as dark on one side of the door as the other.

We removed the curtain from the mouth of the ablutions area. The trench over the running groundwater was our one source of fresh air, and we didn't want to cut it off and maybe asphyxiate. If any smells came from that part of the cave, we grew immune to them.

On the subject of nasty things, it wasn't long before Riah and I both looked like wild Freemanslanders. I doubt we smelled very sweet, either. Glaffcrim wasn't the only thing our benefactor had neglected to stock for us. Also absent were soap, towels, razors, combs, toilet paper—you get the idea.

We tried not to be animals, but it was a lost cause.

Seeing our finite supplies dwindling, we realized we'd have to cut back on heating and food as we'd discussed. And, to keep our clothes from wearing too quickly, we went without them when the room was warm and only dressed when a blanket wasn't enough. But one thing we had no lack of: batteries for the lamp and our torches. We didn't have to spare our torches when we read, and because there was no natural light whatsoever, we left the lamp on all the time.

That was the only thing that kept us alive. We couldn't have survived without light.

I also don't know what we would have done without that Book, which I soon took to thinking of with a capital letter. When one of us lifted it from its cubbyhole in the door, it was with reverence. When we opened it, it was with awe. When we read it, it was with amazement.

But we didn't understand a word of it.

Well, maybe a word. The more we read, the more we understood, until after a while, whole sentences made sense. And then whole sections.

We got through it once and then started again. The second time, we began to see how it was all connected, how one part related to another.

The third time through, it all seemed alive. So vibrant the words almost glowed on the page. Yes, much of it was still perplexing. But by then, we realized that the words were not the problem. Our lack of understanding was due to our human inability to comprehend the divine. We read truth, but could only see small glimmers of the glorious whole that shone beneath.

In his copy, Grey had included the marginal references made by the earlier transcribers. "We are uncertain of the exact wording," it said now and then. Or, "A passage in the original is missing here. None of us can recall it, and the Spirit chooses not to bring it to our minds at present." I marveled at how much I felt the loss of those precious words.

His copy was also marked by a sudden and dramatic difference in handwriting. There was no question when his work was interrupted by the shooting and when it resumed. I wept to see the change. To remember the other changes he had undergone. Even my brother seemed moved by the thought.

Every time we got to that part, he patted my arm. "He finished it, though. He set out to do this, and he did it."

Every time he said that, I nodded. "Yes. He did it." But every time, in the back of my mind, I remembered his vow, "I will fix it. I swear by the death beads around my mother's neck. I will fix it," and thought, *But he never accomplished that.*

Our fourth time through, we were at about the three-quarter mark. It was Jeriah's turn to read Grey's large, uneven scrawl. The God-man Jesus was speaking. "All you who continue in my word, you are truly my disciples."

Jeriah paused, and we looked at one another. We loved this Book. We "continued" in it. It revealed the one whose word it was, and we couldn't help loving him too. Were we his disciples?

I could see in his face that Jeriah's mind followed the same path. Then he looked down at the page and continued reading. "And you shall know the truth." He swallowed. "And the truth... shall make you free."

"Jeriah!" I grabbed my brother's hands in both of mine. "Jeriah! Did you hear that?"

Tears flowed from red-rimmed eyes into his whiskers. "I heard that."

We rose from our chairs and shouted together. "We're free! We're free!"

❧ Chapter 20 ❧

MY FOURTH LIFE

O NE DAY MANY months into our confinement, we pushed the door open and stepped outside.

As in the last fifty times we'd done that, all we could see was a wall and ceiling of icy snow. But today, the snow was wilting.

Jeriah threw his shoulder into the wall, but it didn't yield. I went back in, grabbed two pieces of stove wood from our near-depleted store, and hurried outside with them. "Here." I handed one to Riah.

Together, we battered the wall with our miniature rams until a portion fell outward. Breathing heavily from our unaccustomed exertions, we shielded our eyes against the first sunlight we'd seen in months. We leaned into the opening and pulled the fresh air into our lungs. We couldn't get enough of it.

The snow that still covered the world beyond sagged and puddled. Trees dripped. Rocks protruded from the white seas.

Birds sang. I'd never heard such marvelous music.

We wept. I was so overcome by it all, I doubt I could have stood without the wall's support. Neither of us said anything for long moments.

"I think we should eat," I said at last.

Without taking his eyes off the sight before us, Riah nodded. "I think we should."

With our liberation imminent, we no longer had to make our stores stretch as long as possible. Now, gaining strength was top priority. So we ate our fill, then attacked the snow wall again, enlarging the window into an open door. Then the ceiling fell onto us—if we hadn't put our arms over our heads, we may have been knocked out—and the sky, even the whole world, lay open before us.

Months before, when we were strong and the ground was free of snow, it had taken us two days to climb up here. Given the conditions now, how long would it take us to get back down?

And was it even safe to come out of hiding?

Jeriah got his phone and powered it up. We stood together in the sunlight—the glorious sunlight—while he made a call.

Or tried. Before he could connect, the phone died and refused to come back to life.

We stared at the useless object in his hand. If we stayed here much longer, we'd starve. If the Purification Order was still in effect, we'd be killed soon after re-entering civilization. No matter what we did, there was a good chance we wouldn't see our next birthday.

But we couldn't hide any longer. We'd found something we needed to share with the world, and, like Grey, we were prepared to die trying.

Riah interrupted my thoughts. "I think we should pray about this."

And so we did.

The brother and sister who'd come up this mountain last fall would never have considered such an action, but we were not those people. The old Jem and Jeriah were gone. Grey's God—the God of our forefathers—the God who created all that exists, had re-created us. We were new people, and we were His.

We left the next morning, carrying the last of our food as well as the Book, the Bread of our new lives.

FOUR LONG DAYS later, we found a town and stumbled in wet, thoroughly chilled, and near the end of our endurance. I doubt the sight of two people in our condition was an everyday thing, but we didn't seem to arouse much interest as we passed through the village.

When we went to buy essential supplies, we were deeply grateful that Riah's Urex card had not expired along with his phone. Happily burdened with good things, we crossed the road to an inn and rented two rooms, where we indulged in leisurely baths.

Later convening in Riah's room, we ordered take-out from a local restaurant—roast duck with dumplings and fermented saltcabbage, with a side of fruit fritters. Fresh, wholesome food, delivered to our door! I could scarcely contain my delight.

Only after eating did we have the courage to turn on the videoscreen and check the newsfeeds to see what we could find out about the Purification Order.

We quickly learned that while we'd been metamorphosing in our snow cocoon on the mountaintop, the world had undergone a change of its own. Daig Lar was out of the picture, having been assassinated months before. The High Priestess was also dead. The resettlement communities had been taken over by City forces and were now properly managed with the goal of actually resettling the residents in their ancestral homes.

As what I heard and saw began to sink in, I struggled for words.

Riah ran his hand along his newly shaved face. "How in the world did all this happen?"

"I can't imagine." I picked up the controller. "I've got to see something." I did a search for past news items containing the keyword J. S. Freeman—and found roughly 23 million of them.

"Give me that." Riah snatched the controller from my hands and narrowed the search criteria to include "Purification Order." Though it yielded fewer results, the number was still in the thousands.

The euphoria of escaping our confines fizzled, leaving me drained. "I can't deal with all this." I got up from the sofa. "With Lar and the High Priestess both gone, the Order's probably no longer in effect. I'm going to bed."

I went to my room—a whole big room, warm and clean—and went to bed. In a bed. And slept like I hadn't slept in years.

※

TWO WEEKS LATER, Riah and I sat with Aunt Lanie and Uncle Rhe at their home at Moll. It was the first time I'd seen them since my wedding.

They had grown old. They also seemed to have shrunk, though I may simply have forgotten how short they were. In any event, they were delighted to see the both of us.

We'd talked on the phone earlier, so we knew some of the highlights of what had been going on in one another's lives. "I'm so sorry to have caused you such trouble," I said almost as soon as we'd sat down.

Aunt Lanie shook her head, but before she could speak, her husband guffawed. "No trouble at all! We're just glad you're both safe."

Lanie's head shake turned to a vigorous nod. "That's right. We were so worried about you we could hardly stand it. Thank you so much for coming to see us! This isn't the first time you've been back to Freemansland since you went into the service, is it?"

Riah took his traditional role as spokesperson. "Believe it or not, it is. I'm not sure why we never visited before—" He cast a sideways glance at me. "Different reasons, I guess. But we're glad to be here now. It's been too long."

"Your wife and children are on Freemansland, as I recall," Uncle Rhe said.

Riah nodded. "They came back some years ago. The kids both left to go to university in the City for awhile, but—"

I spoke up then. "It's all my fault. All the investigations into my disappearance. I can't believe the City came to Moll and turned this place upside-down."

Uncle Rhe chuckled. "Nothing was turned over. I offered them a cup of crim and then showed them everything they wanted to see."

"A little more than they wanted." Aunt Lanie grinned. "He made them walk up and down the sharpfalls, saying, 'There's no one hiding here. Let's see if they're camped up there.' By the time they got back, those poor fellas could hardly pick up one foot after another."

Uncle Rhe nodded. "Your aunt insisted they spend the night. 'We'll give you the best guest room,' she says, and takes them into the stack you kids slept in when you first came. Let them sleep on floor mats. They were too tired to argue."

"When they contacted us the first time," Lanie said, scowling, "we told them plain as plain that we hadn't heard from you, had no idea where you were. But they had to come out and see for themselves."

Riah chuckled. "I'm afraid Seena wasn't so good-natured about it when the City came knocking at her door. Neither were KJ and Jeo when the same thing happened to each of them. They were all so shook up that Seena insisted the kids come back to

Freemansland and stay with her in case—well, I'm not sure what they were concerned about." He sighed. "I guess they were afraid I'd suddenly appear, and then they'd have to decide what to do about it."

Aunt Lanie was all concern. "Have you been to see them yet?"

"They've agreed to meet me at Freeman Park this evening."

I put my hand on Riah's arm but spoke to our aunt. "I think he should be alone for that. Okay if I stay here? I'll keep out of your way."

"Oh, for glish's sakes. Of course you can stay here. But please don't stay out of the way. We want to see as much of you as we can."

We had a lot of catching up to do. I was happy to see how the plantation thrived, but not as pleased as our aunt and uncle were that Riah and I were alive. I knew she cared about us, but I'd never appreciated how much until that visit.

Their love helped ease the lingering sting from my recent contact with Pearl. She wouldn't even let me talk to Bark. The furor over my disappearance had terrified her. The authorities detained her and Bark and demanded to know what was going on. Pearl honestly knew nothing and so told the whole truth: she was as surprised at the developments as anyone else, and had no idea what was going on. Bark answered honestly as well, but less completely. He didn't know where I had gone, but he didn't blame me for wanting to disappear.

They were detained for three days, and although they were not mistreated, they were both shaken by the experience. Even a year later, Pearl wasn't inclined to forgive me for putting them through all that.

I was thankful my own family was more willing than Grey's to overlook the trouble we'd caused, and I told Aunt Lanie as much when she and I were alone.

"What's to overlook?" She smiled. "You did nothing wrong. You're simply caught in a whirlwind of circumstances. But I hope you know you're both welcome to stay here as long as you like."

"Thank you, I appreciate it, but—"

"But don't think of it as charity. Your uncle would be happy to put you both to work. There's always plenty to do around here."

I sipped my premium Moll. "I love this place. And you have no idea how much I missed glaffcrim!"

"I think I can imagine." She shook her head. "Pretty sure I'd die if I had to go a week without it, let alone several months."

"But I can't stay. Riah might, but I've got to get back to the City and straighten out the mess I've made of my personal affairs."

The repercussions of my vanishing act were more complicated than you can imagine. At the time I spoke with Aunt Lanie, the City was on the verge of revoking my citizenship—both my CFC status, as I was no longer married to Grey, and my Merit status, as certain parties deemed I no longer had merit. It took almost a year before that was resolved. I had to submit statements under oath to countless agencies and, like Bark and Pearl, Riah and I were subject to questioning. My literary agent dropped me and sued for damage to her reputation. My attorneys and accountants all charged exorbitant fees for having to manage my affairs "under unusual circumstances." Riah's landlord sued for a year's worth of rent, late fees that nearly doubled the total, and cleaning and repairs. To my knowledge, nothing was damaged, but I think they wanted to do a complete remodel and so billed me for it. The City confiscated everything from his apartment as evidence, then required me to pay storage fees before they would return it. And those were just the big things. For several months, it seemed I was slapped with something new nearly every day.

"Something I've got to ask you, though," I said to my aunt. "When we were growing up, you said our mother followed the

Sonmanism faith. You said you didn't get into it like she did, but if Jeriah and I wanted to learn more, you could tell us what you knew."

She nodded. "Neither of you ever had an interest, so I didn't push it. But it was very important to my sister. I understand that's why you both have such unusual names."

After seeing all those Jeriahs in the front of the Book, we'd suspected there was a connection, but we never found anyone with that name in the text. "How did she name us both if she died when I was born?"

Lanie's face softened into a sad smile. "Heelo must have known she was having twins, but she couldn't know if you'd be two girls, two boys, or one of each. So she wrote down names for two boys and two girls. When your grandmother carried you up to Glaffit as new babies, she brought the list." She stood. "I kept it. Hang on."

Hang on? Not likely. I got up and followed her into the home office where she unlocked a fireproof file cabinet.

"I'm not sure why I never showed you this before," she said.

"Probably because I never asked."

She pulled a scrap of banroo skin from a file folder. "It was pretty crumpled by the time your gran got up here with it, and it's faded over time. But you can still make it out, I think." She turned on the desk lamp, then spread out the paper under its glow. "Take a look."

I touched it gently. My mother had written this. She'd torn the page from something, I had no idea what. I turned it over. There was nothing on the back.

"I think it's from the flyleaf of a pamphlet. Your gran told me your mother had gotten some booklet about herbals for things like morning sickness and to improve the quantity of breast milk."

The writing appeared to have been done with charcoal. It was badly smeared, but as Aunt Lanie had said, still mostly legible. I read it aloud, as best as I could make it out: "Boys, Jeriah = God will instruct. Jakim = he will raise. Girls, Jemima = warm and affectionate. Cassia = a sweet-smelling fragrance."

I looked at my aunt. "How did you know which names to use for us?"

"We thought your mother would have chosen the first names listed, the first boy's and the first girl's name."

"Are these supposed to be the meanings, then? Jeriah means God will instruct, and Jemima means warm and affectionate?"

"That's what it looks like."

"Neither one's very fitting. Especially mine."

Something else was written after the list. I squinted and held the paper closer to the light as I read, "These are some of the seven sons and three daughters God gave Jobe to comfort him in his loss. I will use two of their names. These babies will be my comfort."

If Lanie noticed my tears, she pretended not to. "Your grandmother told me Jobe is the name of a person in an ancient Sonmanism legend. But I don't know what the rest of this means. Does it make any sense to you?"

I nodded, wiping my eyes with my sleeve. "It kind of does. Let me tell you what Riah and I have learned."

It was hard to explain, and I did a terrible job. I wished Riah were there to speak for me. He was better at this sort of thing.

After trying to relate the whole story of the Book, I picked up the paper again. "The Book did give the names of the three daughters of Jobe, and two of them were Jemima and Cassia. But it didn't name the sons. I don't know where my mother could have gotten these. She never even had a copy of the book, did she? As far as I know, it only exists in fragments the archaeologists found. And the copy Grey made, of course."

Lanie shook her head. "I got the impression it was some oral legend. I've never heard of a book like the one you describe. But when she came back after her military career—"

"Her what?"

Lanie smiled. "You didn't know about that?"

"No. Our mother was in the military?"

"Yes." Her smile faded. "But let me back up. When Heelo was fifteen, she had a baby."

My stomach churned. "Ibro."

"Yes. When she found out she was expecting, she moved in with Jeo and his mother. That is, your father and gran. And then—I was just a child myself, and I can't say firsthand what happened, but a couple years later, she left Freemansland. She left the baby and everything."

I frowned. How could a mother abandon her child?

"I gained a pretty good idea of all this from your grandmother much later, but I was very young when it happened, and I was pretty much in the dark. My father was shocked when Heelo left home and moved in with Jeo. Papa had depended on her to help care for me, and he was so angry about that, he had nothing to do with her or the baby. We didn't even know she'd left Freemansland until she'd been gone for almost a year."

I ran my hand over the scrap of banroo skin, trying to envision the woman who wrote it. Did she look like me? I tried to imagine me looking pregnant.

"Jeo and your mother had been sweet on each other from childhood, which is why she went running to him when she got pregnant the first time. But the baby wasn't Jeo's. Another man had forced her." Lanie hesitated. "Well, I don't know if she was a willing participant or not. Your gran wasn't sure about that either. But I don't think there's any question that Ibro was another man's son, a man named Vin Freeman. But that doesn't narrow it down."

"No. Not exactly." Vin was a common first name, and half of Freemansland was named Freeman.

"Jeo and his mother were willing to take Heelo and the child into their home out of love for her. But one day Vin came around and attacked Heelo, tried to take her away and make her his wife. She somehow fought him off, but she knew he'd be back. She stole all the money she could find at your gran's place, left a note saying what had happened, and took off. Before going up to Coldclime to catch a flight, she dropped Ibro off at the nearest school barge—just put him on the deck and took off without saying anything to anyone. "

My poor mother! That Vin character must have been truly horrible, if she preferred my father to him.

"Jeo tracked down Vin and killed him. Then he went looking for your mother. Took him a couple of years to find her. She was in the Naval Authority Services. He eventually convinced her to come home to Freemansland with him, and when her term was up, she did. They'd gotten married by then, and they moved back in with Jeo's mother and Ibro. But I never knew any of that until your grandmother came up the stairs from Freedom carrying you two little babies. It was all quite a shock, I can tell you. How I regret never reconciling with Heelo when I had the chance."

That answered many questions, but others remained. "Knowing my father, I don't understand why she married him. She should have sent him packing as soon as he showed up."

Aunt Lanie sighed. "According to your gran, he truly loved her. That's why he took her death so hard. He started drinking the day she died and might never have been sober again the rest of his life."

The old familiar guilt swelled up within me. I had killed her. By doing so, I had driven my father to drink.

But then I remembered: I was forgiven. Of everything! After carrying the burden of guilt my whole life, it was a hard thing to grasp.

With my finger, I traced the name *Jemima* on my mother's list. She had chosen it for me. "How did you know she was interested in Sonmanism? Did Gran tell you that too?"

"Yes." Lanie nodded. "Your grandmother was religious herself. I'm quite sure she had no writings to refer to, but she knew many of the traditions. She told Heelo about some of the things you were just telling me, about the man who was a god of sorts, and how if you were somehow tainted, he could make you clean again. I didn't understand it then and, quite frankly, I don't now. But your mother apparently grabbed onto it and never let go."

I wondered just what Gran had told my mother, how much of the truth she knew. From what I'd learned of Sonmanism in Grey's Introduction to World Religion class, a great deal of what the Book taught had been lost over the years. There was much I still didn't understand, but one thing was certain: the God Man had made me a new person. His love had changed me more fundamentally, more radically—and, as time would prove, more permanently—than even Grey's love had been able to do.

Had God done the same for our mother?

Had she prayed for Jeriah and me as we grew in her womb? Had my mother actually loved me?

I read the smeared words on the banroo skin. "These babies will be my comfort."

She was wrong. We had been no comfort. We—or at least, I— had been her end. But when we are "in Christ," as the Book put it, the end of one life is the beginning of another, a better one.

Perhaps I hadn't killed her after all. Maybe God had simply allowed her to go to him.

That would have been her greatest comfort of all.

❧ Chapter 21 ❧

CHANCE MEETING

IN AUNT LANIE'S dining room the next day, I stared across the table at Riah, amazed. "There's a citizens' inn on Seaview?" It was just the two of us having a late breakfast that morning, as our aunt and uncle were working.

Riah took a sip of crim before answering. "Not just an inn. A resort. Freemansland Seaview Citizens Resort. We didn't see it from the air when we flew in yesterday because it's on the east side. But it's huge. A hundred and fifty suites, four restaurants, two spas, three swimming pools, plus they've shipped in I don't know how many tons of sand and made a fancy beach."

I couldn't fathom it. "What sort of citizen would want to come to Freemansland?"

"Fans of yours, maybe. Pigeonheads who've seen everything else the world has to offer and are looking for a something new." He shrugged. "I don't know who comes. It's only been open for six months or so, but Seena says they're doing quite well."

"And she's the restaurant manager?"

His face radiated pride. "She manages the two smallest ones."

"And Jeo works there too? As a guide? What does he guide?"

"The resort property climbs all the way up the sharpfall, from the beach below to the stillwater above, with a scaler going between. He takes guests up to the rim and gives them a boat tour of Freedom's stillwater. Shows them a dragon den, lets them do a little fishing if they want, tells stories about how people lived before the City came in and changed things."

"Tells stories?" I chuckled. "Like his auntie."

"He says they eat it up like a bowl of Mini SweetGels. After he's shown them the designated sights, he takes them to the barge for a little shopping and lunch–"

"What barge?"

"The one connected with the resort. The Barge Restaurant is one of the two Seena manages. It's all traditional Freemansland food."

I laughed. "Yeah, I'll bet."

"Okay, so maybe it's not quite authentic." He grinned. "But their rappu legs and bicio blossoms are as good as you'll find anywhere on the island."

I smiled to see Riah so happy. "And how do you know how good it is?"

"Because they use Seena's recipes."

"Her cooking truly is fit to serve the fussiest pigeonhead." I tried to catch an annoying gnat out of the air but missed. "And KJ teaches at the Academy?"

He nodded. "Literature and Language Arts at West."

"Not East?" I pretended to frown. "She doesn't like our alma mater?"

"I didn't ask."

The gnat lit on the table, and I squashed it with my thumb. "So you're staying here, then. You're not going back to civilization with me."

"Seena won't take me back, but Uncle Rhe and Aunt Lanie could use my help."

"It's a shame their own kids aren't interested in the business. I can't believe they all left Freemansland for good. We had no reason to stay, but they had no reason to leave."

He shrugged. "Well, now I have reason be here. And since Lanie and Rhe are willing to have me..."

I knew what he was thinking. "Don't worry about me, Ri. I'll be fine."

He studied my face with concern. "Will you?"

"If I could do anything I wanted, I think I'd stay too. But I've got too many things to take care of." A smile crept out. "For now. I might come back one day."

His face didn't produce a matching smile. "I can go with you. If you'd like. So you're not alone."

"No. You need to stay. Work on mending your relationships with your kids. And you know as well as I do that I'm not alone. I'll never be alone again."

We'd brought the Book to Moll with us, photographed all the pages, printed off one set for each of us, and put multiple copies on speks. Spek technology stored documents on a paper-thin disc less than three millimeters in diameter. Because of their small size, space was limited, and it took three speks to hold the entire Book.

We stored Grey's copy in a safe, but we had no intention of keeping the contents secret any longer. The world needed to know these things.

All the world, but especially Freemansland.

I SPENT TWO weeks on Freemansland. I couldn't believe the changes. The City's influence had touched nearly everything in the twenty-some years since I'd left. But I couldn't say what had happened on the second level, Freedom, because I never set foot there. I wasn't ready to revisit those memories.

When it was time for my brother and me to part, it proved more difficult than I'd imagined. For both of us. He accompanied me to the aircraft barge, helped me with my luggage, and saw me to the air stair, where he held onto me for several long moments.

"I've got to go, Riah," I said into his shoulder.

"I know." He gave me one more squeeze before he released me. "Take care of yourself."

It was a windy day, but that wasn't the reason for our running eyes.

I forced a smile. "I'm not alone, you know."

"I know." He hugged me one more time. "I know! Keep reading that Book."

"Every day. You too."

"Every day." He kissed my forehead.

I mounted the stair, took my seat, and didn't look back. My roots were in Freemansland, and so was my family—all the family I had, now that the Standtalls rejected me. But I had work to do in the City.

≈⩔≈

IF A COMPUTER could have a bad attitude, the one in the reception area at Brick House Publishing would have been a prime example.

"I am sorry, but no one is available to speak with you. Goodbye."

Fighting down a wave of fury, I stared at the screen. How could they do this to me?

The reception offices were big and posh by any standards, even a Standtall's. The company could afford the rent in this building and the high-end décor only because of me, J. S. Freeman, the author who put Brick House at the top of all the publishing houses on Book Boulevard. In fact, it was my success that got them on the Boulevard to begin with. Before they published my Stillwater series, they were on a side street several blocks over.

And now, I couldn't get anyone to speak with me. Not even the security guard.

I couldn't just leave. There were other people in the reception area, all watching me out of the corners of their eyes. And they'd see I was refused at the door.

My heart raced and my face flushed. I'd met with the same rejection everywhere I went in this district and should be used to it by now. But every time, it hurt like a backhanded slap.

I pulled on a façade of calm control and, feeling countless eyes boring into my back, headed for the exit. The security guard looked straight ahead as I passed on my way out. Didn't give me so much as a nod.

On the street, the air seemed heavy and stale, as if too many people breathed it. Too many vehicles exhaled. Too many buildings blocked the sun. Someone jostled me as he passed, and I didn't even check to make sure he hadn't picked my pocket, because my pockets were empty. I carried a small bag, and it was tucked under my arm.

I stood on the street trying to decide where to go. I was out of options.

I was also hungry—small wonder, as I hadn't eaten for more than twenty-four hours—so I headed for the park six blocks away. I didn't have the money for any restaurant in this district, but I could probably afford a bite from a food cart.

About halfway there, I waited at the corner with six or seven others for the "Safe to Cross" signal, when a woman's voice worked its way through my foggy gloom. "Miss Freeman?"

I turned to see a thirtyish woman about my height, dark-haired and blue-eyed, in a professional jacket and culottes set.

"I'm sorry, I was in a daze. Were you speaking to me?"

She extended her hand. "Oh, you *are* Miss Freeman! I wasn't sure. It's been quite awhile since we met."

I shook her hand, struggling for a few desperate moments before the memory clicked into place. "Oh, of course. You were an intern at Etimos Agency. Oneta, right? Oneta Pimtim?"

A smile brightened her face. "That's right! I can't believe you even noticed me let alone remembered my name."

"And I'm surprised—" The signal lit up, and we crossed the street. "That you'd speak to me. All I've been getting here on the Boulevard is cold shoulders."

"So I've been hearing."

Just what had she heard? If I asked, would she tell me? I was trying to decide how to respond when she said, "Have you eaten? I'd love it if you'd let me buy you lunch."

I must not have heard her clearly. "Are you serious?"

"Of course. If you're okay with it, I mean."

"Well, all right, you talked me into it." I tried not to sound too eager, though I might have drooled a little.

"Great! There's a mirtositi place right around the corner. You like mirtositi?"

"Love it. You sure about this? It'll set you back a bit."

She laughed. "I'm not an intern anymore. I don't do anything so fancy on a regular basis, but a lunch with J. S. Freeman is worth the splurge."

We rounded the corner. Sure enough, there was a mirtositi bar halfway down the block. "Well, I certainly appreciate it."

It was a busy place, and I knew the quality wouldn't match Jano's. But hungry as I was, that didn't matter.

We got a booth in the back and I ordered a glass of Allock, hoping the carbonation would fill me up so I wouldn't eat like a swamp hog when the food arrived.

We chatted about mundane things, like the weather and movies. When she brought up grappleball—what self-respecting woman talks about grappleball?—I changed the subject.

"I appreciate the lunch, Oneta. You have no idea how much. But what can I do for you? Is there something you wanted to talk about?"

She turned her head as if to look at something across the room but then angled her eyes back to me. "Um, yes, now that you mention it. But I'm not sure—that is, I saw in Publishers Update that you're no longer represented by Etimos Agency."

"That's true."

"Who are you with now? Anybody?"

My rueful chuckle disturbed the surface of my Allock. "No." I took a sip of the drink, then set it down. "Nobody on Book Boulevard will even talk to me these days. They tell me I'm bad for business. But then, you're in the business, aren't you? So you should know all about that."

"I'm in the business, yes. And I know— Oh, here's our food. Umm, it's beautiful!"

The server put a platter of mirtositi in front of us, and beautiful was too weak a word. It took all my will power to wait for Oneta to take the first piece. I didn't want to seem too ravenous. Salivating, I silently thanked God for providing this wonderful food.

Oneta dipped a piece of mirtositi in one of the sauces. "They look wonderful. What are you waiting for?"

I didn't need a second invitation.

After she'd finished her first piece, she picked up the thread of our conversation. "So the rumor is that City Revenue Equity's impounding all the proceeds of your book sales. Payments to Brick House, your agent, your publicist, everybody, are all on hold until Equity can decide how it should be portioned out?"

I nodded and finished chewing before I answered. "Book sales, income on my investments, everything. Until all the lawsuits are settled, nobody gets paid. Everyone who feels I've wronged them has a year to submit claims against me—that is, a year from the time I came out of hiding, which means ten more months. Once the charges are submitted and all the lawsuits are decided, Equity will divide the funds they're holding. In the meantime, Brick House has discontinued all my titles. They don't want to invest in the production costs if they're not going to make any money on them."

"That's more or less what I've heard. But that's crazy. Of course they'll make money on them! They can afford to wait for the sort of pay-off they stand to get." She dipped another piece of mirtositi, then took a nibble, still talking. "Your books are in higher demand than ever before. I've heard of used copies selling for hundreds of urexi, and there's a thriving market of pirated electronic versions." She finished her bite, then wiped her mouth with a napkin. "Umm, this white sauce is delicious."

"Everything is. My stomach is jumping for joy."

She laughed. "I'm glad. But if our friends at Revenue Equity are holding all your money, what are you doing for income?"

"I get a small allowance. Or at least, that's what they say. I petitioned for living expenses over a month ago, but it hasn't been approved yet. In the meantime, I'm begging and borrowing." I gave her a grateful smile. "And accepting the kindness of strangers."

She smiled back, but her mouth was too full for speaking.

"Honestly, though, the bottom line is, I survive by the grace of God."

Her brow lifted. After swallowing, she said, "Never heard that phrase before. What's it mean?"

"God provides for me. Not because I deserve it, but because he is good. And because he has a reason for keeping me going."

"Again, you speak of something foreign to me. But listen. I've got a proposition for you." She paused as if considering. "Hm. I thought my seeing you on the street corner was a random accident, but maybe there is something to this God thing. I don't know." She shrugged. "Anyway, I'm an independent literary agent. I used to work for Diadem Agency, but I recently branched out on my own."

"You're not suggesting you represent me, are you? If you're just starting out, you need an income. Until this mess is cleared up, if it ever is, no publisher will sign me. You can't afford to get mixed up with me."

She grinned. "That's where you're wrong. What I can't afford is turning down the chance to work with a genuine hero."

I almost choked. "How do you figure?"

She leaned forward and spoke quietly. "Everybody knows it. But not many will say it."

I narrowed my eyes. "Everybody knows what?"

"Your plan to overthrow Daig Lar? It was brilliant. Every detail plotted better than any novel. And the timing was impeccable. The whole thing was just perfect."

"Whoa. Wait a minute. What are you talking about?"

"Okay, I get it." She gave me an exaggerated wink. "You had nothing to do with it. Of course you didn't. It just happened all by itself after you turned down the Centre Award."

I stared at her. "That's got nothing to do with anything."

"Now, you can't deny the way you pulled *that* off was brilliant. Standing up there at the podium with the award in your hand, accusing the Awards Commission of collusion with subversives? And then disappearing, like you'd put on some sort of cloak of invisibility or something?" She shook her head. "You're not going to convince me all *that* never happened. Too many witnesses. And there's footage besides. Those presentations aren't broadcast, but they are all recorded, you know."

"I know." I answered absently, trying to follow her line of thinking. "I saw the cameramen. But–" Once I realized what she was talking about, I gasped. "You don't honestly believe I had all that planned, do you? Because I didn't. I hadn't decided whether or not to accept the award until I was sitting on the stage. I had my acceptance speech written and memorized. Want to hear it? Pretty sure I still remember it, if you give me a minute–"

She smiled. "No need. I get the idea. In the absence of any actual proof to the contrary, I'll take your word for it. But here's the thing."

She really *did* believe I'd planned everything, right down to Lar's assassination, didn't she? How could she?

"My family is from Arkentak. We were Stridentans, but it was a culture for us, not a religion. We did the things we did because it was tradition. We didn't actually worship the goddess of womanhood, we didn't revere a great High Priestess. So when we were, shall we say, encouraged to take our practices to the extreme, it made my parents uncomfortable. They became truly alarmed when the holy sisters started punishing people for not going with the new flow. My mother had a good position with the news services, and when she put in for a transfer to Centre City, we were allowed to move. That is, my parents, my sisters, and I. But the rest of our family was still there."

"I'm sorry."

"So am I. And so were they. I had many cousins. Now I have three. Three that I know of, anyway. Some died in the war, some in the refugee camps. And I blame Daig Lar for all of it. For the changes that drove my family out to begin with, and for all the deaths afterward. He was every bit the monster you said he was, and more."

I shook my head. "I don't think it's that simple. There were many people involved, forces at work we don't know about."

"He was behind it. And once you had the courage to stand up and say it aloud, it was like the blinders fell off the rest of the world. The Kentans he'd oppressed all that time shook off their stupor and rose up against him. When that happened, the City Fathers realized they could no longer pretend. They quit turning a blind eye to what he was doing. And all of *that*—" She pointed at me. "Was your doing. It was your declaration of his guilt that caused the rest of the world to see. Your courage that sent the City forces to investigate the refugee camps and finally give real help to my people. It was you who started Arkentak's return to wholeness. We're not there yet, but we're on the road, and you put us there. Deny it all you want, but I know it is true."

By this time, my appetite was gone. I leaned back in my chair, stunned by her false assumptions and the passion with which she voiced them. "I am sorry about your family. And I am not the least bit sorry Daig Lar is dead. But you give me too much credit. All I did was speak my mind. What happened after that was beyond my control."

"You spoke your mind when no one else would." She crossed her arms on the table. "And I'll bet you still have more to say." She paused as if waiting for me to blurt something out right there. When I didn't, she went on. "Do you? Do you have more to say, but no agent will take you on, no publisher will give you a voice?"

I thought of the Book, and a burst of energy flowed through me. "Oh, yes. I have much more to say."

"Good!" She beamed. "I want to help."

"You should hear what it is before you make that kind of decision."

She pulled out her phone. "I've got an appointment this afternoon, but I can cancel it. After we eat, we'll go back to my office. I want to hear everything that's on your mind."

❧ Chapter 22 ☙

THIS ONE THING I DO

I F I LOOKED hard enough, I could find a number of benefits to spending my nights in the indigent cells.

For one thing, they were safe. Though barely big enough for the 220 x 65 centimeter bed shelf, they were private. No bunkmates, and the doors locked from the inside. They were all hard surfaces, cleaned daily. And they were abundant, readily available in the less-prosperous parts of Centre City, and inexpensive. For one urexi, I could hunker down for the night without a care.

I had few possessions—no more than I could carry with me, for the indigent cells were only for sleeping—but one of those possessions was a phone.

The night after I met Oneta Pimtim, I called Jeriah. I listened while he filled me in on what was going on at Moll. Not only Aunt Lanie and Uncle Rhe, but some of the employees as well, were interested in the Book of God. "You know how in the Book, believers would get together on the first day of the week to pray and learn about God and worship him?"

"Yes..."

"I suggested to Uncle Rhe that we do something like that, and he liked the idea. So we're going to try it this Firstday. Aunt Lanie's writing a couple of songs based on some of the Psalms. We'll pray, and someone will read from the Book, and we'll discuss it, like you and I used to do. None of us have ever done this before, but we'll figure it out."

A strange longing washed over me as I lay on my bed shelf and envisioned what he described. "I wish I could be there."

"I do too."

We both grew quiet, missing one another, then he said, "I get my first pay tomorrow, and I'll recharge your Urex card. Check the balance day after tomorrow and let me know if you don't see the addition."

I frowned. "I hate to keep taking your hard-earned money."

"Yeah, I know. I didn't like taking your money, either, so let's just call it even."

We'd had this conversation before, and it never went anywhere.

Just when I was about to change the subject, he saved me the trouble. "Still enjoying your posh accommodations?"

I chuckled. "They're lovely." I winced at the sound coming through my vent of a neighbor's hacking cough. "But maybe my fortunes are about to change. Guess what I did today?"

"Ate three meals?"

"No, I haven't progressed that far yet. I signed with an agent."

"Huh?" It sounded like he was chewing something. That's probably why meals were on his mind. "Why would you do that? I mean, why would an agent do that? All your earnings are still impounded, right?"

"That's what I asked." I told Riah about running into Oneta, our conversation in the restaurant, and the meeting in her office that followed. "She's very interested in the Book, and I gave her one on spek."

Yes, Riah was definitely eating. He finished chewing, then swallowed. "She thinks she can get a publisher for it?"

I nodded, though he couldn't see it, as my cut-rate phone only had voice capability. "I was there when she made the call. It's a small press. In Arkentak."

"I thought all the publishing houses were in Centre City?"

"Oh, my, no. Those are just the major ones, the ones you hear about. But anyway, they're probably going to hire me. Not as a writer, but as a remote clerical worker. The board has to vote on it, but the editor we spoke with saw no reason why they wouldn't go for it. I'll be an independent contractor working from Oneta's office, reading the Book into an electronic document to be transcribed and then published."

"The City's going to take those earnings too, you know."

"I don't think so. The way the Equity order reads, they can confiscate my interest and dividends, rental income, salaries, pension, and publishing royalties. But I've never worked as an independent contractor before, and I guess it never occurred to the lawyers to include that type of earnings in the list of my impoundable income sources."

"Somebody dropped the round on that play."

"That's for sure. And I'm not above picking up the missed grapple and pitching it in. I'll prepare the manuscript just as I would if I were the author, but it will be credited to one of the editors at the publishing house. Oneta will write a foreword explaining where the book came from, and they want to include a note from me as well, because they think my name will make it sell. But the City won't be able to impound the proceeds, because I won't be getting any royalties from it."

"I'm surprised you got the grappleball reference." Riah chuckled. "Just how certain is this scheme?"

"Like I said, I was there when she called, and she had it on speaker, so I was part of the conversation. The editor's confident the board will be as interested as she is. Apparently the Kentans think I'm a hero."

"Vague rumors to that effect are trickling my way too."

That took me by surprise. "Really? What have you heard?"

"Nothing substantial. That's why I said they're vague. But if that publisher can't make this work, I'll be surprised. What about the other projects you have in mind? Did you get a chance to talk to the agent about those?"

"Yes. And she's excited about all of it. Nothing will be published until Equity releases my finances, of course, but I can get started on the writing, and she's going to see if she can interest a high-profile publisher so we'll be ready to move when the time comes."

The hacking sound through the vent must have been loud enough for Riah to hear, because he asked, "Is that you coughing?"

"No, it's coming from one of the other cells. Even with the ventilation fans running all the time, you can sometimes hear what people are doing."

I could envision Riah's frown as he went silent for a moment. Then he said, "You mean other people can listen in when you talk to me?"

"Maybe. But I don't care. I'm through hiding. If Revenue Equity wants to take my earnings, then so be it. I'm coming to learn, like the apostle Paul, that whatever my situation may be—"

Riah finished for me. "To be content with it."

"Exactly. I just need to keep doing what I have to do, and God will take care of the rest. And for right now, what I need to do is transcribe that book so people can read it."

ONCE I RECEIVED the funds from Riah and a little advance pay from Oneta, I was able to rent a furnished room and get out of the indigent cells.

My new home reminded me of the apartment Grey and I had in Yarapit, but worse. It was only one room, not a suite. In Yarapit, the furniture was nice because it was Grey's. But here, the furniture was so disgusting I couldn't bring myself to sit on anything upholstered. The neighborhood didn't seem very safe either, but at least the windows were barred, and the sturdy door had good locks. I never left for the office until daylight and made sure I was home before dark.

I'd been traveling back and forth between my room and Oneta's office—and wearing out my one pair of shoes with the twice-daily walk, as I didn't want to waste my meager funds on tram fare—for several weeks when I decided to approach Oneta with something I'd been thinking about for a while.

She was busy with meetings the first part of the day, but in the afternoon, she stopped by my tiny office where I sat at a desk comparing a printout of what I'd just read into the computer with a copy of Grey's handwritten book. It was a painstaking process, but I took my time because I wanted to make sure it was accurate.

"How's it going?" she asked.

I looked up. "Oh, hi. Making good progress, all in all." I rubbed my eyes. Once I had some money coming in, I'd see about getting my vision checked. "I'm thinking about a change in venue."

She tipped her head. "What do you mean?"

"I should finish up here this week, and then I'll want to start on some of those other projects we talked about."

She nodded. "Yes, and..."

"And I know you said I can use your office as long as I like, but I think I should go to Cararre."

Her brows rose. "What's in Cararre, other than the Zavazda?"

"Probably lots of things, but the Zavazda's what I had in mind. I need to talk to Dr. Simelum."

She pouted. "What for? I'm going to miss having you here."

"And I'll miss being here." It was true. I valued her friendship. Not only because she was my sole friend at that time—other than Jeriah, who was on the other side of the world—but because she was intrigued with the Book, both with its history as well as its content.

When she was able, she helped me proofread my transcriptions. I would read Grey's copy to her, and she'd follow along with my transcription, fixing any discrepancies. Then she'd read the corrected copy back, and I'd compare it to the original.

The discussions that sometimes sprang from that stimulated me to look further into the Book to answer her questions. I'd read it through several times by then, and even though I was no longer young, my mind was still retentive. Often something in one place would remind me of similar wording elsewhere, and I'd locate the related part to see how the two passages shed light on each other. It was amazing how the entire book was so intricately connected, numerous beautiful nuances to one unified story.

"I'll miss our talks," I told Oneta. "We're learning so much together."

She sat in the spare chair. "It's beginning to make a little more sense to me, but I still can't decide what to think. I *want* to believe it, but..." She shrugged.

"Promise me that after I leave, you'll keep reading the Book. That's how my brother and I came to believe. We just kept digging into it, and then one day, we realized it was all true. Every word of it."

She nodded. "Oh, I will. It's fascinating, really. And I look forward to being able to read it in the form of an actual bound book, instead of a photocopied sheaf of handwritten pages. Though that format does have a certain intimacy about it, doesn't it? The personal touch adds, oh, I don't know, authenticity or something."

"Love," I said, and took a deep breath to compose myself. "Grey wrote all that out for me because he loved me."

Oneta gave me a sad smile.

"But even more, the God of the universe caused those ancient people in another time and place to write it because he loved them. And because his love so filled them, other people brought the book to this planet. I'm coming to see more and more that nobody loves like God. The greatest love we see and experience in this world is just a weak imitation of his."

Oneta shook her head. "I don't know about that. But why the glish do you want to go to Cararre? You can write your new stories here just as well as there. Better, in fact." She grinned. "Because I'm here to inspire you with our deep discussions. From your description of Dr. Simelum, I didn't think you much cared for his company."

I laughed. "I didn't, really. But I need his expertise. I want to tell the world the truth about what life was like in Freemansland before the City came—what the people believed, and why. I need to get it right instead of just making it all up like I did last time. And Dr. Simelum knows more about those things than anyone else."

"I figured that was what you had in mind. You're right, of course. You need to do your research." She sighed. "I guess I'll have to let you go to Cararre."

I faked a stern expression. "I don't need your permission."

She chuckled. "Seriously, I wish I had a way to keep you here. In the meantime, though—" She stood and reached for some of the papers on my desk. "Would you like some help with that?"

I handed them to her. "Thanks, I could use it. I just finished checking this sentence." I pointed to the place on the transcription.

Seeing where, a couple lines above, I'd corrected the phrase, *yet from them all the Lord rescued me*, which the computer had misinterpreted as, *yet from the mall the Lord rescued me*, she giggled. "I've never felt the need to be rescued from a shopping mall. Okay, so you're starting at, 'But as for you…'?"

"That's right." I found the place in Grey's copy and slowly read aloud. "But as for you, continue in what you have learned and have firmly believed, knowing from whom you learned it…"

THREE YEARS LATER, I sat at the patio table on the balcony of my apartment in Zapad overlooking the Eel River. In another chair, Meidlu Therody, a reporter from *Publishers Update*, recorded our conversation. Unlike some of the interviews I'd done in the past, I didn't permit her to bring so much as a personal camera, let alone a film crew.

"So when you came back from hiding—from your spiritual retreat, as you put it—" Meidlu smiled, as if indulging me. "You found all your assets had been seized by Revenue Equity, and it seemed half the world was suing you. How did it feel to be suddenly penniless? Didn't it make you want to run back to your retreat? I'm sure you lived simply there, but at least you had food and a roof over your head. How could someone used to the CFC lifestyle sleep in an indigent cell?"

I shrugged. "I started life with nothing, so I knew I could do it again. And I was aware it was temporary. I still had assets, I simply couldn't access them until I'd gone through the necessary steps to get back on my feet. And I did have some help along the way."

"Your family in Freemansland?"

I nodded. "They were willing to give more than I was willing to accept. I only took enough to keep me from starving, and I paid back every bit as soon as I was able."

"You felt too proud to accept charity?"

"In part, I suppose. But mostly, I remembered what my husband used to say, that the role of the CFC was to provide for the rest of the world. By accepting money from friends and family, I felt as if I was failing them."

Meidlu tapped away at her tablet, then looked up. "I seem to remember the title character in *Mimma's Song* saying something to that effect. 'Our urexi support the world.'"

"Sounds about right."

"But now the lawsuits are settled, Equity has distributed the funds they'd been holding, and you're solvent again, if this lovely flat of yours is any indication."

"It's taken some time, but God provided my every need through the thin times and blesses me graciously now."

The interviewer squirmed as if sitting on something uncomfortable. "Ah, yes. But these new books you're writing now. We're having a hard time figuring out what you're doing."

My brows lifted. "Who's *we?*"

"Who?" Her expression was puzzled. "The publishing industry in particular, but the whole world, really. Tell us about this Book of God, for instance. Is it for real? Was it really an old manuscript that your late husband uncovered? Or, as some people suggest, did you spend that missing year writing it yourself, and now you're trying to pass off your own fiction as historical fact?"

This wasn't the first time I'd heard that accusation, and it wasn't always phrased as a question. "All that is explained in the foreword. The book is a word-for-word transcription of the texts found by archaeologists in Freemansland. How it came to be in Freemandland is explained in the introduction by Nedla Rotide, the editor who put the whole thing together."

"And you're saying it's not fiction."

"That's what I'm saying, yes. The Book of God is as real as the balcony we're sitting on."

"Oh-oh." She chuckled. "Now I'm afraid this whole thing will collapse and we'll fall seven stories to our deaths."

"I doubt that, or I wouldn't be out here. But my faith in the Book is greater than my faith in this balcony."

"That's quite a statement. What makes you so sure?"

"Have you read it?"

She gave her head a rueful shake. "I started, but—" She sighed. "It's a long book, and it's so very strange. I just couldn't get through it. It seems so foreign, so—I guess you could say, other-worldly?"

"Other-worldly. I like that. The Book did, in fact, originate out of this world, but it's applicable to Umban nevertheless. The same God created all worlds and governs all things by the same immutable laws and principles."

"I see." Miedlu cleared her throat. "What about your other new books? *Journey to Freedom*, which came out a year and a half ago, and your latest release, *Living in Freedom*? It seems a little unusual for an author to contradict her own previously published works. What were you thinking when you began the Freedom series?"

"It is a little unprecedented, but then, I'm not known for doing the usual thing."

She chuckled. "I should say not."

I leaned back in my chair. "I received criticism from more than one source that the Stillwater stories had a historical setting but were not historically accurate. I wasn't concerned at the time, but now? After learning the truth and seeing how very far we have strayed from it, I feel compelled to tell the truth. About everything. About the past, the present, the world we live in. About who we are today and how our history has shaped us."

"So what are we to believe, then? That you were lying about what Freemansland was like in the Stillwater series, or that you're lying about it now?"

I smiled. "In the Stillwater series—which I never claimed was anything other than fantasy, by the way—I portrayed historical Freemansland as I envisioned it, as I believed it was. In the Freedom series, I portray it as the historical record shows it to have been—and that historical fact involves the original inhabitants' belief in the Book of God."

She looked confused, so I said, "Let me put it this way. When a child looks at the sun—" I gestured toward it. "She sees a ball of light. But as she matures and learns more, she discovers it is much more than that. It is not part of this world, but is a celestial body of its own. It is made of flaming gases too hot to be approached, supplying us with heat and light and energy. Its gravity holds our planet in place. It determines night and day, regulates our seasons, and influences everything in our world in ways we cannot fully fathom. All this, while remaining that simple ball of light that even a child can understand."

Miedlu gave a thoughtful nod.

"In a similar way, the Papevine Twins in the Stillwater series were ignorant about the true realities of the world they lived in. The new books don't contradict the early ones, but rather enlighten them. Enhance them. And so, they enlighten the reader."

Miedlu smiled. "I'm impressed. You not only created the whole elaborate story of the Book of God, but you've managed to make it weave throughout the stories you wrote earlier. As if you had all this in mind from the beginning."

"I didn't, but God did. And now that He's blessed me with a small glimpse of His truth, I feel compelled to tell the world about it. It's too wonderful to keep to myself, and God's already given me a forum for sharing it, through my stories."

"Your Stillwater series was eight books altogether. How many do you envision for this new endeavor?"

"I plan to wrap it all up in the third book, which I'm currently drafting."

"Is it too soon to ask what you plan to work on when the Freedom series is done?"

"Not too soon, no." I shook my head. "I have only one goal these days. To tell the truth to the world. It's the only thing worth doing."

❧ Chapter 23 ❧

TO FREEDOM

DESPITE MY DARK glasses, I squinted against the sun reflecting off the stillwater as the boat carried me toward Moll.

Jeriah, still lean and strong, was at the helm, gray hair fluttering back from his sun-creased face. "Oh, hey." He shouted over the wind and engine noise. "I brought something for you. In there." He pointed toward the cooler beside me.

I opened the lid and grinned. Two bottles of Allock nestled in ice, just like the day Aunt Lanie first brought us to Moll forty-five years before.

"Thanks!" I pulled out a bottle and handed it to him, then twisted open the other and drank. "Tastes like old times."

Savoring the memory's flavor, we rode in silence, the wind in our faces, the sharpfall looming nearer until it blocked the sun's glare.

About the time our Allock bottles were empty, he slowed the boat and approached the pier at the foot of the arch at Moll. I looked up at the lettering. "That's a new sign."

"We replaced the old one five years ago."

The boat glided toward the dock. "It's new since the last time I was here." I grabbed a cleat and tied the boat's rope to it.

"You've been gone too long."

"I have. But I'm home now. For good."

"We've only been begging you for the past ten years." He handled three of my bags, and I took the other two. Though it was more than I owned when I first walked that dock, it wasn't much to show for such an eventful life.

I eyed the long, zig-zagging stairway. "I'm glad there's a cargo scaler. I'm not as young as I used to be."

"No, we're not."

I smiled.

We dropped the luggage on the scaler floor. Riah powered up the vehicle while I took a seat on one of the benches and looked out over the stillwater, fingering my bracelet. Fifteen years a widow, and I still ached for Grey. "I wish he could have come here with me. He'd have loved it."

Loved it because it had birthed me. Not because of its natural beauty. Freemansland was many things, but natural was not one of them.

Riah didn't answer. Just pulled the lever, and the scaler began its ascent.

⁓⁂⁓

AFTER DINNER, WE sat and sipped glaffcrim with Uncle Rhe and Aunt Lanie. My nephew Jeo was there too, along with our aunt and uncle's great-grandson, Repplif.

It had been several years since Uncle Rhe had turned the plantation's day-to-day operations over to Riah. Jeo was now learning the ropes as well. But when twenty-two-year-old Repplif expressed an interesting in getting involved, Uncle Rhe and Aunt Lanie were delighted to let him come and see how he liked it. He'd been there only a couple of months, but they said he was a hard worker and eager to learn.

Uncle Rhe crossed his legs. "Did I ever tell you about the time I met the City's Agriculture Minister, Cago Talpin?"

Lanie gazed at him over her cup. "Jeriah and Jemima were there, remember?"

He nodded. The few wisps of hair remaining on his sun-dried scalp wagged with the motion. "But the young ones weren't, dear." He turned his pale blue eyes on each of us in turn, including Riah and me, and spoke slowly. "Yes, I had the privilege of meeting the Agriculture Minister himself. You'd think he'd be all high-and-mighty, being a high-ranking CFC. But the man was very cordial. Unassuming. And intelligent. A very smart man." He smiled and seemed to be gazing off into the distance. "Your mama and I were at a wedding once, years ago, and he was there. A relative of the groom."

Of course I knew that. It was my wedding.

Riah and I exchanged glances.

Repplif set down his cup. "That musta been a long time ago, Great-Grandpap. Prace Plodin has been the Agriculture Minister for as long as I've been alive."

Uncle Rhe seemed to calculate in his mind. "Yes, you're right. This was long before Plodin took over. Plodin seems to be competent, but he's not the man Talpin was. Yes, sir, Minister Talpin was willing to listen to people like us, the ones who get our hands dirty with the work of feeding the world. I met him at a wedding, years ago, and we kept in touch ever since. Up until the time, after Minister Standtall was murdered and there was a big shake-up in the Council—"

When we were young, he always had a ready supply of stories to tell, and they were good ones. Nowadays, he wandered off point more often than not, and he often combined one story with another until neither made sense.

At eighty-five, Uncle Rhe still clambered up and down the sharpfall inspecting the plantation and wandered around the processing and warehouse facilities. He also liked to visit the employees and their families in their stacks, inquiring if they needed anything and if they were happy with their jobs. Sometimes lately he would lose his bearings, and whoever found him would escort him gently home. Once there, he'd fall asleep in his favorite chair.

Though it saddened me to see him decline, it was touching the way everyone treated him with love and respect. He'd earned the privilege, for he had always treated everyone, young or old, with that same regard. But we don't always get what we deserve in this life.

He rambled on. "Yes, Minister Talpin was a good man. He's been gone for some years now, long before the Book was found. I'm sorry he never had the opportunity to know the Lord."

That led to a conversation about how, a decade after its publication, the Book of God was sweeping across the world like a hungry fire across a dry plain. It had already been published in a number of different editions, and the demand for print copies kept the presses going around the clock.

At first, people read it out of curiosity, believing the rumor that it was a fabrication, as my interviewer had alleged. Some remained scornful after reading it. Perhaps most. Others, though, became believers, and churches were popping up all over the place.

The truths of the Book were particularly well received in Arkentak and Freemansland. The Kentans, beaten down by war and disillusioned by the duplicity of their leaders, were looking for hope, and this new faith offered redemption. The Freemanslanders embraced the Book as their own, for obvious reasons. Unfortunately, many of them as well as the Kentans didn't seem to grasp the concept of forsaking their old gods to worship the One

True God exclusively, but tended to incorporate their old traditions into their new beliefs.

This was a matter of great concern to many of us. Some of the first believers now traveled about, like the early church fathers, preaching and teaching. Others, Riah and me in particular, confined our edification efforts to writing. To his own surprise, my brother turned out to be a talented writer, and a prolific one, despite his busy job managing the biggest glaffcrim plantation in the world.

In the sitting room that evening, I followed the discussion around me but didn't have much to contribute. Instead, I marveled at the changes in the world since Grey's death. He was the one who had started all this with his insistence on copying the book and introducing it to me.

As the conversation went on around me, I looked down at my bracelet, which I had been fingering. He would have been happy to see the Book becoming so well read and so many people coming to know his God. I doubt even he had foreseen this, and it filled me with an indescribable delight—a combination of sorrow and joy, regret and hope, all within a sense of pervading peace.

What direction the world would continue to go, only God knew, and I was content to leave it up to him. But I did still puzzle over the mystery of who had killed Grey, and why. It couldn't have been for the Book, that much seemed certain. Why had he been seen as a threat, and by whom? Had he possessed another treasure I never knew about?

I realized Aunt Lanie was speaking to me. "...intend to work with us here at Moll? Jeriah and Jeo are doing a wonderful job overseeing production, but if you'd like to get involved in the office administration, I could step away from my duties there and keep a closer eye on things here at the house."

I knew what she meant—keep a closer eye on Uncle Rhe, who was now dozing in his chair.

"I'd love to help you. But I can't. At least not right away. Before I do anything else, I need to go back to Freedom."

Jeo snorted. "Who'd want to go there?" Earlier, he'd remarked that he didn't miss giving tours of Freedom's stinking stillwater, so his disdain didn't surprise me.

But Jeriah's frown did. "That's the one place the City has left pretty much alone. It's hot and steaming as a witch's kettle, and just as dangerous. Why do you want to see it again?"

"I'm not sure." I sighed. "Ever since the day our papa died and the City took us away, I've wanted to go back. At first, because it was home. Then later, I thought about going back because I was in the habit of thinking about it. And now, I just want to see it." A sudden sob stuck in my throat.

Aunt Lanie's eyes filled. "Oh, hon, this is your home now. But if you've been wanting to go back and see Freedom all this time, then I think you should do it."

"I will." I nodded. I didn't need anyone's permission, but I appreciated her support. "My trip wore me out, though. I'll stay here a couple of days and rest up, adjust to the time change, and then I'll go." I sought my brother's gaze. "Want to go with me?"

He pursed his lips. "If you really want me to, I'll try to get away for a day."

AS IT HAPPENED, I waited almost a week before I felt up to going, and by then, Jeriah couldn't spare the time. So, carrying only one bag, I went alone.

Aunt Lanie piloted the boat, and Uncle Rhe went along to keep us company. On the scaler down the sharpfall, he'd kept us entertained with stories from when he was a boy growing up on Moll, when his grandfather ran it. Once we got on the water, he gazed quietly through narrowed eyes at his ancestral plantation climbing in neat, green steps up and down the rocky cliffs, a smile softening his weathered face.

It surprised me how much I loved him and Aunt Lanie.

On the dock at the catamara, I hugged them both, then picked up my bag and disembarked.

Lanie called after me. "Let us know when you're ready to come home, and we'll send the boat for you."

I turned and waved. "Thanks, I will!"

At the depot, I bought a scaler ticket. I had no wait. As Riah had said, most people don't go to Freedom. I boarded the car, the operator closed the door, and down I went. Alone.

The car smelled sour, and a dank patina of grim lay over everything. Memories of my childhood home were equally stale. I remembered the Freedom I'd created for the Stillwater stories, and I was familiar with the history I'd studied for the Freedom series. But what was it like now?

While I rode, I wrapped my wrist in a bandage to conceal my marital bracelet. I'd be immediately spotted as an outsider on Freedom as it was, but I didn't want to draw more attention to myself than necessary.

The car reached the bottom of the sharpfall with a long shudder, and I waited several anxious moments before the door groaned open. As soon as it did, a familiar, unwholesome odor eeled up my nostrils and made itself at home in my mind.

No attendant greeted me when I exited, and no line waited to get on. Apparently people didn't often leave Freedom, either.

The depot here looked nothing like the ones I'd traveled through on Glaffit and Coldclime. Rain pattered on the roof and seeped through in places, leaving the high ceiling black and rotting. The bare wood floors showed a century's worth of wear. If any sort of finish had once been applied to the walls and doors, it had long since peeled off, and I could put no confidence in the wobbly railings.

Up ahead, a barefooted attendant in a stained uniform shirt with ragged shorts instead of the standard culottes placed an empty bucket beneath a rivulet coming from the holey roof. Then she carried the full bucket to the door and tossed the contents outside. I smiled at her as I passed, but she never looked my way.

Neither did another employee coming out of the ablutions shed, fastening his pants, when I stepped out of the depot. I walked through the warm rain along the rickety dock and chose the least leaky-looking of the public canoes stacked there. Straddling a hole in the dock left by a rotting plank, I opened the waterproof lid on the pay box and dropped in a five-urexi token. Then I wrestled the canoe off its rack and tried to ease it into the water. Mostly, though, I dropped it in.

I hadn't paddled a canoe since I was a child, and its instability surprised me when I stepped in. I was careful to not tip it when I grabbed my bag from the dock. Then I sat on the seat, unhooked the paddle, and pushed away.

Though soaked to the skin and grimy, I couldn't help but grin. After more than forty years of daydreaming about it, I was back on the stillwater of Freedom. The murky water smelled of sewage and fish. The air was heavy, hot, and humid. Water already puddled in the bottom of the canoe. But I hadn't felt this alive in years.

The guest stacks were a short distance from the scaler depot—even in the downpour, I could see them—but they were only accessible by water, as no one had taken the trouble to cut a roadway to them. There may have been a footpath, but I was too old, and had been gone too long from this place, to risk walking a slick, muddy trail along the edge of a precipice. A leaky canoe was safer.

I tied up the rustic craft at the guest stacks and entered the lowest building, where a woman sat behind a counter chewing an occabot stick. Her thinning hair looked like it had seen neither wash nor comb for a month, and the scalp that showed through was speckled with scabs.

Her gaze shifted toward the door when I darkened it, and she spat a gob of dark green occabot juice onto the floor. "Ya want somethin', lady?"

I dripped across the planks toward her. "A piece of floor, if you've got one to spare." In this last remnant of old Freemansland, one didn't sleep in a *room*.

"Got a couple." She stood and peered at me as I approached. "Who wants one?"

"I do. For four nights, at least. I can pay in advance."

She narrowed her eyes and grunted. "Pretty fancy lookin' fer these parts, ain't ya? Slime, you look genuine City." The teeth that pinched the occabot stick were the color of the gob she'd just spat.

I wore no make-up and had on a mismatched blouse and culottes. With bare, unpainted feet in sandals and my gray hair pulled back in a knot, I wouldn't have been taken for even the lowest citizen in Centre City. But here, I stood out like a brilliant white bird scratching in rotting seaweed. "I was born here," I said. "Coming back for a visit." I pulled my purse out of my bag. "You prefer cash?"

She frowned. "I do, yeah. But the City makes me do things their way, or they'll shut me down and tear down my stacks. This place's been in the family since before the City came, and I ain't about to let 'em ruin it like they done down on Seaview."

"Yes, I heard about that resort they have down there." I pulled out my Urex card. "Freemansland has sure changed since I was here last. What's the charge for four nights?"

She eyed me up and down, probably intending to base her answer on what she guessed I was able to pay despite the faded, handwritten schedule of fees posted on the wall behind her. "Thirty a night. But I'll give you four nights for one ten."

I almost laughed. The sign said the rate was twenty a night or three nights for fifty, but I merely smiled. "I'll give you an even hundred. That's still twenty more than the price posted." I gestured toward the sign behind her.

She didn't even blink. "One ten's the best I can do. " She turned and yanked the poster off the wall. "This is outdated. Just didn't make a new one yet." When she turned back to me, her expression defied me to argue.

I shrugged. "One ten it is, then." I handed her my card. "Hey, you know what? I have a friend who's a printer. He can make you a new sign for ten urexi."

She scowled and took the card. "I can make one myself." She placed the card in the tray of her reader and poised one finger over the keypad. "I need your name. Y'know, for the City records."

"Freeman."

She poked at the keys until she'd spelled it out. "Ya got a first name?"

"Jemima."

She frowned. "Couldya spell that?"

I did, slowly, as she laboriously typed it. "J. Freeman. Kinda like the writer?"

"Kinda like that, yeah."

She finished without further comment, then handed me back the card. "I hope you don't need a receipt, 'cause I'm outta paper."

"Don't need one."

"Good. Top stack's yours. I just cleaned it this morning. Everything you need should be in there. City requires an indoor bathroom, so if you don't want to go out to the ablutions shed, there's a can in the closet you can use." She reached under the counter and produced a metal key dangling from a large wooden T. For Top, I guessed. "Oh, here you go." She got out four glaffcrim discs and handed them to me. "You'll want these too."

"Thanks." I took the items, picked up my bag, and went outside.

The rain had stopped, and the scorching sun raised a putrid steam from the stillwater. The path to the upper stacks—paved with a process we called *pounded*, which was a combination of stones, rubble, and sand embedded into the mud so it didn't readily wash away—was in surprisingly good repair. That is to say, it had only a few deep puddles amongst its many small ones, but it wasn't very muddy. I climbed the zigzagging path to the stack about twenty meters above the office. I breathed heavily for the last half of the journey, and by the time I arrived at the top, my legs felt like lead.

I was definitely not a kid anymore.

After some experimentation with wiggling the key and the knob, I unlocked the door and entered. My new quarters were clean, as she'd promised—the first clean thing I'd seen on this level. I changed into dry clothes and hung the wet ones on the drying rail outside, under the overhang of the roof.

Rolled up on a shelf on one wall, the bed mat looked nice and thick. I sniffed it. Only a little musty. The floor and walls were fragrant hairpine, giving the space a pleasant smell. Beneath the mat shelf was another holding a glaffcrim maker and a large bowl. Above the bowl, a spigot projected from the wall—rainwater from the roof piped into the structure in the classic Freemansland manner. I laid the crim discs beside the bowl. I'd had many excellent cups of crim in my day, but it would be a rare treat to drink a cup made with Freemansland rainwater in a room faced in hairpine. My mouth watered at the thought.

What had she said about a closet? There was a door at one end of the area, and I opened it. It held nothing but a bucket with a seat on it. I chuckled. Probably not the sort of facility the City regulations had in mind.

I sat on a bench—the only furniture in the room—and prayed for quite some time. I wasn't sure why I'd felt compelled to come here. It was all very strange. Familiar as home but alien as the world on which the Book had originated.

When I got up to check, my clothes outside were no longer dripping, so I brought them in. If a sudden wind came up, I didn't want my belongings scattered across the sharpfall.

I draped everything on the bench to finish drying, then slung my purse across my chest, locked the door, and went down to my canoe.

❧ Chapter 24 ❧

FINDING HOME

PADDLING A CANOE didn't used to be so strenuous.

By the time I reached a set of merchant stacks, my arms ached, especially the shoulder broken in the war. I floated to the dock and tied up with several other small boats. Then I climbed out stiffly, ignoring bystanders' suspicious glares, and headed for the nearest shop, a typical Freemansland allsorts—elsewhere, they'd call it a general merchandise.

The door was open, and three shadowy shapes moving within told me I wasn't the only customer. My flat sandals made little sound on the planking as I climbed the steps and entered the stack.

The bare electric bulbs couldn't compete with the bright sun outside, and it took my eyes a moment to adjust. I didn't know which of the three men standing around was the proprietor, so I addressed them all. "Anyone know where I can rent a boat? I need something small, with a motor."

All three stared as if trying to understand my request. The oldest—a wrinkled, loose-skinned man about my age who wore nothing but scraggly gray hair longer than mine and thin shorts that left nothing to the imagination—finally spoke. "You lost, lady?"

"No, I just need a boat."

A green-toothed man grinned around his occabot stick. "How'd you get here, then?"

"I have a canoe. But I'd like something with a motor."

Gray Hair spoke again. "You wantin' to trade?"

"Can't." I shook my head. "It's not mine."

He scratched beneath his beard. Green Teeth walked to the door and spat into the stillwater outside. Man Number Three stared off into space.

Finally the first man summoned an answer. "I got a little skiff out there that might suit you, if ya got somethin' to trade. I don't deal in no sliming City urexi."

I wished I'd anticipated that and brought something for barter. I wasn't about to part with the clothes on my back, nor my purse or its contents. What else did I have?

Then I saw the rack of footwraps. Made from scraps left over from dragonskin processing, they gave a small measure of protection against rough rocks as well as parasites, and were the closest thing to shoes worn on Freedom. Gran used to put me in them sometimes after digging the mudworms out from between my toes, but they never stayed on very long.

I pulled off a sandal. "How about I trade you these for a set of foot wraps and four days' use of your skiff?"

Gray Hair snorted. "What am I gonna do with them slimin' City shoes?"

"Trade 'em for somethin', 'o course." I pulled off the other and offered them to him. "Anyone else you know got anything like these?"

He reached for them with evident reluctance. With Green Teeth looking over his shoulder, he examined them. "Slime. Good quality stuff. Where'd you get these?"

"Bought 'em in Arkentak."

Gray Hair looked up in surprise. "Arkentak?"

Green Teeth took the stick out of his mouth. "You been there?"

I nodded. "I lived there until recently."

Gray Hair turned the sandals over and studied all sides. "These might have some value."

Green Teeth studied me, not the shoes. Man Number Three remained in his own little world.

"Yeah, these'll do." Gray Hair carried the sandals to a table and set them down. "Pick out a couple of footwraps for yourself. You can use the first skiff, there by the piling with the axe stickin' in it."

I stepped to the doorway. "I see it." It looked sound enough. Wasn't full of water, anyway.

He handed me the key to the motor. "Four days only. Know what that axe is for?"

"Of course. To cut off the hand of whoever steals the boat."

He grinned, showing numerous gaps in his dingy teeth. "Or the finger of the slime who keeps it longer than agreed."

I didn't return the smile. "I'll have it back in time without the threat. I keep my word."

"Not sayin' ya don't. Just pointin' out I got a security system."

I chose a set of footwraps from the rack. "Can't be very effective. A person stealing the boat could just take the axe too. Or use it on you." I tucked the footwraps under my arm and left the shop barefoot. "Thanks."

OVER THE NEXT couple of days, I circled the whole circumference of Freedom. Other than the general look, feel, and smell of things, I didn't recognize much. It was time that had wrought the changes, though, more than City intervention.

I found the pile of rock and mud my family had lived on, but no buildings could be discerned among the heaps of rubble. The only thing still upright was the table in what was once my father's skinning shed, the site of my first life's ending. A dragon sunning itself on the table snapped its jaws as I motored past.

Numerous residence stacks and a few commercial ones climbed the sharpfall here and there, but none looked familiar. Over the course of my visit, I passed four school barges, all more modern than the one I remembered. In my dragonskin footwraps, I stumbled around the sharpfall where I thought my cave was, but I never found it.

I partook of Freedom's bounty, catching small fish and mollusks, harvesting fruit and greens, and digging kittel roots. I drank rainwater captured in cups of bolli leaves. Though most of my meals weren't very tasty, I never went hungry. I didn't eat that way for old times' sake, but out of necessity, as none of the vendors I spoke with accepted City urexi. The only thing I could purchase with money was an overnight charge for my boat motor at the guest stacks where I slept.

The third day, I found the last place on my mental list of things to locate: the home formerly occupied by Four Four Freeman. Though empty, it still stood solid, even the roof. When I tied up at the little dock, my trained eye noted fresh scuffs from a boat having been recently docked there. As I exited the skiff, crushed foliage between the dock and the pounded path also gave evidence that someone had been there recently, probably just a day or two before.

It was a steep climb, but the path was not muddy, and its many switchbacks made the ascent more gradual than most around here. Or maybe I was just getting used to the sharpfalls again.

I enjoyed the climb. Whimsical statues stood at the points of the sharp bends. In one place, colored rocks spelled out, "Out of breath yet?" Generations of Four Four's family had shared a creative sense of humor, and I was glad to see the relics still in place.

Here and there, a rustic chair invited climbers to rest. One was a flat rock with a natural, buttock-shaped indentation in the top.

At the halfway point, Four Four or a predecessor had set up a rainwater catch basin. A charcoal filtration system prevented contamination. If you stepped on a foot pedal, water spurted from a tube, like a drinking fountain. I paused for a drink at the homemade fountain, but never sat in any of the chairs.

There were more statues than I remembered, and a few other quirky additions. This puzzled me, because Four Four was old when I was a child, and he was the last of his line. He had to have been gone for years, but it was obvious someone had lived here and maintained it until fairly recently.

The footwraps' bindings had rubbed my ankles raw by the time I got to the house. Though proud of myself for climbing the whole way without stopping to catch my breath, I didn't relish the long walk back down.

I intended to sit on the bench at the top and adjust the bindings. But a sign on the door made me forget everything else. The notice read: "Lease Available. Access from both Freedom stillwater below and Glaffit above. Contact City Properties Manager, Coldclime."

I hadn't seen a Lease Available sign anywhere else on Freedom. And why was this on the front door way up here, rather than near the stillwater, where people could see it?

Pondering the matter, I sat and undid the wrappings. My ankles were chafed, and both my little toes were rubbed red. I put my feet on the pounded pavement and took a few experimental steps. How sore would my soles get walking down that long path barefoot? A stone dug into my left arch, and I winced. It was doable, but I'd have to be careful.

I sat back down and took in the view. Directly ahead stretched an endless blue expanse of sky, dizzying in its immensity. Below, the sun-spangled stillwater. Against my back, the house that had sometimes sheltered me as a broken, desperate child, still solid and welcoming. To either side, lush, life-giving flora and familiar fauna growing together in the warm, fragrant soil.

The longer I sat, the more I wanted to stay. To live out the rest of my days here. The bird songs, the insect chirps, the scent in the wind all called to me. *Home. Come home. This is home.*

I rubbed the bandage on my wrist, feeling the bracelet beneath it. "You always knew I belonged here, didn't you, Grey? That's why you called me Freeman."

I picked up my footwraps and carried them down the path. "I'm a barefoot Freeman. And I'm going home."

EARLY MORNING ON the fourth day, I returned the boat to Gray Hair.

He chuckled when I brought him the key. "You got the whole day yet. Afraid of losing a finger?"

I chuckled. "I'm done here for now. Thanks for the use of it."

He put the key in a drawer. "If you ever want it again, I could use another pair of those sandals. They went real quick."

I headed for the door. "I'll keep that in mind."

Relieved to find my rented canoe where I'd left it, I got in and paddled back to the depot dock. In the building, I bought a scaler ticket and rode alone to Glaffit, but I didn't call Lanie for a ride to Moll. Instead, I took a water taxi across the stillwater to a catamara on the opposite side and bought a ticket to Coldclime.

As soon as I got off the scaler on the fourth level, the damp chill reminded me why they called it Coldclime. But the cold wasn't the only thing that shocked me. Modern buildings spread east and west and climbed the sharpfall, made accessible by roadways cut into the rock, bridges, stairways, and short scalers. Other buildings floated on the stillwater, connected to land by sturdy boardwalks. The wild landscape was tamed. The water didn't smell. On land, people bustled about, fully dressed, and heavy boat traffic plied the water.

First, I found a shop that sold ready-made clothing. The selection of up-to-date fashions surprised me. In addition to comfortable but stylish shoes, I purchased a modern dress—not culottes, but a full-length, legless version—in a jade green and gold print with a cream colored underskirt, as well as a warm jacket.

I had plenty of time to return to Moll for the night but wasn't ready to go back yet. Wanting to shower before putting on my new clothes, I rented a room. I inquired about the location of the Properties Management office and arrived there five minutes before my appointment, looking fresh and professional, my hair in a dignified chignon, and my marital bracelet no longer hidden.

My reflection in the mirror told me I looked like a woman to be reckoned with. The respect with which I was greeted at the Properties Management office confirmed it.

"Good afternoon, ma'am." A woman came out from behind her desk. "I'm Rava Obor, Deputy Properties Manager for the City here on Freemansland. How may I help you?"

I gave her my friendliest smile. "Hello, Ms. Obor. I'm Jemima Standtall. I believe I have an appointment with you at fifteen hundred?"

"Oh, yes, Mrs. Standtall! I'm so very pleased to meet you!" She beamed at me with the look people tend to give celebrities.

She clasped my hand. "Welcome back to Freemansland. When is the last time you've been here? Does it look the same as you remember it?"

"I haven't been to Coldclime since I graduated from the Academy, and I can't believe how much it's changed."

"You were at Academy East, were you not? I graduated from West in seventy-four."

"Yes, I was at East." I chuckled. "Somewhat before then."

We chit-chatted a little over crim, and then she got down to business. "So, you're interested in leasing a property? We have a number of units available on the south side in two of the new rim-scrapers—" She must have seen my puzzlement. "That's what we call the architecture that goes just over the rim of the upper stillwater. The units at the top of those buildings have marvelous vistas on both sides. You have a view of Coldclime and even to the distant ocean in the front, and from the back, you can see out over Thinair's stillwater. On a clear day, at least."

I made an exaggerated shiver. "Sounds cold up there." Despite my hot shower and warm clothes, the chill on this level was unrelenting. It even made my nose run, and I rummaged in my purse for a handkerchief. "You'd have to keep the heat running full on without a break. Not to my liking at all." I wiped my nose and cleared my throat.

"I understand." She broadened her smile. "But of course we have other units available. I just mentioned those at first because many people consider them desirable. Do you prefer the east side, perhaps, for nostalgia's sake? We have—"

I shook my head. "West side. But the property I'm interested in is on Freedom."

Her smile froze. "I'm sorry, did you say Freedom?"

"Yes. I just came from a visit there."

"Did you now." I got the impression she thought it was a joke and was looking for the punch line.

"Yes. I traveled around looking at places I remembered from my childhood, and one of them has a notice on the door, saying it's available. That's why I called you. I'd like to lease it."

"I see." She frowned. "Well." She went back to her desk and consulted her computer. "We don't have many things available there. What few buildings are habitable are already occupied."

I went to the desk hoping to see what she was doing, but she angled the screen away from my view, talking all the while. "In fact, a great many that aren't habitable are occupied. I really can't imagine what could have interested you there."

I told her the location of the house and added, "When I was a girl, the man who lived there was named Four Four Freeman. It had been in his family for generations."

Her brows rose. "Ah, yes. I know the one. But I believe..." She frowned again. "Yes. That's the property. It's in fairly good shape, for Freedom. But it's hardly suitable for a woman of your position, Mrs. Standtall. Don't you think you'd be more comfortable on Coldclime, where it's cleaner? And there are *many* amenities you won't find on Freedom."

I shook my head. "With Mr. Standtall gone, it's just me now, and I'd very much like to live out the rest of my days where I was born."

"Oh, please, that's no way to talk! What do you mean, live out the rest of your days? You can't be much over sixty, and you're still the picture of health."

I was only fifty-five, but I may have looked older because I didn't color my hair or wear make-up. My surprise at her assessment of my age must have shown in my expression, for she hurried on as if to cover her flub. "And Freedom is so unsanitary. After a few weeks of breathing that rank air, you'll start to suffer, I'm sure. And there are so many dangers on that level, from dragons in the stillwater to—"

I grew suddenly impatient. "That is the house I want, Ms. Obor. What is the cost of the lease?"

She sighed. "It's no longer available. The contract hasn't been finalized, but someone has put down a good-faith deposit and is seeking financing."

My heart lurched. "What? Who? What have they agreed to pay? I'll better their offer."

"I'm sorry, but I'm not at liberty to disclose the potential leaseholder. And as far as making a higher offer, you should know that's not the way it works. The City sets the amount, and it's not subject to negotiation."

I sought frantically for a solution. My mind was made up. I was going to live in that place, one way or another. "You're right, I do know that. But, okay, who's the owner? I'd like to buy it."

She shook her head again. "I cannot disclose that either. You'll have to ask your attorney to find the owner. But of course you know contracts protect the lessee from being removed from the property without cause. Owning it wouldn't give you the right to live there until the lessee gave up possession. And the party in question seems as intent on having it as you."

What could I do? My throat constricted with frustration, and the drainage from my nose made me cough. I pulled out the handkerchief again, and something lying in my bag beside it gave me an idea. It was a wicked one, but the old Jemma, the one trained in deceit, took over. "There's nothing I can do to change your mind?" I asked between coughs.

"All I can do is notify you if the party loses interest or can't come up with the money. Until then, why don't you let me show you some places here on Coldclime? I really think you'd be happier on this level anyway, and I'm sure I can find something you'll love. Or even Glaffit?"

I coughed the whole time she was talking. The tickle in my throat was gone, but I used it as a distraction. "Definitely not Glaffit. The temperature's better there than on Coldclime, but—" I coughed some more. "I'm sorry, but could I trouble you for some cold water?"

"Of course! I'll get you a glass."

I coughed again. "Thank you."

The instant her back was turned, I opened my bag and pulled out a small instrument that Jeriah had given me a few years back to scan for listening devices, as I still tended to worry about that. Called a Weaselstick, it could also be used to grab whatever information was pulled up on a computer even if the screen had gone dark.

The IA specialist in me noticed that Ms. Obor had not exited the window after having located the property listing. The name of the person who wanted it would still be there. And though the Weaselstick was no longer state-of-the-art, the computer was even older. It would have no safeguards against the device's technology.

It took only a few moments to set the stick for download, touch the back of the screen with its sensor, wait a second for the transfer, then slip it back into my purse. As soon as I was done, I made sure to cough again so Ms. Obor wouldn't think her mission was a waste of time.

She returned a moment later. "Here you go, Mrs. Standtall. I hope you're not coming down with something."

"Thank you." I took the water and sipped it. "I think it's just from the change in temperature. Coming up here after being on Freedom is a shock to my system."

Then a thought struck me: I'd just committed a criminal act, stealing restricted information from a City computer. The old Jemma would have thought nothing of it, but now, a wave of guilt almost made me choke on the water. At least it made my cough convincing.

I didn't know yet what sort of information I'd acquired, nor what I'd do with it once I found out. Maybe I shouldn't look at it. I should destroy the device without seeing what I'd downloaded.

But even as I had the thought, I knew I wouldn't do it. The fleshly rut I'd slipped into was too deep, and my motivation to escape too weak. No, I would see who was taking Four Four's house from me, come up with a plan to put a stop to it, and seek forgiveness later.

❧ Chapter 25 ❧

CONFESSION

IN MY ROOM at the Freemansland City Inn, Coldclime—a clumsy name for a hotel if there ever was one—I kicked off my shoes. Funny how three days on Freedom made me want to go barefoot. Only then did I look at the data I'd stolen from City Properties Management.

I scrolled through the legal gobbledygook until I found the name of the applicant.

You may have guessed it already, and I did too, in a far, dark corner of my mind. That is to say, the name, when I saw it, didn't surprise me.

Dabo, Mayne. Citizen by Merit. LAST LtCdr, Ret.

What did surprise me was my reaction. I gripped the device with trembling hands, my eyes devouring that name, especially the first name. Mayne. How I used to try not to think of the man who bore it. I'd buried him for good, I thought. But now here he was, risen from the grave.

Our conversation on the dock at Tenney's restaurant played through my mind. *That house captured my imagination. And when I say I want to come back and live on Freedom, I have that very place in mind...*

Did he remember that night as clearly as I did? I could still taste the rappu legs and feel his warmth in his jacket when he'd put it on my shoulders. I heard the songs of the night insects, smelled the stillwater below our feet dangling off the dock.

Whether or not he remembered the details, he obviously remembered the house we'd talked about.

My heart raced as I located his contact information. Light-headed and flushed, I sank onto the bed and closed my eyes. *I shouldn't have stolen this information, Lord. I confess that. And having stolen it, I shouldn't have looked at it. I confess that too. This whole thing is wrong, wrong, wrong. But now that I know what I know, would it be wrong to give him a call?*

Not willing to wait for an answer, I pulled out my phone and called the number.

He picked up after the fourth ring. "Dabo."

The way my heart pounded, I wondered if it would explode. "Mayne?"

"Yes?"

"This is, um, Jem. Jemima Freeman."

Pause. Then, "Oh, yeah, I think I've heard of you somewhere. Did Riah give you my number?"

My brother was still in touch with him? He hadn't mentioned him for years. "No, I—well, long story. Are you in Freemansland?"

"Why do you ask?"

"Because I am. And I understand you want to get that house on Freedom we once talked about, the one up near the top of the sharpfall on the west side? And we need to talk about that."

Another pause. "And just how did you—? Oh, wait, let me guess. Long story, right?"

"Um, yes. That's one of the things we have to talk about. Where can we meet?" A sudden thought almost made me faint. "If your wife is with you, she's welcome to join us..."

His answer was unemotional, matter-of-fact, and just what I hoped-against-hope to hear. "I have no wife. It'll be just me."

I hoped he couldn't hear my sigh of relief.

"And yes, I am in Freemansland. Would it be convenient for you to meet me at Tenney's? Say, nineteen hundred?"

I wasn't sure I could wait that long, but I didn't argue. "Okay. Tenney's it is. See you in two hours."

☀

THE SETTING SUN splashed the stillwater with orange and yellow when I approached Tenney's. The place had been updated since the old days, and the open-air dining room now extended further into the water than it used to. But the sign still said Tenney's, and its cheery lights beckoned.

Mayne stood by the door. Though his physique was thicker and his hair grayer than last time I saw him, he was the same Mayne I remembered. Same posture. Same quiet strength.

I greeted his shadowy silhouette. "Good evening."

He turned, and those same lively blue eyes lit up along with the old Mayne smile. "Jem!"

The sight of him made me warm all over despite the chill night air. "Thank you for agreeing to meet with me."

"Like I'd say no."

I almost wanted to hug him, but he kept a respectful distance as we shook hands. "You look great. Better than your publicity headshot."

I laughed. "That's really funny. I was fifteen years younger then, and dressed to impress. Now, I'm just me."

"That's what I mean. You're you." He gestured toward the entrance. "But are you hungry?"

"Am I ever."

He opened the door, and we entered the restaurant. Though not much taller than me, his neck was thick, his shoulders and chest broad, his manner confident. I had never met anyone more thoroughly manly.

He had called ahead to request a specific table, and we talked as we waited for it. I had many questions, but I didn't ask them. I just let the conversation flow, feeling as if I had no right to ask anything of him after hating him for all those years. Hating him for no reason.

I studied every detail of his face as he talked, his hands as he gestured, the short gray beard that he'd missed a spot in trimming. The more I saw and heard, the guiltier I felt.

A construction security specialist, he now worked as a freelance consultant. "I travel all over," he said, "and it doesn't really matter where I call home. So a little while ago, I decided to call home 'home.' I've been here a couple of weeks now, looking for a place. Thought I might take an apartment in Coldclime, but nothing grabbed me."

"I'm surprised Four Four's house wasn't your first choice."

"It was." He shrugged. "That was the one I really wanted. But it wasn't the first place I looked at."

I waited for him to explain, but then he said, "I shouldn't be talking about myself all the time. I want to hear about you."

"You already know about me. My life is a best-selling book."

He chuckled. "I doubt the public face reveals much about the real J. S. Freeman." He sobered. "Although I will say *Mimma's Song* made me sit up and take notice. I got the impression much of that was the real Jemima speaking."

"You read it?" I envisioned him reclined on a sofa in reading glasses, holding a book in his hands, the table lamp behind him casting a warm glow on the page.

His brows rose. "Of course."

The host announced our table was ready, and we followed him to the last table at the far end of the dock.

I took a seat. "This is the table you requested?"

Mayne nodded. "The very same."

The host asked for our wine preference.

Mayne looked at me, brows lifted. "What would you like?"

I shook my head. "Whatever you want. I won't have any."

He looked up at the host. "No wine, thank you. Do you have Allock?"

"Yes, sir." The host turned to me. "And you, ma'am?"

"I'll have the same. Could you put a shot of cheradan in it?"

The host hesitated. "Umm, we have cheradan in the bar. Sure, of course, I see no reason why we can't put some in your Allock, if that's what you'd like."

"It is."

"We'll bring those out to you right away."

The colored lights strung along the edge of the canopy made Mayne's eyes sparkle as they studied me. "Since when do you drink Cher-Allock instead of wine?"

"So you've heard of it before?"

"It's not all that uncommon."

"I guess it was Jeriah who introduced me to it. Since when do *you* turn down wine?"

"I don't drink crim, either."

I gasped. "You don't drink wine or glaffcrim, but you call yourself a Freemanslander? What's the matter with you?"

"I like to limit my addictions."

"Limit them to what?"

"There was a time when I was addicted to painkillers. Once I finally broke free of that, I swore off everything."

"Thankfully, the painkillers never got their hooks into me. Alcohol, yes. I'm best off avoiding that. But crim?" I shook my head. "I've been cut off from glaffcrim a couple of times, but I always go back to it. I think it's in my blood."

The server not only brought our drinks, but also an appetizer of bicio blossoms.

I objected that we hadn't ordered the blossoms, but Mayne said, "I ordered ahead."

"I didn't know Tenney's lets you do that."

He shrugged. "I don't think they usually do, but they agreed when I asked them. Mind if I thank God for the food?"

"Not at all. But please don't pour your Allock on your head."

He chuckled. No, it was a giggle. Just like I remembered it. "I don't wet my head like that anymore. That was an ignorant superstition. Now, thanks to the Book, I know who I worship, and why."

I hardly knew what to say. "You're a follower of Jesus?"

"I always was, you know. Or at least, I always wanted to be. As soon as I learned about the Book, I knew it would hold the answers I'd been looking for all my life. Thank you for that."

My hands were under the table, and I fingered my bracelet. "It's not me who is to be thanked."

"You're right." He lifted both his hands shoulder high, palms out, closed his eyes and prayed, "Thank you, Father God, for your bountiful blessings. For this food, for the renewal of this friendship, and for all we have in Christ our Lord."

We both said, "Amen."

"Okay." Mayne wasted no time picking up a bicio blossom and dipping it in the sauce. "I'm hungry." With the blossom, he gestured toward the plate. "Dig in."

I was already reaching before he'd spoken, but decided not to eat the blossom I held until I'd broached the subject I wanted to discuss. "As I said on the phone, we need to talk."

He swallowed his first bite. "We've been talking, haven't we?"

"Yes. But we need to talk about the house."

He wiped his hands on his napkin. "The house you have no business knowing I put an offer on, you mean?"

"Yes. That's the one."

"Okay. So what did you want to say?"

He seemed amused, somehow, and that irritated me. "I want to say that *I* want that house. It's not fair of you to sneak in and take it just when I was about to get it."

He snorted. "So that's why you contacted me after all these years. Makes sense now. But let's back up a bit. Before we talk about the house, why don't you tell me that long story you mentioned on the phone, about how you got my number, and how you know my business."

I flushed. Deeply. I laid down my uneaten blossom, and words fled me. I felt like the old Jem again.

He picked up another blossom and held it, eyes glittering. "So what's the story?"

I leaned back in my chair with a long, "Aaaach."

He scraped up some sauce with the blossom and put it in his mouth, chewing and saying nothing.

I leaned forward again. "Okay. Here's what happened. Yesterday, I went to see if the house was still there, and I saw the Available sign. So I had an appointment with the Properties Manager this afternoon, and after failing to convince me I was too good to live on Freedom, she told me someone had already claimed that property."

He nodded as he wiped his mustache with the napkin.

"So, I—I had an old Weaselstick in my purse. Habit, you know. I asked for a glass of water, and while she was gone, I— Well, you can guess."

He laid his napkin on the empty blossom plate. "I'm sure I can, but I want you to say it."

I looked at him with narrowed eyes. "You're not recording this conversation, are you?"

He smiled. "No. I have a supply of fun gadgets too, but I didn't think to bring any."

"Why do you want me to spell it out?"

"Because we can't be forgiven of our sins if we refuse to confess them."

A shiver shook me.

"Are you cold? Would you like my jacket?" He made ready to stand and remove it.

I shook my head. "I'm already wearing a jacket. And if you gave me yours, I'd just get rappu juice all over it. You ordered rappu legs, didn't you?"

"How'd you guess?"

I wrapped my arms around myself. I couldn't look him in the eye.

Patient as a snake, he took another sip of Allock. I had little doubt he'd sit there all night if he had to.

"I'm ashamed of myself. Not only because I took the information off the Properties Manager's computer with my Weaselstick. Not even mostly, though that was illegal. What I did earlier was far worse. That's what I'm most ashamed of."

He leaned back in his chair and crossed his arms, saying nothing.

"You were never anything but good to me, Mayne. Looking back on it—I couldn't see it at the time, because I was too stupid, but later—much later—I realized how much you cared for me. You were my savior at the Academy, the way you stepped up and said I was spoken for. If I'd had the capacity to love back then, I'd have loved you for it. But instead, I hated you. I hated you when I boarded the plane on the transport barge and flew out of Freemansland. I hated you more with every tortured step I took in Foundational. My hatred grew when Jeriah got married and I was left with nobody. It got more cold and bitter every time I thought of you, which was often, because you were part of my life. A part that, deep down, I didn't want to lose." I choked up then and had to stop, though I had more to say.

Mayne's blue eyes glimmered. "I'm sorry."

"Don't. You have nothing to apologize for."

The server came then, bringing a bucket of rappu legs, an empty bucket to hold the shells, and a pile of napkins. Then he picked up a platter of seaweed salad from his cart and set it on the table along with a bowl of roasted kittel roots and water asparagus.

I picked up a napkin and dabbed at my eyes. Good thing I wasn't wearing any makeup. "Oh, my, this looks wonderful." I sniffed. "You're too good." When the waiter was gone, I added, "I don't deserve it."

"Granted. But do you still hate me?" He hadn't changed his position. Still leaned back with arms crossed, gazing across the table at me with a benign expression.

I shook my head. "No. Not at all."

He uncrossed his arms and sat upright. "Good. Then let's eat."

I hardly knew what to make of this conversation, but I was hungry, so I pushed up my sleeves and dug in.

Rappu legs never tasted so good. We cracked open the shells, pulled out the meat, and ate without talking for several minutes, though my mind was plenty busy.

Probably his was too, but I was the first to speak. "So, what can I do to persuade you to let me have that house?"

He reached across the table, picked up my glass of Cher-Allock, and took a taste. "Mm. Pretty good. I'll have to try that sometime."

"You just did. But you didn't answer my question. How can I convince you to let me have the house?"

He returned my glass to its place in front of me, lining it up in the same ring of condensation on the table. "You can't."

"I can buy it, you know. I can find out who owns it and buy it."

"You want to strut your CFC stuff, go ahead. I still get to live in it."

I dropped a rappu shell in the bucket. "Four Four and his wife let me stay there sometimes, you know. I was practically their daughter, but you never even met them. The house should be mine."

He took a bite of the water asparagus. "These roasted vegetables are delicious. What are they seasoned with?"

"Tenney's secret recipe, I don't know." I licked a bit of seaweed from my lip. "It might take me a while to figure out how, but one day, I'm going to live in that house."

"It didn't take me any time at all to figure it out."

I'd been bringing a fork full of salad to my mouth but paused and looked up. "What?"

"I know how you can have the house."

I continued eating. "Sure. You could just let me have it. I'll reimburse you for the down payment."

He put down his fork and leaned back in his chair. "You know what my LAST name is?"

"Dabo."

He crossed his arms. "I mean my nickname in Land Air Sea Tactical. We all have nicknames, you know."

I shook my head. "No, I didn't know. What's yours?"

"Mountain Man Mayne. Mounty, for short."

"And is that what you want me to call you?"

"You know how I got that name?"

He must have had a reason to be changing the subject like this, but I couldn't guess what it might be. "No. Why do they call you Mountain Man? Because you grew up climbing the sharpfall, so you're good at mountain climbing?"

"Because I'm like a mountain. I don't move. I hold my ground. Once I've taken a position, I don't budge for nothin'."

Tenacity had been a trait of his even as a kid. "This is your way of telling me you're not going to give up the house."

He nodded. "I'll tell you any way I have to. But you're not going to move me."

I glared at him. "But didn't you just say a minute ago that you know how I can have it?"

"That's what I said." He uncrossed his arms. "If you marry me, we can both have it."

You knew he was going to say that, didn't you? So did I. But even though the same thought was in my mind, I struggled to make it fit in the realm of reality.

"Why don't you already have a wife? Are you divorced? Widowed?"

"No."

"Oh, please. Do NOT tell me you waited for me. Riah told me you did, and I didn't believe him. No man would do that, not even you."

He sighed. "If you don't want me to tell you, I won't. But if it makes you feel any better, I did succumb to temptation. I was actually engaged at one time. For several years, in fact. But I couldn't bring myself to marry her, and she finally dumped me. Said she was wasting her youth on me."

"You're pathetic, you know that?" Sitting there like a manly lump of gorgeous rock, he looked anything but pathetic, but the situation embarrassed me. "You didn't have to do that. You knew we weren't really promised. And that I'd married someone else. You deprived that poor woman of an excellent husband. That was cruel of you."

He shrugged. "She married a year or so later and had a couple of kids. They all seem to be doing pretty well, so I don't think I deprived her of anything."

"Then you shouldn't have deprived yourself. That was foolish."

"So I've told myself, over and over. But here we are." He gestured between us. "You and me. We both want the same thing—the house. And each other. So what do you say?"

He was absolutely right. About all of it.

Fighting a grin—I didn't want to seem too eager—I pulled out my phone and dictated a text. "Hey, Bark, about that promise I made after your brother died? I need to introduce you to somebody. Where can we meet? Let me know the place and time, and we'll be there. Oh, and bring the key to Ashgrey's bracelet."

Mayne cracked open another rappu leg as I spoke. After I put the phone away, he asked, "What was that all about?"

"Another long story. Do you have the time?"

He pulled the meat from the shell. "I've got the whole rest of my life."

❧ Chapter 26 ❧

SUNSET ON THE STILLWATER

MAYNE AND I sat on a balcony at our Freedom home, watching the sun sink below the water in a blaze of orange. He yawned. "Long day."

"But a good one."

We'd been married a year, and had just that day put the final touches on our home renovations: installing screens on the balcony, so we could sit outside without every blood-sucking insect on Freedom making a meal of us.

We loved the character quirks Four Four's family had built into the stack of sheds over the past several generations, and we left them in place whenever we could. These included the hollowed-out stone sink in the kitchen with running water—a feature few houses on Freedom could boast, though this house had had it for almost two hundred years. The water poured into the stone basin from a spout shaped like an open-mouthed fish. The ablutions shed held another innovation otherwise unheard-of on Freedom—a bathtub. This one made from a small rowboat. Mayne's favorite feature was a carved wood dragon that appeared to be coming through the wall just inside the main entrance. Someone had done a skillful job of covering it with genuine dragonskin to make it look like the real thing.

We couldn't keep everything, though. First off, we had to tear down the whole sleeping stack where Four Four's widow had died. Her body had lain there for several months before it was found, and I won't tell you the mess that made.

Many extensive repairs were necessary, but Mayne knew so much about building that I wondered if there was anything he *didn't* know. We made the plans together, I shared the labor with him, and I marveled at his skill, his patience, and his ability to solve any problem.

And now, at last, the work was done. We figured we'd probably make small changes as long as we lived there, but all the most urgent things were accomplished.

He yawned again. "Now that we're finished, are you going to invite all your friends and Standtall in-laws to visit us?"

I tried to imagine Grey's family visiting Freedom and laughed at the mental picture. "Don't think so. Why?"

"Why not? We have a guest stack."

"That's for your family. And your LAST buddies. I think Grey's family will be happy to never see me again. They were very kind to me—most of them, anyway—but I'm an aberration. That disappearing act I pulled strained their tolerance to the limit."

"Grey's brother seems to like you okay."

I nodded. "Bark's all right. But he can't afford to be too friendly without upsetting Pearl. She still hasn't forgiven him for helping Riah and me slip out of Ottava Xenio Hall in the middle of the Centre Awards. She was mad at him even before then, for helping Grey with his sneaking around. Though he was never in any actual danger, Pearl had a fit when she found out what they'd been doing."

"I guess that's why she wasn't with Bark when you introduced me to him last year."

"That's exactly why. She probably only let him see us because my taking off Grey's bracelet meant I'd be out of the Standtall family for good."

Mayne's brows puckered in a little frown. "I don't understand what she has against you."

"I'm not sure either." I shrugged. "Even before I knew him, Grey was the odd one in the family. Maybe she's upset I didn't make him settle down and live like a normal CFC. I didn't keep him out of trouble like a good wife should."

"Could you have? Would he have stopped putting himself in danger if you'd insisted?"

I chuckled. "I don't know. It never occurred to me to try. But all in all, from her point of view, I guess I was a bad choice for him from the beginning. Even so, she was always nice to me. I never suspected her real feelings until after the Centre Awards debacle."

We sat in silence for a few minutes, holding hands and watching the insects crawl and flutter on the other side of our new screens.

Mayne squeezed my hand. "Pearl can't forgive because she doesn't know what it is to be forgiven."

How could I love him so much, but still hold Grey in my heart as I did before? "That's true. God's love expands us."

I regretted that I hadn't understood Grey's faith when he was alive. We could have had this sweet communion at the end of the day instead of being at odds those last few years. Why hadn't I listened when he tried to talk about it? "I'm so glad you and I both know the Lord. I hope Pearl will come to faith too. I know it weighs on Bark's heart that she hasn't."

"I'm sure it does." After a sober pause, he broke into a grin. "What would you have done if Bark hadn't approved of me?"

"How could he not? We're made for each other. Anyone can see that."

He chuckled. "Took *you* long enough to see it."

I let out a long sigh. "True enough. And I'm sorry."

"That's okay. It's been worth the wait. But—" He clapped his hands on the arms of his chair, then pushed himself out of it. "I'd better hit the mat. We have to get an early start in the morning."

I rose too. "Yes, we do."

He was flying out for a job the next day, and I was going with him. Not to help with the job, because I didn't know anything about construction security, but to keep him company on his trip.

We left the balcony and passed through the stack, up a stairway, and then across an outdoor covered bridge into the ablutions shed. While we washed up, Mayne asked, "What's your next writing project? You haven't mentioned what you're working on."

"That because I'm not writing anymore. I've already said everything I have to say."

He looked up from his tooth cleaning to catch my eye in the mirror, which was shaped like a boat oar. "Hmm?"

I unpinned my hair, then brushed it. "I don't think I have any stories left in me."

Mayne emptied his mouth. "You can't stop yet. You've got one very important one left to tell."

I put my hair in a braid. "And what's that?"

"The story of your life. You've said yourself that all the world knows your name, but nobody knows who you really are. That's the story you've been working on all your life, and I think it's worth sharing it with the world."

I frowned. "Sounds pretty self-serving. Besides, people are tired of hearing about me."

He put his arms around me from behind and rested his chin on my shoulder, watching me in the mirror. "I'm not. And I don't know the whole story, do I?"

"Probably not." I tied off the braid and turned to face him. "I'm not hiding anything, I just tell you things as I think of them."

"Well then, don't write it for the world, write it for me. I want to know everything about you."

I kissed him. "I'll think about it."

I DID THINK about it, but I had a hard time with the idea of opening the dirty windows of my life and shining a spotlight on myself. These days, I preferred to talk about redemption and the transforming power of the God-man Jesus, not the foolishness I once believed and the godless ways I behaved.

Though I never discarded the idea, I didn't do anything about it for the next three years. I sometimes traveled with Mayne. When he went on a job alone, I often went to Moll and did what I could to help there, including working with Jeriah on his writing projects. Mayne and I both were active with the two churches nearest our home, one on Glaffit and one on Freemansland. I spent time with KJ. I even visited Seena once. Every now and then I thought about writing my life story but didn't know when I'd find the time.

After Mayne brought it up for the umpteenth time, though, I finally started working on it. It went quickly, but I was only about halfway done by the time he went out of town just after my sixtieth birthday.

He'd only been gone a couple of days when Jeriah called to say Uncle Rhe had taken a tumble down the sharpfall.

I packed a bag and headed for Moll.

RIAH AND I sat on the floor beside Uncle Rhe's mat. Aunt Lanie was there, along with their three children and as many of the grandchildren as could get there. Sixteen of us sat in the sleeping stack, not counting our uncle. After lingering for three days, he'd taken his final breath a few minutes ago.

His older son, Arn, wiped his eyes. "So tell me again why we're not going to do the usual?"

Arn's wife, Tosa, answered. "The City considers it a health hazard to dump a body in the stillwater. Nowadays it has to be taken to the crematorium on Thinair."

"Or buried under rocks," added the youngest son, Kane. "The law says he can stay here on Moll if we put at least a meter of rock on him to keep him from washing down the sharpfall."

Lanie had been holding her husband's hand since he passed, but she let go now and turned to the rest of the family. "I don't like the idea of burning him, and I especially don't want him hauled up to Thinair. He was born at Moll, he died at Moll, and he should be buried here."

"I agree." Repplif rose. "I'll go start collecting rocks."

Jeriah stood too. "I think we can all do that. But first, we need to get someone from Records to verify the death. And they want someone present at the burial to confirm that it was done according to law."

While waiting for the official to arrive, we selected a burial site and gathered rocks together, sharing our memories of the deceased. I found comfort in the simplicity of it, the lack of empty ritual, the physical exertion and sense of purpose. The Records Deputy noted the cause and time of death—being a native Freemanslander, he was content to take our word for that—and accompanied us as we carried the body to the chosen site.

While we laid the rocks gently around and upon him, we sang one of the first hymns Aunt Lanie had written based on one of the psalms in the Book:

The Son heard my cry, my cry for help. He lifted me out of the mire.

He brought me up from the horrible pit, he set my feet on a rock.

I sing the new song he put in my mouth, it flows from my heart to my mouth,

Praises to God, I sing praises to God, the new song he has put in my mouth.

The man who makes the Lord his trust, his faith, his joy and his song,

The man who makes the Lord his trust will rest ever in the Son.

When I sing the new song he put in my mouth, that flows from my heart to my mouth,

Many shall hear it, many shall see, and many shall trust in my God.

Oh, let's sing the new song he put in our mouth, all we who have been made new,

So that many shall hear it, many shall see, and many shall trust in the Son.

When the workers who lived in the stacks got wind of what we were doing, they came to help, each bringing a rock or two. When the first song ended, Aunt Lanie started a different one, and we sang one hymn after another until the last rock was laid.

Hundreds of people filed by the body, singing, tears streaming, laying a rock on the pile, until it was a small mountain. After depositing their contribution, they gave a nod to the family and then went home.

It was a fine memorial. Uncle Rhe would have approved.

The next day, everyone went back to work, and it was time for me to go home as well. I said my goodbyes to Jeriah, Aunt Lanie, and the rest, feeling blessed beyond measure. They were my family. My own flesh and blood. They knew me—the bad and the good—but loved me anyway. And I loved them the same. No matter what.

Instead of taking the cargo scaler, I walked the long, zig-zagging path down the sharpfall, remembering Jeriah's and my first time climbing it with Aunt Lanie. We were scared kids, torn from our home, having known nothing but fear and pain all our lives until Aunt Lanie and Uncle Rhe showed us love. I remembered our caseworker, Miss Orange, telling us that day that Uncle Rhe would be good to us, because he was a good man. She was so right.

I thought of how God had used so many people to keep me alive, to nurture me, to teach me, to protect me—my eyes blurred as I added in my mind, *to love me*, as I pictured Grey—and to put the Book in my hands. To give me a platform from which to deliver it to the world. Why would God take a battered little girl out of the stinking stillwater and give her such a privilege?

Because he loved me. I didn't deserve it, but he loved me, because he's love.

I paused to compose myself, leaning on a rail overlooking the stillwater. A boat motored toward the dock. Though still a good way out, I could see it was a water taxi. We never used to see them on Glaffit as kids, though they were already common on Coldclime long before we were at the Academy.

I continued the rest of the way down without any more tears— or rather, not many—but by the time I reached the bottom, I felt drained. I was eager to get home. Even more eager to see Mayne. He was due home day after tomorrow. What I wanted more than anything else at that moment was to be in his arms.

As I passed beneath the arch, the water taxi approached and slowed. There was always a good bit of traffic in and out of Moll, so I didn't pay much attention until I had boarded my own boat. That's when someone called, "Excuse me? Ma'am?"

I turned toward the voice.

A man exited the taxi, a little clumsily, as if he wasn't used to watercraft. Once both feet were on the dock, he strode toward me, his stylish, very-unFreemanslandish boots clomping across the boards. "Ma'am? Excuse me, but I'm looking for someone. I'm told she's visiting Moll." He looked up at the arch towering above us. "And it looks like that's where I am."

I stayed on my boat. "Yep. That's where you are."

A wide-brimmed hat of the sort popularized by the Steefren cattlemen shaded his eyes, and his suit was of the Streefrenian cut as well. "Could you tell me if—" His eyes narrowed. "Well! I think you're the very person I'm looking for." The water taxi roared away from the dock, and he had to shout. "Are you Jemima Standtall?"

I wanted to say, "No," and cast off. I wasn't, after all. I was Jem Dabo now, and I had little patience for anyone City or anything that prevented me from going home. But as a child of God, I couldn't be dishonest. The fire in my conscience after the incident at the Properties Management office had brought that lesson home to stay.

Being trustworthy, however, didn't mean I had to be trusting. "Who's asking?"

The man pulled out his ID. "Kenlan Fren, City Marshal. I'm here on a more personal matter, though, not in an official capacity."

"Oh?"

"I'm sorry to bother you, ma'am." He put away his ID. "I understand you've just suffered a loss in the family, and I'm sorry." He seemed embarrassed suddenly, or uncertain how to begin. "I hope I haven't come at a bad time."

"You have. But here you are. What do you want?"

He flushed and lowered his gaze. "Yes, ma'am, and I do apologize. My condolences on your loss. I hear your uncle was a fine man."

"He was. Thank you."

Fren lifted his head. "But as you said, I am here now, all the way from Streefren, which is really quite a distance. So I might as well ask what I came to ask, if I may."

I fought a rising annoyance. "Please do."

"Did, ah—" He glanced down again and then, seeming to summon the words from somewhere near his boots, lifted his head and looked me in the eye. "That book your late husband gave you before he died. The one that was later published as *The Book of God*. According to the foreword in the first edition, the book Mr. Standtall gave you was done in his own handwriting?"

What was he getting at? I leaned forward against the poles supporting the boat's bimini top. "Yes. That information is public knowledge."

"By any chance, was the handwriting on only one side of the page? Were the backs of the pages blank?"

I didn't answer right away. Though his manner was earnest, everything about this situation made me suspicious. However, in the letter that accompanied the Book, Grey had prepared me.

In my mind, I saw the scrawl across the page: "There is more here than you can see. I have written on one side of the page. If anyone asks, tell them this: There is more here than you can see." Jeriah and I had wondered what he'd meant by that. Later, I showed it to Mayne, and he couldn't figure it out either.

If anyone asks... And now, someone was asking. So I answered as Grey had instructed. "There is more there than you can see."

Fren cocked an eyebrow. "Pardon me?"

Okay, so maybe this wasn't what Grey had prepared me for. Or if it was, Fren didn't know the code. I clarified. "The writing is only on one side of the page, as you said."

"What do you mean, there's more than you can see?"

I shrugged. "You can't see anything on the backs of the pages."

"Do you—" He took a half-step forward. "Do you still have the book? Would you allow me to see it for myself?"

If not for Grey's letter, I never would have let the conversation get this far. Who was this guy? An off-duty City Marshal? Was he one of the ones who'd killed my husband, torn up my home, and maybe even cut my father-in-law in half? Grey's letter hadn't told me to *trust* a person who asked, only what to say. But this one didn't seem to know what I was talking about.

Though I couldn't trust him, there was something even more special about this book than any of us understood, and I didn't want to miss the chance to find out what it was.

"Ma'am?"

I felt incapable of making a decision. I had to talk to Mayne. "I don't know." I shook my head. My thoughts seemed to be slogging through jelly. "I don't know. I'll have to find out."

He reached into a pocket. "If I give you my number, will you call me?" He extended a card to me.

I leaned forward and took it. "Yeah, I'll call you. Once I know something. You gonna be around for a while? In Freemansland, I mean?"

He bobbed his head. "I can arrange to stay for a few more days. Not sure how long, probably less than a week. Can you get back with me before then?"

Why were my thought processes so sluggish? It must be grief. My mind had been wandering in the past so much these last few days.

"Ma'am? Will you know something soon?"

I blinked, and the sun seemed to shine brighter and my thoughts grew clearer. "Yes, I should be able to get back with you in two days, three on the outside."

"Thank you, ma'am. I'm much obliged."

I started the boat's engine, then reached over to untie the lines. Fren stood on the dock, looking about him with an uncertain expression. But of course, his taxi had left. He had no way to leave Moll without calling for another and waiting in the sun for it to arrive.

Though I wanted to put distance between us as quickly as possible, I couldn't very well leave him standing there. "Could I give you a ride somewhere?"

He perked up. "Yes, ma'am. If it wouldn't be out of your way, could you deliver me to the depot where I can get that rail car thing up the cliff to the next level?"

"You want the scaler to Coldclime?" I nodded. "Certainly. Climb aboard."

I grabbed a dock cleat to hold the vessel steady while he carefully stepped on. He was definitely not used to boats. "Have yourself a seat there, and we'll be under way in a minute."

Once he was sitting, I pushed away from the dock, then went and sat at the controls. "Do you care which catamara I take you to?"

He rubbed his chin. "Which what?'

I chuckled. "Which station where you can get up to the next level. Each level has three. Closest one good enough?"

He nodded. "The closer the better."

With the dock safely behind us, I opened the throttle and skimmed across the water faster than I'd ever taken this boat. Mayne loved to make it fly. I didn't, ordinarily, but I was in a hurry to deliver my passenger and be free of him.

Fren held his hat on with one hand and grinned, so apparently he liked speed too. I remembered Grey on our honeymoon, wanting to race around on Personal Trail Vehicles and motorcycles. I didn't like speed then, and I didn't care for it now, but it bothered me less on the water than it did on land.

I dropped him off at the dock by the depot with a promise to call him in a couple of days, then took off at a more sensible pace for home.

Our place was technically on Freedom, but because it was so near the top rim, it was easier to access from above. Mayne had repaired the old dock on the outside edge of Glaffit's stillwater. From there, we could climb a short ladder over the rim, then down a stairway to the house. It was easier than taking the scaler to Freedom, boating to the house, and then climbing up the zig-zag path.

But our dock was on the opposite side of Glaffit from the depot where I'd dropped off Marshal Fren, and by the time I got there, the sun was low enough that it would be dusk on the other side of Freemansland.

As I neared my destination, I was puzzled at how hazy everything seemed. I blinked and rubbed my eyes, but my vision didn't clear as I shut down the motor and secured the boat.

I picked up my bag and disembarked. By the time I'd climbed over the rim and walked down to my door, the world had brightened again. How strange.

I carried my bag into the sleeping stack and dropped it, then went into the kitchen to look for some supper.

I had a headache.

❧ Chapter 27 ❧

FREE INDEED

IN MIDAFTERNOON THREE days later, Mayne met Kenlan Fren on our dock on Glaffit. The water taxi that took him there must have cost the marshal a shining urexi, as we were far out of the usual route.

Mayne had the taxi wait until he'd spoken to the marshal to get a feel for his character. I'm not sure just what that interview involved, but I figure most people would find interrogation by a veteran LAST an unnerving experience.

The marshal passed the test, though, so Mayne sent the driver away and escorted Fren over Glaffit's rim and down Freedom's sharpfall as far as our home's main entrance.

I sat in the first stack with the shades down, as the sunlight aggravated my headache. I heard their voices as they approached. Mayne opened the door as Fren was saying, "So when we leave, we'll have to climb all the way back up there? You do this sort of thing all the time?"

Mayne answered, "It keeps us young," and they stepped in.

Fren let out a shriek and grabbed Mayne to pull him away from the dragon coming out of the wall. Then he let go and sagged in relief. "Oh, my GLISH, that got my heart going!" He stepped toward the statue and examined it. "That looks as real as you do."

Laughing, Mayne rapped the dragon's head with his knuckles. "It's wood. But you're right, it looks real. First time we came in here, Jem and I both did the same thing."

I laughed too as I rose and went to greet him. "Even now, I jump every time, but I seldom use that door."

Fren still seemed a little shaky as he looked about. "I must say, this is a very unusual house. Even for Freemansland. I mean, I haven't visited any other private homes here, but this has got to be unusual."

"It is," I said. "Would you like some crim? I just made a pot."

"I'd love a cup, yes. I've noticed the crim tastes better on Freemansland. Why is that?"

I put on a pair of dark glasses and opened the shades. Even with the glasses, I winced at the light. "Because it's born here, I guess."

After only about a minute of chitchat, I couldn't wait any longer. "I'm glad you're enjoying your visit to the land of many mysteries, Marshal, but I understand you'd like to see the Book Ashgrey gave me."

He nodded. "If you have no objections, ma'am, yes, I would. I believe, as you said, there's more there than meets the eye."

Mayne and I exchanged glances, then he rose. "I'll get it."

He went through a passage to the next stack, and I turned my attention to our guest. "How do you know about this? About there being more to the Book than we can see, I mean?"

He took a sip of crim and savored it before swallowing. "An old friend of mine—a colleague, my mentor—was also an associate of your late husband's, though I wasn't aware of it until recently. His name was Brose L'Nee. Ever hear of him?"

My eyes widened with surprise, then I closed them because of the pain. "Yes, of course. We both knew Brose. His wife Nelia and I were friends as well. But then—" I rubbed my temples. "We lost track of each other. I don't recall why." I picked up my cup and guzzled the remaining crim. "You knew Brose? But I don't understand. What did he know about the Book?" I poured myself a second cup. Sometimes it seemed to help a headache, but it couldn't touch this one.

Fren crossed his legs. "I'm not sure. I never spoke with him about it directly. But after he died, his family gave me—"

My breath caught. "He died? Oh, I'm sorry. What about Nelia?"

"She's been gone for a number of years. The family gave me an envelope they found among his things, directed to me as City Marshal and addressed to the office where we once worked together, Brose and me. The envelope wasn't sealed, and it didn't seem to have anything important in it. But it had my name on it, so they thought it might mean something to me."

"What was in it?"

He shrugged. "Not much. A program from a grappleball game Brose and I went to years before, a couple of ticket stubs from a jekko match, and a print-out of a newsfeed brief about amateur pugilists. Some names were written on the program and the stubs. It meant nothing to me, and I'd have thrown it away, but I had a feeling Brose was trying to tell me something. It's taken me three years to sort it all out. But one thing led to another, and without telling you the whole sordid tale, I'll just say it brings me here to your, um—" He looked around him. "Your living room."

"First stack."

He lifted his eyebrows.

"It's the first part of the stack of buildings that make up the house. It's our first stack."

"Yes. Well, here I am. A place I never, in all my life, expected to be." He eyed the dragon by the door. "Ever."

Mayne returned with the Book in its plastic case. "Why don't we go into the kitchen where we can lay it on the table."

We rose and followed Mayne up a stairway.

Fren examined the carvings on the stair rail, commented on how the steps looked like lily pads, and once in the kitchen, exclaimed about the fish-shaped water spigot. "Yes, indeed. A most unusual house."

Mayne laid the book on the table. "It's homey."

"It's delightful." Fren watched Mayne open the lid and remove the Book from its case. "So this is the Book, is it?"

"The very same," I said. "It's the copy Grey made from the fragments archaeologists found here in Freemansland. But the original text didn't originate anywhere on this planet."

Fren nodded. "I read about that, and frankly, I don't know what to make of it. But what I'm concerned with is this volume right here. The Standtall original." He reached a hand toward it, then paused and looked back and forth between Mayne and me. "May I?"

Mayne nodded, and I said, "Of course."

He opened it carefully and ran his hand across the frontispiece. "Unusual paper. It's of Freemansland origin, isn't it? What's it called again?"

"Banroo skin," Mayne answered.

"According to what I've learned," I said, "the process for making it was developed by the Arkentakian prisoners on the top level of Freemansland for the purpose of preserving these very writings."

Mayne watched Fren's every move. "It was very fitting that Standtall used the same material when he put it all together."

Fren turned the first page. "I agree. This is really quite amazing."

He looked at the writing, but mostly, he examined the backs of the pages, both visually and by running his fingertips across them. Then he pulled out a small device from his pocket. "Is it okay if I put a little more light on this? It won't damage the material."

Mayne went and stood beside him. "Is that a greanlight?"

Fren nodded.

"Go ahead, then."

I didn't know what they were talking about, but Mayne was definitely interested.

Fren ran the device slowly along the blank backs of several pages. The light it shed was dim, and it certainly wasn't green. About the time I began to think the whole exercise was pointless, Mayne and Fren both went stiffly alert, and then I saw what had caught their attention. About a quarter of the way down the page, a tiny dot glowed orange.

Trying to ignore the pain in my head, I leaned closer. "What is that? A spek?"

Fren nodded. "It is indeed."

"Are there more?" Mayne asked.

Fren continued his search. "I aim to find out."

While he went over every page, Mayne and I sat at the table and watched. By the time the marshal had finished, he'd found a total of fourteen speks embedded in the pages. Then he closed the book. "I know this is very precious to you, Ms. Freeman."

"Mrs. Dabo," I corrected.

He smiled. "Yes, ma'am. But would you grant me permission to remove the speks and take them with me?"

I frowned. "What do you think is on them?"

"I hesitate to say."

"But you have a pretty good idea, don't you?" Mayne asked.

Fren nodded. "Pretty good."

"So do I," Mayne said. "And yes, you have our permission."

LATE MORNING OF the next day, Mayne sat beside me on the bed—yes, we were of the age that we chose to sleep in a bed, not a mat—where I lay, towels covering the window in order to block the sun.

He rubbed my back. "Come on, time to go."

I pulled the sheet over my head and groaned.

"I'm taking you to the hospital."

I uncovered my head and peered at him with narrowed eyes. "They can't do anything, you know."

"You don't know that. Come on, get up."

"They can't. They never could." Then I remembered. "Oh, but you know that, don't you?"

I'd forgotten Mayne's father had been a stellasede. In a violent rampage, he had killed Mayne's little sister and the grandmother who defended her while six-year-old Mayne took refuge in the stillwater.

I sat, slowly. "But you're right. They've done a lot of research on stelli in recent years. I should make an appointment with Dr. Pigeon."

Mayne stood and helped me up, then held me after I'd risen. "I already called." He hugged me tighter. "You have an appointment, but with a different doctor. Somebody named Colom."

He handed me my clothes, and I put them on. "Why not the Pigeon? I just talked to him a few months ago, and he didn't say anything about retiring any time soon."

"He didn't retire. According to the person I spoke with in his office, he died."

I jerked my head up to stare at him, and winced. "What happened?"

Mayne shrugged. "I wasn't told the details."

Later, I learned from Dr. Colom that Dr. Pigeon had been killed by a stellasede patient just two weeks before. I felt an odd sense of loss. I could never stand the man, but Dr. Pigeon had been a part of my life for forty-five years, and it didn't seem right that he should be taken from it.

I don't remember going to the hospital. The next thing I was aware of was lying in bed and listening to Dr. Colom give Mayne the results of the tests they'd just done. One of the stelli had begun to move and was eating its way through my brain, growing as it went. The surge of trioxydiosmicoline stellase flooding my system would likely wake the other worm as well.

I could tell Mayne struggled to keep control of his voice. "Is there anything we can do?"

"We can't stop the stelli from doing their damage, but for now, we can relieve the pain. When sedation becomes necessary, we can help you with that too. But I'm sorry. The best we can do is help with her comfort and safety." The doctor shook his head. "She's already lived with the stelli far longer than anyone else we've ever tracked." As if that should make it easier to bear now.

AND SO THEN it was I who had a port behind my ear, and Mayne whose lot it was to inject me with chemicals to dull my pain and keep me calm. I used to think it would be Grey who'd take care of me. I never imagined it would be Mayne.

But it was Mayne. He who loved me from the beginning would bear the burden at the end.

Even now, though, Grey is not out of the picture. He, too, was ever faithful. Remember when he vowed to fix it? Well, he did. He fixed it. Even from the grave, he fixed it.

Three months after I came home from the hospital, KJ came to stay with me for a couple of weeks while the Academy was on break and Mayne was away on a job. She came into the room where I reclined on the sofa in the dark, dictating my manuscript to my computer. "Auntie Jem! You've got to see this!"

I looked up. "What?"

"I know you don't follow the newsfeeds, but this, you have got to see!" She sat on the floor in front of me, turned her tablet around to face me, and played the report.

"At four this morning, Centre Standard Time, a sweeping series of simultaneous arrests were made by military authorities and security forces primarily in Centre City and Arkentak. In an unprecedented move, ten high-ranking officials were taken into custody, including City Father Janren Stock, who was apprehended at his private retreat in Manarassetan Cove, along with Merjan Strong, Minister of Domestic Peace, Prace Plodin, Minister of Agriculture, and their respective under-ministers..."

I stared at the screen, then reached down and took the tablet from KJ. "What in the— Am I hearing this right, or is this all in my imagination?"

"It's real, all right. Or if it's not, I'm having the same hallucination. I can't believe it. Just listen!"

I sat up, and she joined me on the sofa so we could listen together after I backed up to start again from the beginning.

The story is familiar to you, of course, but the reality of it took a long time to sink in to my weary, worm-riddled mind. As I gradually figured out, the information in the speks Grey had hidden in the Book provided far-ranging evidence to uncover the covert actions of the late Father Hold. Along with three others, he had created an elite organization of world leaders, which had grown over the years and now was led by Janren Stock. Working subtly to manipulate events, people, and economic development, these villains channeled much of the world's wealth and power into their own hands and for their own benefit. Though the first City Fathers truly wanted to be benevolent caretakers of the world, these men's motive was personal greed. Not only had they ordered the execution of countless individuals, like Stal Standtall, who stood in their way, but they were responsible for the deaths of millions by their support of Daig Lar and his instigating the Kentan war.

Crime built upon crime, deception upon deception, murder upon murder.

Their coming to justice was a slow and painful process. It's plain my noble Ashgrey was involved, but how prominent his role and who he worked with, I'll never know.

Once the evidence was made public, the sorting-out and prosecution was so complicated and prolonged that many of the perpetrators, like Father Hold, had died of natural causes before they could be held accountable. Or perhaps all the causes weren't so natural. Mayne says the number of deaths did seem to defy the odds.

Indeed, the shake-up resulting from the investigation and arrests has still not settled as I write this, and there is unrest in many places. But here in my home in Freemansland, I am unaware of most of it.

I am aware of little, in fact, other than the desire to finish these memoirs before I am out of time. But I am not concerned. The God who has led me every step of the way from the moment of my conception in my mother's womb until this day will see to it that what he has begun will be completed.

Mayne has been a tremendous help, urging me to complete a thought and helping me keep on point. He doesn't even seem to mind hearing of my love for Grey, as he says it's part of who I am. He's grateful to Grey for loving me so well when he wasn't able to do it himself.

That's what he said, but he actually was more present than I realized. I knew he and Jeriah kept in touch, but I wasn't aware how close they were. Remember when the constables brought me the key along with word of Grey's death? After they left, Riah left me with his friend Pettyne while he took off with the key. It was Mayne he gave it to for safekeeping.

It was Mayne who kept the Book after Riah found it in the cold storage locker.

And it was Mayne who'd built the cabin in NaHora—built it for his own use, originally, but stocked it for us when Riah told him of our escape plan.

As I dictated that part of the story, Mayne chuckled.

The interruption annoyed me. "What's so funny?"

"You know whose cabin that was, don't you?" He was still laughing.

"No—don't tell me it was yours!"

He nodded. "Yep."

I thought about it. "Well, that makes sense. It explains why the person who'd brought in all those supplies included everything a Freemanslander could want except for crim. I should be mad at you for that. You made me go a whole year without it."

Oneta, my agent, has hooked me up with an editor who will polish the manuscript once we get it drafted. She promises to make sure the editor maintains my voice and changes none of the facts. She hasn't yet started looking for a publishing house. Mayne suggested she not even try, but simply let the Lord bring the right publisher to her. She seemed to like that idea.

I have other visitors too. Kenlan Fren came by to thank us for letting him take the speks. He also explained a little more about how the information they provided figured in all the crazy things going on in the world today. I didn't understand most of what he told us, but I think Mayne did.

Jeriah comes as often as he can, though his work at Moll as well as preaching and teaching keeps him busy. Jeo comes every now and then, but his wife is afraid to bring their children, even though Mayne's doing a good job of keeping me calm and comfortable. I guess the occasional exception is what has her concerned, and I can't say that I blame her. If I were a mother of small children, I wouldn't want them around me either.

And speaking of children, KJ said the sweetest thing the other day. I told her I was nearly done with the manuscript, and we talked about the eventual publication of the book. I'll leave all that up to Mayne, as I'm already past the point of being competent to make such decisions. But however it works out, I expect the book will sell well. I mentioned to KJ that it was a shame I had no children to leave my earnings to. "There's you and your brother, of course," I said, "and his kids, and any children you might have in the future. Nieces and nephews are wonderful. But I regret that I was never able to give Grey any children of his own."

"Don't be silly, Auntie Jem." She took my hand. "Don't you know what they're saying about you in Centre City? About you and your first husband?"

My thoughts got hung up on that for a while.

"Auntie Jem? Are you with me?"

While I'd been wandering in my mind, KJ had gotten up, made another pot of crim, and poured herself a cup, and I hadn't been aware of it. "What?"

"Would you like some more crim?"

"Yes. Thank you." I took the cup she offered and drank, though it was steaming. I couldn't feel heat and cold anymore. I felt invincible, as if I could run barefoot through the snow or face a dragon's fire without harm. If not for the sedation, I would be a wild woman of the wood by now. A character in one of my

Stillwater stories. I wished I could do that. Run wild and free. But I got the impression it would upset Mayne if I did.

"So do you want to know what they're saying in Centre City about you and your first husband?"

"Is that what I was just thinking about? I'd forgotten."

"I'm not sure what you were thinking about. But do you want to know?"

I took another gulp of crim. "Do I want to know... Oh, yes. Tell me. What are they saying about us?"

"That the two of you gave birth to the whole church of Umban. There are about a million people all over the world who are in the kingdom of God now because of you two. He put the Book together and gave it to you, and you delivered it to the world."

I set down my cup. "That's ridiculous. It's Jesus who builds the church. All we did was—"

"Serve as his instruments, I know. But God used the two of you to bring the gospel to the world. He didn't give you just a few kids from your womb, but a million children through your work with the Book."

I stared into my cup, trying to make the thought take shape in my mind. Instead, I saw a baby in the cup—I know, it was a hallucination, but I saw it all the same—a chubby, naked baby. It smiled at me, all wreathed in steam, and then it divided into two babies, and I thought, "Twins, like Jeriah and me!" and then those two divided, and then those four multiplied, and as I watched, the surface of the crim became covered with babies, hundreds and then thousands of them, growing tiny and tinier, until they all blended together and I couldn't differentiate one from another.

I handed her the cup. "This is no mere cup of crim. It's my children. I have many children. Just like you said. Look! It's full of my children."

KJ took it from me and peered inside. "What are they doing?"

"Just what they're supposed to be doing. Multiplying. You'd better put that down before they spill all over. Maybe you should get another cup to pour some of them into."

If she was puzzled, she didn't show it. "I'll get you another cup and put some fresh crim in it."

PEOPLE COME AND go. Mayne is almost always here.

I dream I'm running down the path to the stillwater, but the water seems so far away. I leave the path and scramble straight down through the brush, through the trees, over the rocks. I pause, standing on a rock in the moonlight. The sweet air flows over me unhindered by clothing. The water calls. *Home. Come home. Come home.* I crawl off the rock—it seems more natural to go on all fours—and continue down the sharpfall. When I reached the next turn of the path, something grabs me. I scream and bite and kick and scratch. I mustn't be stopped! I must get to the water!

Now I'm awake, lying in bed. The towel over the window glows with the sunlight behind it. Mayne sits in a chair a short distance away, head bowed in sleep. He has a bite mark on his cheek. When I stir, he wakes up.

He says something, but I can't hear him. Jeriah comes in with a cup of crim. He sees me, and his lips move, but I can't hear him either. One of his lips is swollen, and his face is scratched. He sets the crim on a table and speaks to Mayne. Mayne rises from the chair with difficulty and approaches my bed.

It's not Mayne, it's a dragon! Fear floods me, and I thrash. I'm tied down. I scream. That, I can hear. The sound reverberates in my head and multiplies itself into more screams. I can't stop screaming, but the sound makes me mad.

They're both near me now—the dragon, and Ibro. I scream and thrash. Ibro throws himself on top of me to hold me down and the dragon shoots fire behind my ear. It burns into my brain.

And then it's Mayne brushing my hair from my face and Jeriah covering me with a sheet. They're both weeping. Mayne speaks. I see his lips move, but I can't hear him.

"One more thing," I say, but the sound hurts. Oh, how it hurts.

Mayne says something else.

I make a typing motion. "One more thing," I say. "To write."

Jeriah brings a tablet and then leaves the room.

Mayne unfastens one of my hands. He holds the tablet for me, and I try to type, but my fingers curl. They won't do my bidding. I must poke each key with the knuckle of my middle finger.

I type what you now read, these last few paragraphs.

Through the distress of my affliction, I revel in the grace of God. I have a hope. I have a future. I have a million children who will never die.

I must hide from the sun, but I walk forever in the Light. The stelli hold my body captive, but my soul is forever free. When I am dead, I will live.

The Son has made me free, and I am free indeed.

If you enjoyed this series, please let the world know with a review on Amazon, Goodreads, Booktopia, and/or your own blog. Readers and authors alike always appreciate reviews.

Thank you!

Telling the old, old story of Jesus and his love, but in surprising new ways…

Yvonne Anderson writes
fiction that takes you out of this world

Fly through the **Gateway to Gannah**
for some serious sci-fi adventure

Book 1: *The Story in the Stars*
(Finalist, ACFW Carol Awards, 2012)
Book 2: *Words in the Wind*
Book 3: *Ransom in the Rock*
Book 4: *The Last Toqeph*

Also, check out "First Love," Anderson's novella in
Coming Home: A Tiny House Collection
Seven stories from seven authors featuring
characters who live in tiny houses.

www.YsWords.com